Ghost of
a Girl

Ghost of a Girl

A Kami White
Para(normal)legal Mystery

E.L. Oakes

CAMEL
PRESS
Kenmore, WA

A Camel Press book published by Epicenter Press

Epicenter Press
6524 NE 181st St.
Suite 2
Kenmore, WA 98028

For more information go to:
www.Camelpress.com
www.Coffeetownpress.com
www.Epicenterpress.com
www.eloakes.com

This is a work of fiction. Names, characters, places, brands, media, and incidents are either the product of the author's imagination or are used fictitiously.

Design by Scott Book and Melissa Vail Coffman

ISBN: 978-1-94207-854-8 (Trade Paper)
ISBN: 978-1-94207-855-5 (eBook)

Printed in the United States of America

CHAPTER 1

⁓

Monday Morning

THE "HAWAII 5-0" THEME SONG MERRILY jingling from my cell-phone jerked me awake from a dream of warm water and perfect waves. I blinked as my office came into focus around me—no ocean, no surfboard. Just a worn leather sofa, a folding table, and a mile of empty oak shelving. I nudged the cat, who was sprawled full-length on the back of the sofa. "Hoover? Answer that, will you?"

Hoover glared at me and stretched one tawny paw over his nose. Hairless Sphynx resemble wrinkly-felted Jim Henson Creature Shop characters. Glaring wasn't particularly effective.

"Lazy-bones." I stretched over and pulled my cellphone off the little folding table. "Hola! No hablo bad sales pitches."

"Is this Kamera White?" My name, incorrectly pronounced as 'camera', not Kam-eey-ra, snapped my brain to attention. *Oops! That sounded official.* When I affirmed with the correct pronunciation, the no-nonsense voice on the other end continued quickly. "This is Detective Ron Brittle from the San Amoro police department. You're the registered owner of a blue 2005 Kia? License plate 4GZT892?"

"My car? My brother has it." *Arg!* If my car was sitting in a tow-lot somewhere racking up fees, I was gonna sell him on the black-market to pay for it. That is, if I could find someone who would pay for a loser brother. Or maybe I could just sell his liver. I read somewhere that they don't even need the whole liver for a transplant, just a portion of it. He would be fine with only half a liver. "Where's my brother?" And more importantly, "Where's my car?"

There was a long pause from the detective. "We've just recovered the car from the South Reservoir."

"My car was at the reservoir?"

"No, Miss White," Detective Brittle corrected. "We found it *in* the reservoir."

Kenny! I was gonna kill him. I was gonna tear him into tiny pieces, boil him and feed him to Hoover one nibble at a time. No, wait. I was gonna feed him to Hoover alive! That is, if I could get the picky cat to even taste him. "I'm sorry, Detective. I know I shouldn't do this, but I need to report a homicide because as soon as I find my brother, I'm going to kill him."

"Don't do that, ma'am. Fratricide is messy," Detective Brittle discouraged dryly, and I pictured an older gent with a sharp wit, someone who looked like a cross between Richard Belzer and Tom Selleck. He continued more warmly. "Tell you what, why don't you let me find him for you? What's his name?"

"Kenneth James White." I had to do quick subtraction to get his birth year. I'm terrible at remembering dates. I gave the detective Mom's number . . . Dad's contact information, too, but since he'd been in the Indian Himalaya for years, it was doubtful he'd heard from Kenny since probably last Christmas. By the time Detective Brittle had the information he needed, I was getting worried—sick-to-my-stomach, never-sleep-again kind of worried. If my car was in the reservoir, then where was Kenny? "Detective, he wasn't . . . I mean, there was no sign of Kenny in the car, was there?"

"We identified your car by license plate, Miss White. The divers brought it up a short time ago, but as far as I know, there was no sign of anyone inside. That spot on the lake is a popular dump spot for joy riders looking to get rid of stolen cars. This our annual clean-up sweep. Cars, motorcycles, weapons, drugs. Last year, we found the Baby Jesus from St. Andrews Church. You name it, it's down there. It might take a day or two to sort everything out. I suggest you call your insurance, and we'll be in touch with your case number after we've towed it to our impound lot. Your insurance company can appraise it there."

"I don't imagine there's much left to appraise?" His silence told me everything I needed to know. "Thanks. I . . . Look, Detective, my brother? He's not a saint, but he's not really a bad kid, either. I just . . ."

"If I find him, you'll hear from me. Come to think of it, you'll hear from me either way."

Like that didn't sound ominous. "Thank you, Detective."

I gave the detective the office address and phone number and hung up. Anger over losing my car was giving way to worry about, and more than a little fury towards, Kenny. Dragging myself off the couch, ignoring Hoover's disdainful glare, I pulled up Mom's number on my phone. It went straight to message, and I glanced at the clock, realizing she would already be at the greenhouse working. I left a brief message. "Hey, Mom. Call me as soon as you get this, unless I catch you at work first. Then just ignore it."

I called the greenhouse and Diane, my mother's partner, answering with a crisp, "Herbs & Greens. Good morning!"

"Diane? It's Kami. Is my mom around?"

There was a pause, and I knew she was standing up to look out the plate glass window of the office. "Oh. You've just missed her. The truck is already gone. She's going to Sonoma to pick up some seedlings."

Mom wouldn't answer her cell if she was driving. I groaned. "No worries. Tell me, though, do you know if she's seen Kenny lately? Or has he been around the greenhouse?" Sometimes he helped Mom out for extra cash. Kenny was perpetually broke.

"Not in a few weeks. Why?"

"Just looking for him." I didn't see the point in worrying Diane until I'd talked to Mom. "Call me if you hear from him, please?"

On Diane's promise, I hung up, hoping Mom would check her messages when she got to Sonoma. After a quick wake-up shower, I pulled on a pair of clean black jeans and a light blue blouse and checked myself in the mirror. Rings under my pale blue eyes made them look even paler and wider than usual, and my blond curls whirled around my face. I didn't know who looked more like a Jim Henson Creature Shop creation, Hoover, or me. Nothing to be done about it now. I dug out my car insurance paperwork and, still barefooted, headed out my door and directly across the entryway to Office 1-B.

Office 1-B is leased to Mallory Kent, 'Insrance Broker.' (The neighborhood sign painter isn't big on spelling.) 1-A is White Legal Services. That's me. Upstairs from me in 2-A is Morri Morrimont, a retired journalist who writes word-puzzles for a little extra income, and, I think, to keep him out of Mrs. Morrimont's flowing silver hair. Across from him, in 2-B, is, well, nobody—just one big empty no-rent-paid office space, abandoned after the husband-and-wife chiropractors were arrested for practicing without licenses. But this morning, I needed my Insrance Broker.

I flung open Mallory Kent's door and stormed in without knocking. He was with a client and I was left to pace back and forth while I waited, formulating in the back of my mind all of the ways I was going to wreak revenge on my brother.

As soon as his client left, I popped into the chair opposite Mallory's desk. Mal is a big guy, rotund is one way to put it, with a smattering of dark hair around a balding head, and deep brown eyes. While his dress shirts and slacks are average business wear from Men's Big & Tall, his taste in ties is downright inspiring. Today's choice was a bright lilac color with a silver-thread paisley pattern. Before he could even say hello, I blurted out, "My brother stole my car and the police just found it in a reservoir."

"Uh oh." Mallory's wide mouth turned down in a frown, lending him the appearance of a pudgy sad goldfish. "Let's look up your policy, shall we?"

Mallory Kent, tie fetish aside, is a good insurance broker. He always shops around to get you the lowest rates and knows all the secrets to getting great discounts. He got me a super deal involving car, life, and business insurance. Not that I was intending to need life insurance anytime soon, but with the auto policy it was cheap, and least Mom would be able to bury me instead of dropping my body in the Bay. Or maybe she could just dump my body in the Bay and keep the money, which seemed more practical to me.

Mallory's fingers were tapping at his computer, scrolling on his mouse, and tapping again. Finally, he looked up with a frown. "Kam? Did you *loan* your brother your car, or did he *steal* your car?"

"I may have handed him the keys, your honor," I said as blankly as I could but quickly qualified the statement. "But I only gave him permission to drive it for a day or two, not two weeks!"

"But you didn't report the vehicle stolen?" Kent was nodding, waiting for his computer to do whatever it was doing, but he knew, and I knew—I'd done insurance fraud filings for him in the past—that I was pretty much screwed.

"Suck time?" I asked, a glimmer of hope in my voice that was quickly dashed by Mallory's nod. I dug my fingers into my tight blond curls, down to my scalp, trying to squeeze out the slowly growing headache that stemmed from my loser brother's latest mess.

"I'm sorry. Because you didn't report the vehicle stolen, the insurance company views it as an uninsured driver incident. That only covers the cost of the car after deductible, according to Blue Book. And the bad news is that losing your car affects the rest of your personal policies. Your business insurance effects the percentage you pay on your auto policy, and both of those rates affect your life insurance. Without the auto, your life premium doubles."

"I guess I'll just plan to not buy the farm until I can get things straightened out. If I do buy the farm, can I insure it through you?" Well, what else could I say? My car was surely totaled, and its Blue Book value was somewhere around the cost of my deductible. I'd never seen a check for zero dollars and zero cents before, so that was something to look forward to, at least.

"If you cash out your life insurance now . . ." There was a long moment and more tapping. "You'll get $332.98, and that's considered taxable income."

That was three hundred more than I currently had in my account. "Do what you gotta do, Mal."

"I'll swing by with the paperwork before closing-time."

I HEADED BACK TO MY OFFICE WITH less fury in my heart, and more frustration. Where was my brother? Why was my car in the reservoir? I needed some hot tea and an aspirin, pronto. My office suite consists of a front reception area, a side office room, and a large open room that had once held beautiful oak filing cabinets full of documents. Juliet Hanford took the cabinets and left the files, which were currently piled on the floor, along with stacks of cardboard boxes waiting to be filled with them. The file room also houses the microwave, mini-fridge and electronic tea kettle; the sole bastions of my homemaking abilities.

Over the fridge was a fancy hand-drawn map of Europe, in a faux-antique style, with landmarks and places of note sketched on it. Criss-crossing the map were other lines, drawn in green and red felt pen. It isn't mine, The Map. It belongs to my lawyer, Reginald Burroughs, willed to him by my previous boss. I'm just the Keeper of The Map, but I love it all the same. I love the beautiful little land-mark sketches; tiny castles, intricate flowers, and beasts both real and mythological. One of my favorite hobbies was researching the locations and trying to interpret the pictures. In the South of France was a phoenix with its wings unfurled, the symbol of a medieval artist's association that still exists there today. In Germany, a dainty trio of unicorns danced around in the Black Forest. A white cathe-dral marked Santiago de Compostela on the pilgrim trail in Spain.

While I waited for the tea kettle to boil, I traced my finger around Italy's boot, reminding myself to call Reginald Burroughs and let him know I still had the map if he had a place for it. I knew he still wanted it, but I suspected that his grief had held him back from asking for it.

I was jolted from my moment's meditation when the front door jangled open. I glanced at the clock: 10:30? Miss Mairfax wasn't due until 11:30. *Mallory!* He must be working fast today!

"Coming!" I called out as I switched off the teakettle. I dashed into the other room. "That was fast! I didn't expect you for . . ."

"I'm . . . You were expecting me?"

There was a guy standing in the doorway. I didn't know who he was, but he sure wasn't Mallory Kent. He wasn't much taller than me, and he was the kind of skinny that said ill or undernourished, with thinning brown hair and round watery eyes that gave him a look reminiscent of Yoda. He waved both hands in the air in an 'oh wow' gesture. "I can't believe that! You're incredible!"

"Uh huh." I didn't have the heart to tell him that he wasn't who I was expecting at all. "Please come in. What can I do for you?"

"You mean you don't know? I thought, since you knew I was coming . . ." He was kind of ping-ponging around the office, checking out the empty shelves and the barren walls. Then he started to reach out for the suit of armor.

"Don't!" I might have screamed that, just a bit. I dove forward to plant myself between him and Sir Evrett. The guy jerked his hand back from the suit of armor as if burned. I muttered apologetically, "Sorry, that's 14th Century. Oils on your hands tarnish the steel."

As soon as I was certain he wasn't going to touch Evrett, I continued more calmly. "Please, have a seat. What can I do for you?" Belatedly, I remembered that I only had one chair, so I spun it out towards him with one hand and seated myself on the edge of the folding desk, which wobbled precariously. "I'm sorry, I'm Kami White. You would be?"

"Irvin. Irvin Zettlemeyer."

The name didn't ring any bells. I casually leaned over and tapped Z E T into the clientele database, but nothing came up. "What can I do for you, Mr. Zettlemeyer?"

"Oh, I don't know. Now that I'm here, I'm not sure. It's all rather embarrassing. Very strange . . . I don't know where to begin. I saw your sign, and I think I need your help . . ." His voice lowered and he peered around the office as though someone might be listening. "I need help with . . . research."

"For a lawsuit?" *Yes! A client! A real walk-in-the-door, paying client.* That was what I'd been waiting for. I took a second glance at Mr. Zettlemeyer. I wasn't sure that he was the dream client I'd hoped for. "What kind of research are we talking about? Background check? Property records? Business files? There's nothing to be embarrassed about. We've handled all kinds of research, and we're very discreet."

We, of course, being me and the cat. Hoover never tells client secrets.

"Haunting!" Irvin Zettlemeyer squeaked out, and then clapped both hands over his mouth, his watery eyes seeming to glance in every direction at once.

I glanced around myself, looking for signs that Evrett was active, but all was quiet on the suit-of-armor front. I looked back to Irvin with raised eyebrows. "What is haunting?"

"My house. I mean, *the* house. It's haunted."

"Umm . . . I'm a paralegal." I glanced towards the window to see if this was a joke perpetuated by Nicky, but the FrankenStang was nowhere in sight. She'd been trying to get me involved in paranormal research for a while.

"Exactly. Paralegal Research." He waved at my window sign. "That's what I need."

"Don't you mean *paranormal* research?" I said it softly as silk, leaning back a bit and uncrossing my arms, waiting for the 'duh' moment as he realized he had the wrong word, and the wrong office, and very much the wrong person.

"Paranormal. Paralegal?" His wide watery eyes blinked at me. "What's the difference? You research, right?"

What exactly does one say to that?

More precisely, what does one say to that when they're a broke paralegal with no car, and no solid source of income on the horizon outside of a small stipend that kept the business running while my former boss's entire estate was tied up in a probate dispute?

All I knew about haunting research I'd learned from Nicky when she was trying to help me find out what had happened to Charles. It was also true that Morri from upstairs and his friend, Father Joseph Talbon, had once been involved in a paranormal research group. They had offered to pass on their paranormal research to Nicky and me more than once. But I was a paralegal. I dealt with law . . . not ghosts. I opened my mouth to say so, to say that he was in the wrong office and good day, when, in the corner of my vision, Evrett's gauntlet twitched. My mouth slid shut. I had been working in a haunted office for years now. I had a ghost for a personal friend. How hard could it be?

I smiled my best smile, grabbed up a legal pad and my last working ballpoint pen, and said, "Of course, Mr. Zettlemeyer. I'd be happy to help you."

CHAPTER 2

Monday Morning Goes On

It turns out that an initial interview for a paranormal investigation isn't all that different from preparatory interviews for paralegal investigations. In the course of standard questioning, I learned that Mr. Irvin Zettlemeyer was a twenty-nine-year-old computer programmer. A start-up business he and his ex-wife started together had collapsed and resulted in a nasty divorce with ongoing financial difficulties. Now he lived with three housemates, in a house owned by the computer firm they worked for. Housing in the Bay Area is at a premium and offering rental incentives helped companies recruit the best.

"Must be nice." I muttered, glancing around my barren office. "My employer left his house to cancer research."

Zettlemeyer's eyes went wide and he leaned forward, his voice deep with amazed wonder. "His house had cancer?"

"Yes. Fortunately, it wasn't terminal." *Oh, god. Someone save me.* "Tell me about your house, Mr. Zettlemeyer. Why do you believe it might be haunted?"

"I think people must have died there or something." He blinked emptily. "Isn't that where ghosts come from?"

"People dying doesn't necessarily mean it's haunted, I don't think. If that was the case, just about everywhere would be haunted, right? Hauntings can have other sources. Ghosts can be attached to objects, for example." I took a deep breath and glanced at Evrett again. The former crusader knight was two continents and an ocean away from where he'd died. That didn't stop him from doing as he pleased. "What kind of symptoms are you noticing? Are your roommates having experiences, too?"

"House."

"Excuse me?"

"House-mates. We don't *room*. I don't want to give that impression. We're just guys who share a house. House. Mates. Well, one of us is a girl. We're girl and guys housemates."

"Oh, right. I'm sorry." I grew up in the Bay Area. The idea that anyone might care if someone else thought they might be rooming, not housing, hadn't even occurred to me. "I'm still curious why you think the house is haunted? Can you tell me about that?"

"Things move. You put them one place and find them somewhere else. There's cold spots all over. I mean, it's cold one minute and warm the next."

"And those cold spots? They aren't near windows? Or air vents?"

Zettlemeyer gave me as much of a withering look as his pallid gaze could muster. "I came here for help."

"And I would like to help you, Mr. Zettlemeyer. That's why I have to ask these questions. I'm not mocking you." No matter how much I might really want to. "I need to know so we don't waste our time chasing down faulty air conditioning vents instead of ghosts. *Eliminate the impossible, and whatever remains, however improbable* . . ." I let the Arthur Conan Doyle quote hang in the air unfinished.

"Oh. I . . . Well. That's all right then," he stammered with his eyes focused on some spot on the wall behind me. Suddenly he flung himself out of the chair, his slender pale fingers pointing shakily somewhere over my head. "Omigod! Alien! An alien!"

"Alien?" Startled, I glanced back over my shoulder. Hoover, unbeknownst to me, had slipped from the file room and jumped to the bookshelves behind me. Standing tall on the empty shelf, he was surveying the office with an amused kitty-grimace on his wrinkle-nosed face.

"Nono. He's a cat," I tried to explain, standing up to gather Hoover in my arms, scratching his long ears. "Look? See. Just a cat. His name is Hoover."

"Cat? That's *a cat*?" Zettlemeyer recoiled, squealing in disbelief, and more than a little bit like a five-year-old girl. "What's wrong with it? Why is it *naked*? Is it sick?"

"He's a Hairless Sphynx. They're rare. Wanna pet him?" I tried to hold Hoover out for petting, but apparently neither Zettlemeyer nor Hoover were keen on the idea. Zettlemeyer scootched the chair backwards so hard he almost fell. Hoover clawed a six-inch long stripe down my arm as he used it for a launching pad to the top of the empty shelves, where he crouched with his ears back, glaring viciously.

"Bad kitty!" If only he knew how ridiculous the glare of a hairless cat looked. I turned back to Zettlemeyer. "I'm so sorry! He's just a bit temperamental. Things have been kind of difficult around here lately." Zettlemeyer was staring warily at Hoover so I tapped my notepad authoritatively, trying to draw his attention back. "Now, tell me about this haunting. What kind of experiences are you having?"

"Doors open and close. At night, we hear crying. At first, I thought it was one of the other guys watching TV, but we've all heard it, even when the television isn't on. Knocking. Banging. You put something down, and when you come back, it's gone. Drinks knock over, books fall off shelves. All kinds of stuff. All four of us have seen it." Zettlemeyer's voice was a little calmer, but his eyebrows kept twitching and he hadn't stopped watching the cat.

I glanced down at my notes, mostly a jumble of single words: cold, door, crying, knocking, banging. My arm was dripping splatters of blood from the traces of Hoover's claws. *Great.* At least Zettlemeyer wouldn't have noticed, so intent was he on watching for Hoover's next attack maneuver. I tugged my sleeve down to soak up the mess. "All right. When's a good time for me to come by? I'd like to see the house for myself, and I'd like to talk to the rest of the household."

"Tomorrow? Can you come tomorrow night?"

"I'll have to check my calendar," I lied, knowing full well that the only thing on my schedule was hunting down my deadbeat brother. "Now, there's a question of contract. Initial consultation is a hundred dollars. If you need a full investigation, there's an hourly rate fee. I'll be honest. Most of the time we find logical explanations for issues, with no supernatural event involved. If it is paranormal and we help purge it, that service is free." In the corner of my vision, I witnessed the visor of Evrett's sallet helmet slipping another quarter inch and stammered swiftly, "If you want it purged, that is. I mean, some people don't."

"Why wouldn't they?" Zettlemeyer shoved to his feet. "I mean, yeah, yeah, the fees are no problem. Do you take Apple Pay?"

"Venmo or PayPal," I answered, trying to remember the current balance in my Paypal account.

He pulled out his phone, transferred my fee, and then texted me the address before scrabbling out into the street, casting a last wary glance back at Hoover.

"Bravo! We have a job!" I waved phone with the text and did a little victory dance. Okay, so it was a weird job, and I had no idea what to do with it, but I had a job!

Hoover stared disdainfully and Evrett was silent behind his steel-riveted façade.

I had to admit that for my own sanity, I was rather flabbergasted by the entire situation. I picked up my phone and texted Nicky. "Wanna hunt ghosts? Whatcha doin tomorrow night?"

My interview with Irvin had only left me a half hour to prep for meeting with Miss Maifax, but by the time she arrived, I had her paperwork ready to go. I reminded her that she had to be in court on her scheduled dates to win the suit, but it was unnecessary. I suspect that Miss Maifax sees spurious small claims as a hobby, the same way some people golf, or surf, or do quilting . . . and she was an avid hobbyist.

CHAPTER 3

Monday Afternoon

WORK OBLIGATIONS FINISHED, I SENT AN email to my father in India asking him if he'd heard from Kenny, and another to my cousin Patrick, currently in Oregon healing from a car accident, asking the same. Kenny and Patrick were closer as cousins than I was to Kenny as a sibling. Kenny's best friend, that I knew of, at any rate, was Jude Booder. I don't talk to Jude Booder. I didn't even have his contact information. I texted Nicky again. "Crazy Q for ya. Do you have Booder's #?"

Then I opened a search engine, looked up paranormal research and started learning what I needed to know for the newest skillset on my resume. I hoped it didn't involve more night classes!

In legal jargon, we us the term "reasonable doubt." When you cannot be absolutely certain of something, even when faced with all of the evidence both for and against it, then reasonable doubt exists. Reasonable doubt is the extension of the law that lets a jury listen to their instincts and trust in their honest interpretations of the evidence. Reasonable doubt has released killers and overruled thin prosecutions. It's a cause of sleepless nights for many legal professionals. In paranormal research, however, *reasonable doubt* was apparently something disregarded with abandon.

As I surfed sites, I realized that reality seemed to be constantly overshadowed by the supernatural, the strange, and the sometimes downright absurd. For every image purported to be ghostly, there were pages upon pages of debate about authenticity. For every claim that seemed legitimate, hundreds more were so completely ludicrous that they wouldn't even make subject matter for lame made-for-YouTube movies.

The sites I appreciated most were full of tips, suggestions, and equipment lists. Equipment I'd never heard of, let alone ever considered owning. A K2 meter? An EMF detector? There were familiar items, though. I had a digital voice recorder for taking depositions; I'd even used it to record Evrett, the only ghost I knew personally. I had digital cameras which could record video. I even had a digital infrared camera for night-surveillance that could upload images directly to my laptop. Thankfully, all of Charles' investigation equipment had been locked in the office cabinet when Juliet did her Dick Turpin impression.

The "Hawaii 5-0" song rang out and I glanced at the caller ID before answering. "Nickydoodle! Whatcha doin?"

She sounded panicked. "What's wrong? Are you okay?"

"Okay? Yeah. Why wouldn't I be?"

"Gurl, you just asked me for Jude Booder's number. Did you have a stroke? A brain seizure? What's wrong with you?" Nicky's words shot out like a thrown piston, and I started laughing. My best friend's voice was distressed as she barked, "Have you lost your friggin' mind?"

I stopped laughing, wiping tears from my eyes. "Yes, I've lost my mind, completely. And my car. And my brother." I gulped down the last giggle. "Have you heard from Kenny? Seen him at all?"

"No. Hold on a sec . . ." There was a long pause, and I heard her call out to someone else in the room before she came back on. "I'm at Surf Surplus, just finished my shift. I asked Rick and the crew, but no one here has seen him in weeks. And what's this about ghost hunting? What's going on?"

"Asked Rick? Are you two on or off again?" I didn't really need to know. Their casual relationship was pretty much beyond my comprehension.

"That is none of your beeswax. Ghost hunting. Talk. Now."

"Impatient much?" I then had to explain it all. Kenny borrowing my car, my car in the reservoir, and, lastly, Irvin Zettlemeyer's misunderstanding.

I could practically see her hopping up and down. "Changing your mind about working with Father Joe and Morri?"

Morri and Father Joe's group had done the initial research on Evrett, and I trusted their judgement, but I wasn't about to ditch my credibility as a legal expert to play ghost chaser. "No. I just really need the work. And Irvin seems genuine, if not entirely sane. I could really use your help. The website I was just reading was talking about K2 and EMF detectors?"

"Oh, yeah. We'll need those," Nicky enthused. "Pretty much any hardware store that carries electrical supplies will have them. Are you sure this guy has a ghost?"

"Not in the slightest. He thought Hoover was an alien. But he's paying for an initial consultation, so I figured it wouldn't hurt to take a look. Is there anything else I need to know about the equipment?"

"Nah. I've seen what you've got for cameras and stuff. You know how to use all that. Look, I gotta get some sleep. Call me tomorrow and I'll help you out with it all."

"Can you come with me tomorrow night to talk to them? It's here in the East Bay." Nicky lived on the outskirts of Santa Cruz in a trailer at her parent's auto junkyard. Her dad didn't want to get a guard dog, and Nicky was a good substitute.

"I have a shift at the marine animal rescue." Nicky sounded truly regretful, but I knew her volunteer responsibilities took priority even before she explained. "We've got an injured seal pup that needs food and meds every few hours. Got caught in a boat prop, poor little dude. I'll try to trade shifts, but no promises. Let me see what I can do."

"If you can manage, otherwise I can do it on my own. This is just the meet-and-greet to scope out the situation and get the lay of the land."

She paused, and then said, "If this guy is that out there, I don't think you should go alone. What if he's a crazy nutjob? You could be the next Hannah Raye . . ."

Hannah Raye, a fellow classmate at East Bay, had been missing since last Thursday, with searches taking place on campus and posters going up all over town. That thought gave me pause and I was about to reconsider going alone when the image of Irvin Zettlemeyer staring at Hoover with his round watery eyes popped into my head and I and tried not to laugh. "I'm pretty sure he's a bit nutty, but not a crazy nutjob."

"Well, if I can't make it, at least see if Father Joe can go with you." Nicky rang off and I did a little more research online. I located the two meters the site recommended on sale at a nearby hardware store and was in the process of bicycling over there when I remembered a tiny flaw with my grand plan. The house was out in the hills. Unless Nicky could come, I had no car and no way to do the job.

Whom could I ask . . . Reese Calhoun? Reese would loan me her van. Just one problem: Reese's van was coffee-stain brown with huge bright green stripes, and read "Eat at Reese's, More Than Coffee" down both sides—not exactly the impression I wanted to give on a job. Mallory . . . would laugh, laugh in my face. At least he'd do it kindly. How about Mom? Oh, god. Mom! I'd forgotten to call her about Kenny! I promised myself I'd call as soon as I got back to the office. After that, if it seemed like she was feeling generous, I'd ask to borrow her Beetle.

AT ACE HARDWARE, I FOUND A K2 METER and an EMF detector. The EMF detector was inexpensive, the K2 meter was less-so. But it was the exact model that many of the paranormal research sites recommended, so I felt good about it. Unfortunately, feeling good about my new career path was short-lived. As I pedaled slowly back to the office, everywhere I looked around town, there were pictures of Hannah Raye. She beamed down at me with her warm smile and glowing blue eyes from telephone poles and shop windows, asking, *"Have You Seen Me?"* Despite her smile, I felt heartsick. Where are you, Hannah? How do you just walk out of class and disappear? My good mood was dissipating.

I was also dreading the phone call I had to make. It's not that I don't love Mom . . . I do. But we have a complicated relationship. She always seemed to have one foot in solid reality and one somewhere in a world made up of daisies and peace and kumbayas . . . and trying to tell her anything negative about her precious baby boy? That was fraught with pitfalls. When I was nine, Kenny cut the arms off my Pretty Princess Barbie. When I ran tattling to Mom, she told me that I was too attached to material things, and to love my brother as my own heart. So, like any good sister who loves her little brother like her own heart, I pinned him down, sat on his chest, and wrote BRAT on his forehead with a red permanent marker. That got me grounded to my room for a week, but it made me feel better.

Right now, I didn't think I could feel any worse. My car was dunked. Kenny was missing . . . and guess who was stuck having to tell Mom? It was me—again. To the rhythmic hum of my bike tires on the hot pavement, I rehearsed, practicing the words Mom would need to hear, working out my oratory for my special jury of one. Kenny probably wasn't really missing. He was hiding from me, right? Not wanting to tell me he'd dumped my car in the lake. Which really, considering my current mood, was probably wise. Kenny was a scrapper. He would be fine.

The more I practiced saying it, the more it felt like lies.

I slipped off my bike and locked it to the bike rack in front of the office building, trying to sort out words to tell my mother and knowing that if I found Kenny before the cops did, I was gonna give him a heck of a lot more than a few letters in red permanent marker.

I was so focused my problems that I missed the small dusk-gray pick-up sitting by the curb. But I couldn't miss the person standing in front of the door to the office. From the back, even at first glance, there was a whole lot to admire. Sleek black Levi's covered a backside that Chris Hemsworth would die to own. Tucked into the jeans was a satiny-looking dark blue shirt, accented by a black leather jacket casually tossed over one shoulder. Even in the afternoon Indian summer heat, he looked cool.

From the back, it was a wowzer moment. My breath hitched for a second before I managed to expel it with what I tried to hope was a subdued, "Hello, can I help you?"

The perfectly even tips of his gleaming straw-gold hair brushed over the collar of his leather jacket, and his hand slid his sunglasses off, revealing twinkling blue eyes as he turned around.

My heart thudded to an embarrassed stop, my face heating up with blistering speed from small flame to furnace force. My voice was nothing more than a squeak. "Jack. Didn't recognize you from behind."

Jack Austin's smile was rippling, as was his voice. "No reason you should."

But my ex's eyes said the rest of the sentence, ". . . notice what you never noticed when we were together." Oh, I'd noticed. Believe me, I noticed. But I wasn't about to admit it to him now. I pushed past him and unlocked the door, ushering him inside. "What brings you to my humble abode?"

"God, you are so . . . " He stood there, leaning against the doorway, his eyes like the pristine waters of the mountain lake where we once vacationed together. It seemed ideal until a storm blew up, tore down our tent in the middle of the night and we ran out of gas. We'd spent the rest of the night huddled on the porch of a roadside gas station waiting for it to open.

That, sadly, is how things with Jack Austin always seem to go—even our wedding, such as it was. Jack stood at the altar in a handsomely cut, perfectly fitted tuxedo, in front of our friends and family, ready to put a ring on my finger and I swear, I'd never seen anything more beautiful. So, I . . . well . . . I ran to the bus station across the street and got on the first bus leaving the terminal. I woke up in a dusty, stained wedding dress somewhere east of Vegas. I blame the bus station. Jack blames me . . . and who could blame him?

"So . . .? What? Grumpy? Sorry, I've had a bad day." I trotted through to the mini fridge. "Want a yogurt?"

"Rude, is what I was going to say." Jack smiled, and I knew he didn't mean it. He'd been about to say something else, something that complimented me. Jack doesn't have a mean bone in his body. *Damn him.*

"How can I be rude? I just offered you my last yogurt."

"That's not polite if you know I don't like yogurt."

"You should eat it anyway. It's good for you." I popped the lid and scooped a spoonful into my mouth—Greek yogurt with honey—not too bad. I held out the next spoonful. "And yummy!"

Jack didn't take the bait. "No thanks. I've got some papers for you to sign. Oslo and Burroughs got part of the business accounts released, enough to manage upkeep on the business until the rest of the inheritance comes through." Jack, in addition to being my ex, was also Charles' accountant, which now makes him my accountant. He smiled mischievously and his eyes, brighter blue than the September sky, twinkled. "But if you don't want your money . . ."

I didn't, however, deserve him in any capacity. Maybe I could blame my blazing cheeks on the bicycle ride? Finally, I shifted to look towards, but not quite at, him. "Thanks, Jack. You didn't have to come by, you know. You could have called, and I'd have come over there."

"Well . . ." He was sorting the papers on my desk, laying them out in the order that I needed to sign. "I heard you didn't have a car."

"What? How! I only found out this morning. Jack Austin! Have you been spying on me?" He hadn't been. Jack was far too honorable for spying; far too honorable for too many things . . . including me.

He shook his head, his brow creased with concern. "The police called me looking for Kenny. I know your car's trashed." Jack rested a file-folder on my pathetically empty desktop. "You can look over those, get them back to me next week?"

"I didn't know Kenny was still working for you." Jack often hired him for odd jobs around the office.

"He's been helping out down at the women's shelter I'm helping build. It's an on-call part-time thing, but Jaxine told the police that he worked for me. Actually, I haven't seen him in weeks."

Jaxine—Mom. Why did it bother me Jack was still familiar enough with my mother to use her first name? I was barely even comfortable calling her mom. But that was my family. Once you were family, you were always family, even ex-fiancés. "Darn. I was hoping to talk to her before the cops got to her. Is she okay?"

"When I called her, she sounded fine." And he cut straight to the heart of the matter . . . as always. "She's okay. Worried, but she's okay."

I felt tension ease across my shoulders. How did he know how to do that?

"Ken's a free spirit. That's what Jaxine said. She seemed more worried about you and how you were getting on with everything, especially without your car." Jack reached out to rub Hoover's back. Hoover purred and curled around Jack's hand with unbridled affection. Even cats loved Jack. Then he dropped a car key on top of the files. "I bought a little used pick-up awhile back, for doing home-repair, hauling lumber, that kind of thing. But I never manage to get around to what needs to be done. The truck's just been sitting in the driveway. If you want to borrow it, take it for as long as you need."

We'd bought the house together, right before our wedding, just a little two bedroom-fixer-upper. When I bailed, Jack bought out my half of the down payment. Now it was something that he wasn't getting around to. He was stuck in a dream we'd housed together. Tears yanked somewhere behind my eyes, and I tried to tell myself that it was just exhaustion and stress. *Say something, you idiot.* "I'm . . . Thanks, Jack. That's . . ." Incredible. Honorable. Generous. Kind. *Loving.* I couldn't meet his eye. "I appreciate it."

"You pay gas and talk to Mallory about temporary insurance. Borrow it as long it takes you to get yours fixed." His eyes narrowed. "It's not charity, Kam. It's getting a wreck out of my way for a few weeks. At least, maybe you can think of it as a present for Jaxine. She's worried about you."

I shifted position, looking past him, out the window to the little dark gray pick-up truck. It was a bit battered and worse for wear, but it had a nice black canopy over the back . . . and I needed a ride. I sighed. "Tell you what? I'll rent it from you? Fifty dollars a week. Is that fair?"

"Seventy." Jack's smile was killer when he was humoring me. I hate that, too. "You can expense it if you use it for the business."

"Sixty."

"Done. Don't let Kenny borrow it."

"Never." *If I found him. If he was even* . . . My brain short-circuited before it could think the word "alive." I reached for the petty cash box in the cabinet behind my desk and found sixty dollars, which I counted out for Jack. "If I still need it next week, I'll pay you when I drop off the papers."

"It's all good. I trust you for it." Jack pocketed the cash and turned for the door. I took a second look at his backside. Ah. I mean . . . I checked to see if he was leaving footprints on the barren floor that would need cleaning up later.

"Jack, wait! How will you get back to your office?"

Jack paused on the threshold. "Oh, I'm meeting the guys over at Magillies on Main, Fisher'll drop me off after the game. Wanna come?"

"Football at the pub with the guys?" I tried to play it cool. Half of me was dying for a nice normal evening, hanging out, having a cider. A quarter of me was dying to spend an evening with Jack, and the last two eighths were warring between finding Kenny, and not risking breaking Jack's heart, or mine, ever again. "Nah, I think I'll give a miss. I've got a ton of work to plow through tonight."

"Baseball. Football doesn't start for a few weeks. It's the Mariners versus A's tonight." He fired another killer grin. "Baseball, chicken wings, and beer. If you change your mind, you'll be welcome." He paused. "I miss you."

Then he was gone, striding out the door, jaywalking across the less-than-busy street. I told myself that hating him so much was the reason I loved to watch him go.

CHAPTER 4

Monday Evening

I RESISTED THE URGE TO TAKE THE PICK-UP for a test-drive and walked across the street to Reese's Café for some dinner. Reese's Café is a two-story coffee-shop, serving pastries, sandwiches, and the usual selection of coffee drinks, teas and smoothies. I was working there as a sandwich maker when Charles hired me to be his legal secretary. It's my second home. Well, it would be my second home if I had a first home.

The after-work crowd mostly consisted of students meeting for study groups and workmates sharing a cup of tea after a long day. Hyperactive late-teen Max with his spikey hair and multiple piercings was working the counter, and behind him, I could see Reese at her small desk in the closet-sized space she called an office.

I settled my brief-bag at an empty table and came back to the counter. "Hey, Max. How's it been today?"

"Just iced drinks and blendeds today. No one wants a plain house roast in this heat." He raised a hand over the espresso machine and waited for my order.

"Iced vanilla latte and a tuna sandwich on rye."

"And a fruit cup!" Reese hollered from her desk. "You too damn skinny, girl! You need vitamins."

Reese is South Oakland tough. She doesn't pull punches.

"And a fruit cup." I acceded, before shifting the conversation back to what was on my mind. "Hey, Max? You remember my brother? About this tall? Looks like me, but more manly? Long hair, jeans and T-shirt?"

Max shook his head, his gelled black hair sticking up straight and stiff. "He the one that's always drawing stuff?"

"Yeah. He's an artist." At least, he was always drawing stuff. I wasn't sure what makes an artist, but it's probably something more than just carrying a sketchbook around. "He's making some kind of comic book, I think."

"Hasn't been in here in a while. Not in the evenings on my nights, anyway." Max shrugged and pulled my espresso. "Reese? You seen Kami's bro lately?"

"Can't say as I have." Reese stood up and leaned in the doorway. She wore her usual brown; brown slacks, brown polo shirt, brown apron. Her long black hair was tied back in a braid, making her narrow features look strict and hard. I knew from experience that if she lost the apron and put her hair down, she was Paris run-way gorgeous, but she once told me that she wanted to be remembered for hard work and honesty, not a pretty face. Something told me that being a pretty face had been a hard thing for her in the past. The only flash of color she wore was the red rose tattoo around her wrist. "Why? Something up?"

I explained shortly about my car.

"Need a loaner? The van's available." Reese pointed to the keys hanging from a thumbtack on the office bulletin board, and I winced inwardly.

"Nah. Got it covered. Thanks anyway." Thank you, Jack, for saving me from the green-striped monstrosity. "I'm just really worried about Kenny. I don't know what to think."

"You think he's officially missing? You want me to put up some fliers or something?" Reese gestured the board where Hannah Raye's picture now hung beside a much older one, Vivian Astor, who had gone missing at the end of last summer. A shiver went down my spine. *Vivian Astor, blond haired, blue eyed, smiling saucily into the camera.* Had anyone else noticed the similarities between her and Hannah? I couldn't remember the details of Vivian's disappearance. I'd have to look it up. I turned my attention back to Reese's question.

"No, not yet." I took my coffee and sandwich plate from Max. I lowered my voice, even though the café was quiet, and no one seemed to be listening. "The police are looking for him, too. I'm hoping to get to him first."

"Oh, lord." Reese rolled her eyes. "Please tell me it's our local force and not those Oakland city bad boys."

"San Amoro." I shrugged. "I'm sure Kenny didn't do anything wrong . . . I mean besides lose my car . . . but I'm worried."

I dug into my tuna salad sandwich. Not as good as if I made it—Max didn't cut the tomatoes thin enough. Or maybe Reese told him to try to force more vegetables into me. I'm the stray cat she keeps putting food out for. Reese came out and stood by my chair. "So, how's everything else going? Any clients?"

"Yeah. It's good," I mumbled around my mouthful of sandwich. Have I mentioned that Reese, in addition to baking the most incredible coffee cake on the planet, can also read me like a book? She whipped out the chair opposite me and straddled it, leaning on her elbows to stare at me with her brows raised.

"And . . .?" she prompted when I didn't answer right away.

"Okay. It's a wacky job, from a guy that's probably made out of wacky, but it's a job."

"Wacky? Is he the thin guy who walked over there earlier today? He was here with some friends. Three of those tech-types. Smart and strange, except for the really hot bro-grammer one. You know the type. Anyway, the skinny one scraped the icing off his iced gingerbread. I tend to notice that kind of thing." Reese looked around then back at me. If her eyebrows raised any higher, they were going to escape from her forehead. "Okay, spill. If it doesn't break confidentiality, of course."

"Um . . ." I pretended to chew for a long time. Reese tapped the tabletop until I swallowed and met her gaze. "Well, the guy thinks his house is haunted."

"And he wants to sue the people who sold him the house?"

"Um. Not exactly."

"He wants you to research property laws to see if he can sell it?"

"Nooooooo."

"He's . . . Oh, god. He wants you to find out if it's haunted for real?" Reese's giggle started low in her throat, and she did me the good grace of trying to swallow it down before it escaped.

I gave a miserable nod. "He misread my paralegal sign. He thinks it means paranormal. That my sign says paranormal research."

Reese was rocking back and forth as she struggled not to laugh. "And you told him yes? Yes? Are you out of your mind?"

"I'm out of my bank-book!" I tried to explain. "My car is destroyed, and until Jack and the lawyers can get Charles' finances settled . . ."

"Did you say 'Jack?' Jack as in *Jack*, not the guy you hate or your 'ex-boy', but just Jack?"

I glared across the table at Reese. "Can I eat my dinner in peace?"

"For now." Reese finally stopped sniggering, wiped tears of laughter from her eyes, and smiled. "As for the haunting thing, you've worked in an office with a haunted suit of armor for years. Ask Evrett to help you."

"Evrett is rarely helpful, and seldom communicative." But did I have any better suggestions? "Still, it can't hurt to try."

Reese had planted a good seed, and I actually felt better. I got a gingerbread (with icing that I didn't scrape off) to go and headed back to the office.

I UNPACKED MY SHINY NEW PARANORMAL INVESTIGATING GEAR and scanned through the instruction manuals, figuring out how it all worked. I ran around the office and took EMF and K2 readings until I felt comfortable with the tools and the terminology. The good news was that it didn't seem complicated. The bad news was that if I was reading the numbers right, I should probably have the wiring in the file room looked at by an electrician before it started a fire.

I didn't really believe Mr. Can't-Tell-A-Cat-From-An-Extraterrestrial had a haunting on his hands, but the key, I determined, was *reasonable doubt.* Right now, he was convinced the house was haunted. I was fairly certain it was no such thing. All I had to do was provide logical explanations until I provided him with enough evidence to produce reasonable doubt of his convictions.

I fed Hoover, scooped his litter box, put on sweat shorts and a tank top and hauled my laptop into the side office to stretch out on the sofa. I had a paper due on Friday, but that would have to wait. It was time to find my moron brother.

THE FIRST THING I DID WAS CHECK MY EMAIL: nothing from Dad, and only a brief note from Patrick saying he hadn't heard from Kenny in months. Nicky sent me Jude Booder's email address from the surf shop mailing list. Since I had long promised never to speak to Jude Booder again, I decided that a formal email constituted typing, not speaking . . . and this was urgent.

Email sent, I looked up the reservoir where my car was found on the internet. My car had about three-quarters of a tank when Kenny borrowed it. My Kia was an older model, so he probably had about two-hundred miles before he had to fill up. He could have gone anywhere. Why hadn't I bothered to ask what he needed my car for?

Messages sent, I stretched out on the sofa with my feet propped at one end and Hoover propped on the other, near my head where he could occasionally reach out and pat my curls playfully with one paw. But my mind wouldn't rest. The image of Vivian Astor, smiling at me, right beside Hannah Raye, her gaze too wise for her age, kept coming back to my mind.

I opened my laptop back up and typed Vivian Astor's name into a search engine. The California Missing Persons website immediately came up with her poster. What were the chances that they were connected? Aside from a similar appearance, what else did they have in common? Vivian disappeared in August of the previous year, last seen at a local restaurant with fellow nursing students; August, which was a year and a month before Hannah. Vivian had been a nursing student at Chabot College, only a few miles from Cal State East Bay. They were both students? She was 25 years old when she went missing.

Surely the cops were already all over this? I found a Facebook page Vivian's family had created and posted a brief note of speculation. Is it possible, could it be possible, that her disappearance was connected somehow to Hannah's?

Finally, I closed my laptop, turned off the light, and pulled the blue afghan over myself. Things would look better in the morning. They just had to.

Watching the shadows play on the wall in the now mostly-barren room, cuddling a purring Hoover on my chest, I lost track of time, and it eventually lost track of me. I drifted into sleep. Suddenly, I was riding my bicycle down an unfamiliar street that turned into a long dirt trail. My bicycle turned into a horse. I've never ridden a horse, but in my dream, I knew how. It was familiar, comfortable, something I did every day. I knew this horse. I was riding with others, and somehow, I knew them, too. The other riders flanked both sides of me, but I couldn't see them properly. My vision was occluded, segregated, everything divided into thin lines, like I was wearing Evrett's helmet.

Sound and chaos erupted around us, and I stood in the stirrups, unsheathing my sword, a practiced motion unmarred by hesitation or fear. I wheeled my mount with a steady hand, paying no mind to its snort of dismay. Screams filled my ears, ringing in the confined helmet. Stench of smoke and blood filled the air as I turned to face the enemy. *Too slow!* A cold steel blade pierced directly beneath the breastplate of my armor, crushing into my chest, steel rings of maille catching on my torn skin. I was falling backwards over the rump of the horse, pain turning to numbness as I landed on my back, staring up at gray, smoke-filled skies . . .

I woke with a scream and sat up, panting in the darkness. Not yet completely aware that the nightmare wasn't mine, I found myself reaching under my ribcage, feeling for the wound that wasn't there. The room felt heavy and cold around me, and Hoover was on the back of the sofa staring into space. Not my dream. Not my life. *Evrett.*

"That was rude!" I barked at Evrett. There was a sudden lifting of the air around me, as though the whole room seemed to grow brighter, though it was the middle of the night and even the streetlamps outside were dim and yellow.

I could feel the emotion of his thoughts like a hammer, a silent whisper at the back of my neck.

I sat in the darkness, listening with all of my senses, but everything had gone completely still. The cat was poised, ears pricked forward, so I addressed that empty spot warily. "So, what were you trying to tell me?"

Nothing. Only silence. Hoover ceased his vigil and curled up with his nose on his tail.

"Oh, for crying out loud, Evrett! Go away. I need to sleep." I burrowed back into the old blue afghan, squeezed my eyes shut, and was just starting to fall back asleep when a thought not my own slid to me through the darkness.

"Raise your visor, or you won't see the enemy."

I jerked upright, panting like a racehorse, uncertain I'd even experienced the words. Evrett had never done that—never spoken to me, not in words, not in thoughts, not in anything more than faint knocks on a recording. I found myself shivering and pulled the afghan tighter around my shoulders. *Had I imagined it? I knew I hadn't.* Raise my visor? What the heck was that supposed to mean? I lay awake after that, but if Evrett had something else to say, he never bothered to say it.

CHAPTER 5

Tuesday Morning

THE NEXT MORNING, I ROLLED OFF THE COUCH and started my day by checking my messages: no word from Jude Butthead Booder, no answer to emails to my brother. Phone calls to him no longer went to voicemail, but to a recorded message that the voice mail box was full. *Come on, Kenny, where are you?*

Out of ideas, I ran criminal and financial checks on Kenny, just in case. Maybe he'd gone out of state and gotten arrested doing something stupid—better arrested than missing, right? No arrests, no criminal record, not even bad credit; in fact, my loser brother's credit score was higher than mine. *Thanks, student loans.* I sent another email to Dad in India, checking the time difference. It was unlikely Dad would have heard from Kenny, but I felt some strange obligation to keep him in the loop. As uninvolved as he was in our lives, he was still our father. He should give a damn that his son was missing.

As long as I was pretending to work, I checked in with law firms that sometimes had contract work for me, but it seemed like there was a lull in the usually rampant litigation of the Bay Area. I reached out to Peter Oslo, senior partner of Oslo & Burroughs, to see if he knew of anyone needing help. He said they had a big estate escrow case coming up, but since it was mine, I wasn't allowed to work on it. I laughed, though I didn't feel like laughing, and Peter, kindly reassuring, promised me that everything was going to work out before he hung up.

There was nothing left to do but homework. I was only taking one class this semester, all I could afford, but it was civil law and working on my paper took all my focus. It was almost noon when a subtle roar sounded on the street outside, and I smiled in relief as Nicky's classic Mustang rolled up to the curb. It was a constant-project car, filled out with so many after-market and spare parts that we affectionally called it the Frankenstang.

Nicky was in a flowy print blouse, denim shorts, and leather sandals. She bebopped up the steps, her long black hair bobbing in a high ponytail. Just seeing her brightened my mood. Nicky might be a flaky surfer type, but she was pure joy in my life.

I grinned. "What about the wounded seal pup?"

"I didn't bring him with me. If you want to see him, you have to go by the rescue." Nicky laughed at her own joke. "Chrissa's taking my turn."

"I'm sure the little dude will miss you." I said consolingly. Then I pointed out my newly acquired ghost hunting gear and let Nicky play with everything.

"This stuff should all work. We're just doing baselines tonight, right?"

"That's the plan."

"Did you talk to Father Joe and Morri?" Nicky had done some investigating work with them since my last and only foray into the paranormal.

"No. But something weird happened last night with Evrett." I filled her on the bizarre dream and strange message. "He's never done anything like that before. I heard him, plain as day. Not archaic French on digital recordings, but more like he thought straight at me. I don't want to use the word psychic, but something like that. And the dream . . ." I shuddered. "I didn't think he remembered his death, but I lived it last night."

Nicky crossed over to Evrett, flipped on the K2 meter and pointed it at him. Nothing happened. "Well, I think he's asleep now. He said it in English, though? Last message we got was in French."

"It wasn't words, so much as . . ." I hesitated, not sure how to quantify it. "More like, just an idea. I don't know. I may have still been asleep, still dreaming. It may not have had anything to do with Evrett at all. I may have imagined the whole thing."

Nicky gave me a skeptical glance and didn't say anything else. She didn't need to.

"I'm keeping regular office hours," I warned her. "So, we're stuck here for a bit longer."

"Are you actually working, then?"

I looked at my empty desk. "Doing homework. And I'm trying to find Kenny."

"I still can't believe he ditched your car in the reservoir. What a little jerk!" Even Nicky seemed to think this was a step too far for Kenny.

"We don't know that yet. It may have been stolen." I muttered to Nicky what I would hardly admit to myself. "I want to go by his place before we head to the job. I'm worried. He may have been carjacked . . . he may be dead somewhere . . ."

"Or he may be just fine, hanging out at some artist commune in Marin or something, and totally forgot he even was driving your car."

I had to admit that sounded more like Kenny. After all, how many times had our mother told us we could be lying dead in a ditch somewhere, just because we forgot to call?

"You've never been dead in a ditch yet, have you?" Nicky knew my mother as well as I did—maybe even better. She abruptly changed the subject—another symptom of knowing my mother, I think. "Do we need burgers?"

"Maybe. And milkshakes."

"I'll be back in ten minutes."

Magillies on Main has great pub burgers but they don't travel well. Nicky came back with Five Guys burgers and fries. Protein, fat, and salt—pretty much the three mainstays of my diet if you don't count sugar and caffeine. Well-fortified, we loaded Jack's little Match Box-sized pick-up truck with my gear, locked the office, and headed across town to Kenny's last known address.

CHAPTER 6

Tuesday Evening

M Y BROTHER HAS A GOOD GIG, with free room and board in an apartment over a garage out on the bay side of Hayward in exchange for taking care of the property and looking after the elderly gentleman who owns the place. It's perfect for my brother, who never seems to be able to keep a job long enough to pay regular rent but can always be relied on for an odd job or two. The main house is palatial, the driveway wide, and the garage is a three-car affair. When we pulled up, the gate to the main house was closed, and the garage was dark. I climbed up the stairs that led to the door of the garage apartment and knocked, but there was no answer. Nicky had followed me up, reached out and gave the door handle a hard shake.

"Locked by the deadbolt." She leaned over and pressed her face to the small side-window. "I don't see anyone."

I pushed her aside and looked for myself. From what little I could see, the studio looked messy and occupied, but there were no signs of life. There was a pile of duffle bags, sleeping bags, and other gear on the floor near the door. "Maybe he went camping?"

"Or went on the run after he dumped your car, knowing you'd kill him." Nicky suggested. "Let's see if his landlord is home."

But the gate was locked, and the house looked empty. The lawn was green but didn't appear to have been mowed in at least a week, maybe more. I wasn't a lawn expert. Nicky clicked the intercom on the gate, but there was no answer from the house. "Weird. I thought Kenny said he was an invalid or something."

"He's not disabled, I don't think. He goes to Vegas a couple times a year, that kind of thing. Just needs extra help keeping up on things." I shrugged. "This is a bust. Let's get to work."

I was disappointed, but I guess I shouldn't have been. It seemed Kenny was really missing. Losing a fellow student was one thing, but how does one lose an entire brother? Mom was gonna kill me.

WE FOLLOWED NICKY'S PHONE'S GPS APPLICATION to Irvin Zettlemeyer's house. The day was still hot and muggy, and even though a low golden haze of pollution and pollen hung over the Bay, I caught glimpses of the San Mateo Bridge, and, across the glittering water, San Mateo's rising towers. The rich scents of warm eucalyptus and drying grass washed up the hills on the late afternoon breeze, and we rolled down the windows and breathed deeply.

The address Irvin had given me was on winding roads up the canyons outside of town. From the road, it didn't look like much. It could be any single-story home with front-side garage and parking. I pulled into the driveway and knocked on the front door.

Irvin opened the front door wearing a UC Berkeley sweatshirt. "Hey, you came!"

"Of course, we did." *Because we're crazy.* I gestured towards Nicky. "This is my associate, Nicky Gratz. She's our tech expert."

Nicky waved hello, but I don't think Irvin saw anything beyond her long, tanned, surfing-fit legs.

Irvin stood back to let us in. That's when it became obvious that the house was far more than it appeared from the roadside. As in, it was way-beyond-my-budget kind of amazing. Irvin gestured me past him into a vestibule, tastefully appointed with ornate Italian tile flooring, a high arched-beam ceiling, wrought-iron coat hooks, and marble benches. Beyond the vestibule was a grand open-floor-plan living room, dining space, and kitchen.

The floors there were hardwood, and the front wall consisted of arched pane-glass windows that offered a full view of the cities of Hayward and Fremont below, turning golden-orange in the coming sunset. Dominating the space was a circular stone fireplace. It was the kind of place that you stored away pictures of in files labeled Dream House, or When I win the Lottery. I wasn't going to win the lottery, and my dream house file had gone the way of my wedding to Jack, so instead of taking pictures, I found myself standing there with my jaw hanging open. Walking to the edge of the dining room, I realized that you could see out the full-wall windows and straight down for three stories. If you looked out, you could see all the way across the bay to the lines of traffic lighting the San Mateo Bridge, and beyond that, the twinkling lights of the Peninsula. From the road, the house looked small, but from downhill it must look palatial.

"Wow," was all I could think to say.

"This is off the chain!" Nicky was standing in front of the plate glass windows with her arms spread.

To the right, a stairway dropped down to another level, that, with beige carpeted floors and a hallway set with doors, looked more like a normal home.

"Yeah. It's cool, huh." Zettlemeyer seemed less nervous on his home turf but still wouldn't quite meet my gaze. He craned his neck, looking around me, and his voice was hushed as he muttered, "You didn't bring . . . the alien, did you?

Fish. Barrel. Why not? "He doesn't go out unless the planets are in the right alignment."

"Oooooh."

"Irvin, I'm teasing. He's just a cat." *Fish in barrels aren't as fun as they sound.*

"Oh." Did I detect disappointment in his tone? He pointed across the room. "Um. The others are in there."

"Lead the way." We followed him through the main room and kitchen area to a breakfast nook where, sitting on stools around a raised island, were the housemates. They were just as Reese had described, smart tech-types.

"Hey, you guys," Irvin said casually. "These are the researchers, Kami and Nicky."

"Robert Daltry, web systems engineer." Robert nodded to us and raised a few fingers in a half-wave. He looked to be in his mid-twenties, short, with close-cropped dark hair and a round face and round glasses that made him look even rounder. Web systems engineer meant he was smart, right?

"Fiora Espinoza. Everyone calls me Fi." The next one introduced herself. She had a thick Latino accent and even thicker brown hair that bushed out in huge waves around her head. She was wearing a bright tie-dyed printed T-shirt and bright pink sneakers. Her smile was friendly, but awkward, like she wasn't used to talking to strangers. I decided I liked her. "Thank you for coming,"

"Hi, Fi. Nice to meet you. . . . And you." I hesitated as my gaze met the deep brown eyes on the far side. Reese's hot bro-grammer description didn't cover it. He was taller than the others, probably six feet tall, topped with an extra three inches. His head was close-shaven and his eyes were molasses-sweet . . . and holy cow, he was handsome. Handsome in a why wasn't he on television kind of way—in a GQ photo-shoot kind of way—in the kind of way that I never would have stood a chance against if I hadn't sworn off men forever after leaving Jack. After leaving perfection, how could anything else compete?

HE STOOD UP AND EXTENDED A HAND ACROSS THE TABLE. The dark skin of his hand contrasted beautifully with the pale white of my fingers when I took it for a business-like shake, and his soft southern accent sounded like melted butter and his welcoming smile nearly melted something else, maybe my shoes. "Dillon Cheshire. Glad you could come."

"As to this ghost-thing, I keep tellin' these guys it's nothin'. They're imagining things, but hey, if it makes them feel any better, you should check it out. You want a cold drink?"

"No, thank you. Not while I'm working." And who could blame me if I smiled just a bit more broadly. Maybe this job wasn't as silly as it seemed on the surface. Nicky's elbow knocked firmly into my ribs. "So, you all work for the same company?"

"They own the house. We get low rent as a perk." Dillon confirmed. "I work systems security."

"For computers? Like firewalls and that kind thing?" What I know about how computers work could fit on a Post-It note. A real one with sticky stuff on the back, not the application that you can download for your smart phone.

He chuckled and I felt my face blaze. Darn my pale skin that pinked at the slightest inclination! Nicky's sandal connected with my ankle under the table. "Sort of. There's a bit more to it than that."

"So, you don't believe in ghosts?" Nicky spoke up, meeting his gaze directly, almost challengingly.

"Ghosts in the machine, maybe. Ghost code that doesn't know it's dead." Dillon chuckled again. "My guess is someone in the house is playin' tricks or something."

"It's not me!" Robert Daltry spoke up hastily.

"Not me." Fiora Espinoza chimed in.

Irvin just shifted uncomfortably in his chair, his pale gaze frank behind his rimless glasses. "I wouldn't have hired you if it was me, would I?"

I gave the anemic programmer a keen look. He couldn't have fooled a half-blind jury with a mad bias for computer geeks. I didn't think he could fool these guys, and certainly not me. "Believe me, I've seen stranger things."

FOR EXAMPLE, A RESPECTED PARALEGAL taking a paranormal research job when it was hardly her area of expertise. I stalled, pulling out my digital recorder and setting it up. Nicky picked up the digital camera and started snapping sets of images of the nearby spaces. "If it's okay with you, I'd like to record this interview. It helps me keep things straight later." I hesitated, letting my eyes scoop up towards the track-lighting fixtures above. "And you never know when activity might be captured on recorder that isn't apparent at the time."

I'd gotten that from one of the paranormal websites. Many of them had entire lists of advice, tips and equipment, and most of it made sense to me. Sasquatch-hunting pointers excluded: Most of those tips seemed to have been made up by a lunatic. Except the part about carrying a compass. Everyone should carry a compass. I had one in my duffle bag, just in case.

They all nodded, but Dillon held up his hand, hovering his fingers briefly over my little digital recorder. "I'd like it in writing that this is confidential, used strictly for the investigation? Not put out on YouTube or one of those fringe fake news sites?"

"Absolutely. Everything that happens here falls under client confidentiality," I agreed immediately, kicking myself for not having thought of that before. "If, after this interview, you no longer desire my services, we'll erase the recording with all of us in evidence. If you do want me to continue the investigation, I'll have proper confidentiality contracts drawn up and delivered tomorrow."

The four housemates exchanged glances. Dillon looked skeptical. Fiora looked relieved. Robert looked contemplative. Irvin seemed to be on the verge of a nervous break-down. So, nothing new there.

They agreed and we continued. I glanced at Nick to see if she wanted to add anything, and then leaped in and started asking all the standard questions, or, at least, what I assumed standard questions should be, knowing she would reign me in if needed. I figured the "what" and the "where" were important, but I skipped the "who" part, since if they knew who they wouldn't be calling me.

"Which doors open and close?"

They exchanged another look, one that said, 'You show her. No, you. No, you do it.' Dillon finally stood up. "Come on. I'll show you what they're talking about."

He led me down the corridor, the other three trailing behind, muttering not-so-quietly to each other, and down the stairs to the second floor. Nicky followed in the back, continuing to take still pictures of the entire space.

"These are the bedrooms. This side," Dillon's fist knocked the wall, "is against the hillside. The bedrooms all face the view and there's an external balcony running the length."

"This is my room." Fiora opened a door onto a messy bedroom full of colors so bright that they made my eyes hurt. If yellow could be arrested for assault, I was pretty sure Fiora's room was on a suspect list. How did she manage to sleep in there? "My closet is wall to wall with Robert's closet."

"Love the décor!" Nicky enthused. I knew she meant it, bless her bohemian heart.

"We'll both leave the house with our closet and bedroom doors closed." Robert explained, not quite meeting my eye. "But when we get back, our closet doors will be open. Sometimes, I'll leave the closet open, go upstairs, get a drink, come back down and the door will be closed again."

"May I?" I opened the closet door, closed it again. I pushed on it, pressed it back and forth to see how heavy it was. No breeze or passing truck might have shifted it. Nicky photographed the door and the hinges and made a note on her yellow pad. "Do you ever leave the balcony door open? Or the window?"

Robert walked to the sliding-glass balcony door and pushed it open. "Air pressure? We thought of that. It happens both when the doors are open and closed. We've tested it."

Of course, they'd tested it. Geeks and science were like chocolate and ice cream. I tried not to sigh aloud as I pressed my hand around the inside of the closet, thinking that space between boards could be causing pressure. If Robert opened his door and Fiora closed hers, there could be counter-pressure. But the closets were dry-walled and then lined with cedar planking with no vents or other openings that I could see.

I took the notepad from Nicky and let her walk around Fiora's room, doing EMF readings and telling me the numbers, which I added to the roughly drawn map on her notepad. They spiked a little around the computer on the desk, but I figured that was to be expected, even for as little as I know about electro-magnetics. Nicky glanced over at me. "Everything seems to be normal right now."

We moved on.

Robert's room was unexpectedly tidy and organized. Even the clothes in his closet were sorted by color, with the exception of what I took to be a large collection of Renaissance costuming. There were long cloaks, doublets, fancy gold-trimmed jackets. I wondered how much of it was similar to what Evrett might once have worn. Not much of it looked authentic. As I checked the closet for leaks and made notes on the ease of pushing the door open and closed, I tried a polite, "Nice cloak."

"The blue? Or the green? The green is for my elf costume, for LARP."

"Larp?" I knew I was going to regret asking. I was trying to imagine the short round systems engineer as an elf. Nicky was holding the EMF reader in front of her face to hide her grin. I was too far away to elbow her.

"Live action role play. Rob's really into it." Irvin filled in as I continued circling around the room with the EMF detector. Nicky followed me, recording the numbers, but her bottom lip was between her teeth and it was obvious she was trying not to laugh.

"Live action? You mean you dress up and play role playing games? Like Dungeons and Dragons?"

Robert cleared his throat, and Irvin nodded. "A little like that, yeah."

"Fun hobby," I tried to say with a straight face. "Maybe I should try it some time."

"Really?" Robert scooted up to my left elbow. "Do you like Elves? We have a whole Elvish clan war going right now in Greenwood Adventures. I also do Vampires of Darkness twice a month and a Steampunk airship thing on Fridays. Steampunk might be more your speed. Here, read these and see what you think?"

He pushed two hand-stapled, ink-jet printed booklets at me. "If you think you might want to come, call me!"

Out of the corner of my eye, I saw Dillon in the doorway, shaking his head, laughter on his lips. Nicky looked like she was about to explode in hysteria.

"Thanks. I'll look into it." I tucked the pamphlets into the pocket of my duffle bag and changed the subject as swiftly as possible. "Now, where else are you having activity?"

They led us through the house step by step. Nicky took more EMF readings and I scribbled more notes along the way. The bottom floor of the house overlooked a small, sloped garden area with a brick patio and a hot tub. The floor itself consisted of three rooms divided by arched doorways. The last one had double French doors with heavy drapes, and its own shower and entrance from the outside; a self-contained granny unit. This was Dillon's room, since he was a consultant and not a direct employee of the company.

Of the other rooms, one was an ad-hoc library with plush chairs, Ikea bookshelves and walls hung with framed comic books—collectors editions, most probably, but I had no idea. You'd have to ask my brother—that is, if you could find him. There were also 1980s movie posters, things like *Breakfast Club*, *Short Circuit* and *Predator*.

"Whoa! Those are the originals!" Nicky squealed as she studied the posters. "Not duplicates. How'd you score those?"

"This is the hang-out room. It has a quiet clause," Irvin told her, pointing to the sign tacked to a bookshelf.

This room is for reading and relaxation. Please keep noise to a minimum, and if you must use electronics, use headphones.'

"We think that's why can hear the crying down here, even when you can't hear it anywhere else. It's quiet." Robert added, and behind him, Fiora nodded. Behind them, Dillon leaned nonchalantly against the stairwell frame, and Irvin slouched with his hands crushed together in front of him, looking terrified.

Nicky was already taking EMF readings, with nothing out of the ordinary that I could tell, but I wasn't an electrician. "It's supposed to spike around the stereo like that?"

Nicky nodded. "You guys might want to check your power strip back here and replace it."

Fixing their electrical issues wasn't our job. I turned to Fiora. "Tell me about the crying."

Fiora shook her head. "It's just a woman. It sounds far away, but very afraid."

"Not 'wah boohoo' kind of crying." Irvin agreed, nodding vigorously. "It's scary. Hopeless sounding. Like nothing you've ever heard."

"I have heard like it before," Fiora insisted quietly. "When I was a little girl, political activists bombed a federal building. My school was on the same street and we saw everything. There was a woman standing in the street, covered in blood, flames all around, and she was crying. Hopeless and afraid. Like this crying."

I'd heard horrible stories taking depositions before, but Fiora's forced me to take a deep swallow. We forget, I think, how lucky we are here in the United States, where political activists can march openly in the streets instead of bombing public buildings in direct view of children to make their point.

"Is there a particular time that you hear it? I mean, could someone be watching TV elsewhere in the house? Could it be coming from another room? Or even from a neighboring house."

"Wait here." Robert waved to me to sit down, which I did, then he ran back upstairs. A moment later, the intercom near the sliding glass door to the balcony beeped. "My TV is on half-volume. Can you hear it at all?"

I got up and wandered around the room, then into the next room, a geek-room full of computer equipment. I shook my head, and Irvin pressed the intercom button and reported, "Nope, can't hear a peep."

"Okay, three quarters volume."

Nothing.

"Full volume." The background noise over the intercom nearly drowned out Robert's voice but downstairs it was still quiet.

"Okay, so maybe not the TV." I jotted down a note, knowing that I wanted to test that for myself.

There was a long pause and footsteps on the stair, receding, then the intercom again, "Okay, I'm in the kitchen and I'm turning on the stereo system."

We went through the same routine: half volume, three quarters volume, full volume. On full volume, you could just hear the bass-beats of the quality sound system, but not the melody, if there even was a melody.

It shut off suddenly and Robert's voice came back through the intercom, "Ow. I'm deaf now. Could you guys hear anything?"

"Barely," I answered back. "How does the intercom system work? Could it be someone playing games with the com?"

"You'd hear it." Dillon pushed the intercom button, a solid beep emitting. "There's one on every floor. Kitchen, balcony hall, and down here by the patio. It beeps whenever you open a connection, whether you call all of 'em, or just one. You hear the beep, then the voice. If someone was messing around with it, you'd hear the beep."

"Thought you were a naysayer?" I gave the Dillon a small frown, wondering if he didn't have some kind of agenda of his own.

"Oh, I am. Don't believe we've got ghosts. But when they told me about the crying, my first thought was someone screwing with the coms. I've been all over it with a fine-toothed comb, but if one of us is messin' with it, I can't figure it out."

"Well, then, that makes two of us." My frown turned upside down. I didn't believe that Dillon was messing with his roomies. For one, they weren't exactly easy targets. They were technical people, with their heads grounded in code and mathematics and science. Sure, they might like a good monster movie, to judge by the collection in the DVD cabinet, and at least one of them liked to play elves and dragons or whatever, but they were the kind of people who troubleshoot and resolve, not blow things out of perspective.

Well, maybe Irvin, I revised silently. But cats can be pretty alien, can't they?

"Make it three," Nicky consulted her notes one more time, then fired a raised eyebrow at Dillon. "I don't see how it can be someone playing a trick, unless all of *you* are involved and *we're* the victims? Is this a prank on the ghosthunters?"

"No! Of course not," Irvin squeaked. The others all shook their heads.

Nicky kept her stare on Dillon. "Then I think you guys might have a problem."

We traipsed back upstairs.

Nicky pointed up the stairwell. "What about lifts? Dumbwaiters? Anything like that?"

They all shook their heads. "Stairs are the only way up and down, unless you want to climb the balcony."

I stepped onto the balcony and looked down—and instantly closed my eyes and stepped back inside. There was no way someone could climb that modern glass and steel façade—not unless they were some super-climber, the kind who scales the Empire State Building for publicity stunts. I glanced at Nicky, and she shook her head.

"No way. No one's going in or out that way."

"So, what do you think, Nick? Full investigation?"

She shrugged and glanced around the room. "I think there may be something here."

"Agreed." I wasn't sure if I agreed or not, but Nicky had more experience in ghost hunting than I did. I turned to our clients with a brief smile. "We can't really say yet whether or not your house is haunted, but we think it warrants a full investigation. That means spending an entire night here with cameras, sound equipment, etcetera. You four can be in the house when we investigate, but to keep contamination to a minimum, we'll need to all plan to be in the same rooms at the same times."

"Saturday?" Irvin suggested, looking at the others.

They all nodded, except Dillon. "I'll be climbing in Yosemite, so it doesn't matter to me."

"Saturday it is, then. We'll send over the confidentiality agreements and contract tomorrow by courier. In the meantime, I'm going to do some research on the house itself."

"What kind of research?" Dillon wanted to know.

"Property records. When it was built, who the owners have been, the blueprints if I can get them. Whether anyone died here."

"Do you think someone died here?" Fiora seemed disturbed by the question—possibly a cultural thing?

I smiled reassuringly. "We don't know and knowing is half the battle."

"We'll look into all the options," Nicky added, waving her notepad. "We'll get to the bottom of things. Don't worry."

We shook hands all around, and me with Dillon last. "Thanks for all your help."

"Don't mention it. Have a good night."

But he was still holding my hand.

"Right, then, thanks. We'll be going."

"Night." His voice was as warm and sweet as a Louisiana bayou evening, but without the mosquitoes.

Nicky grabbed my elbow and yanked. Somehow, I managed to let go of his warm fingers and turn towards the door. I even managed to get it open and escape out into the cool night air, sucking in the breeze sweeping up the hill from San Francisco Bay, heavy with eucalyptus pollen and the last of the summer jasmine. It was better than a lot of things the wind off the bay could smell like this time of year, believe you me.

"Could you be any more obvious?" Nicky pushed me towards the pick-up. "Geez."

"Oh, c'mon. It was a just handshake. And you gotta admit, he's cute."

"He's a computer nerd. I bet he's never been on a surfboard in his life. Prob'ly a total barney." If they didn't know a cutback from a reverse, they weren't worth Nicky's time.

"And the last thing I need is another man in the picture." I rolled my eyes.

"Another? So, Jack is in the picture?"

I pointed to the neon lights ahead. "Oh, look! Taco Rico is still open. And it's Tuesday."

Nicky fired a glance across the car at me. "Tuesday two-dollar tacos are not going to get you out of this."

"If I buy, they might." I pulled into the taco shop, and Nicky didn't mention Jack again; Tuesday two-dollar tacos for the win.

CHAPTER 7

Tuesday Night

I PARKED THE TRUCK IN THE ALLEY behind the office. Nicky promised she'd call me in the morning and took off to spend time with the injured seal. I locked my gear in the back of the pick-up, under the canopy, unlocked the back door of the building and went through from the maintenance hallway. Strange, how one's perspective changes when seeing through the eyes of ownership. Suddenly, things bothered me that I'd never noticed before, things I'd taken for granted. Leaving old paint cans in a maintenance corridor probably wasn't a good idea, and those unshielded light bulbs were probably some kind of building code violation. Building codes—one more thing to research and follow up on. My list was growing long, and my bankroll was increasingly short, but I didn't dare give any excuse for Juliet to report any kind of violations against me.

I unlocked the fire door through to the file room and made my way to the front office. A shadow shifted outside the front window. There was someone outside. My heart skipped a beat, and I flattened my back against the wall. I'd heard Nicky's FrankenStang rumble off, so I knew it wasn't her. I edged into the front office and stared towards the front window. All I could see was an outline, masculine, framed by the streetlights. I reached for my cell phone and had the nine pressed and was reaching for the one as I called in low warning, "Who's there?"

I was seconds from hitting the last number when the shadow spoke up, moving in front of the door to peer through the glass. A shiny badge pressed to the glass. "Detective Ron Brittle, San Amoro Police Department. I'm looking for Kamera White."

He still said my name wrong. I instantly lowered my phone lest he think it was a weapon of some sort. "Oh! Sorry, Detective." I unlocked the office door, switched on the light, and gestured him through. "It's kind of late for detecting, isn't it?"

He smiled, not too politely. "I'm afraid I need to ask you to come with me. There's been a complication with your car."

I dropped my canvas shoulder-bag on the chair and assessed the detective. My superpower for trouble-detecting nudged my next words. "When you say complication, what exactly do you mean?"

"That's all I'm at liberty to say right now."

"Uh, am I under arrest? And if so, what for?" Now that I could see Brittle in the warm yellow light of the office, I had to revise my earlier impression from our phone conversation. He was much younger than I'd imagined; handsome in a tired, receding-hairline law-enforcement kind of way, thirty-something with light hair, crystal blue eyes and nice even teeth that showed when he smiled at me . . . and it was a nice smile, not a mean one. Where I'd pictured a worn older detective in a black suit, he was lean and athletic look-ing, and wore simple black slacks and a blue polo shirt. Without the badge and gun belt, I would never have pegged him for a cop.

"You aren't under arrest. We just need to ask you a few questions."

A few questions. Working for Charles, I'd heard that line a few times directed to our clients. I instinctively glanced to Evrett, but my ghost-knight in shining armor was silent. "Do I need a lawyer?"

"Do you think you need one?"

"Doesn't matter what I think. I'm calling one."

I DIALED REGINALD BURROUGHS FROM THE BACK SEAT of Detective Brittle's unmarked police sedan, and he met us at the station, his Tesla easing into the police lot just behind the detective's car.

"The back seat?" were the first words out Reggie's mouth as he raised his eyebrows. Reginald Burroughs is one of those people that you don't believe exists until you meet him. Oxford educated, law degree from Stanford, he is drop-dead handsome. Despite the late hour, his perfectly tailored suit hung pressed from his tall sturdy frame. His dark hair, with just a smattering of silver at the temples, was waved back from his tanned forehead in elegant perfection, and the faintest hint of a Welsh accent still clung to his voice after over a decade in America. Reginald Burroughs is also unfailingly gay. He's a bit like a special rainbow edition George Clooney. Reggie is the criminal defense expert of Oslo & Burroughs, and his team was the best in the East Bay. I was desperately hoping I didn't need his help.

Detective Brittle did not look happy to see him. "That's where everyone rides."

"I think there's probably a higher chance of surviving an accident back there," I suggested, more to mollify Reggie than for Brittle's benefit. I was feeling confident. Whatever was going on with my car, whatever reason I was being dragged in for questioning in the middle of the night, I was pretty sure I could handle. I've been in a few interrogation rooms, watched the technique as they've tried to get a client to slip and admit something they'd already denied, so I thought I was ready, despite my confusion at being called in at all. I had confidence that I'd done nothing wrong, and with Reginald Burroughs at my side, I was confident that the police couldn't pull anything over on me.

But once we were in the interrogation room with his partner, a somewhat wobbly-looking older detective named Detective Dortman, Detective Brittle's first words ripped my breath from my lungs and stole my ability to think.

"We found a body in your car."

A million immediate responses raced through my mind, but the brain only has so many synapses and the mouth can only form so many words. It homed in on the most important. "Kenny!"

"It's not your brother. The body is a woman . . ."

"Oh god. Not Hannah Raye . . ." I choked.

They both looked sharply at me. Brittle glanced at his notes, and then at his partner, not meeting my eye. "Why would you ask if it was Hannah?"

I gulped, realizing that if I wasn't in the hot seat of suspicion before, I'd just firmly placed myself there. "We're taking the same class at East Bay. She's missing. If there's a body . . ."

Rather than reassure me, Brittle kept his focus. Kudos to the cop. "Miss White, can you please explain to us why there might be a body in the trunk of the car you claim your brother borrowed from you?"

"Of course I can't! Omigod, there's some stranger's body in my car?" I was going to vomit. No, really, I was sure of it. I started scanning for a garbage can. "Whose is it? Where's my brother?"

"We're the ones asking the questions," Brittle said quietly, but his eyes strayed to Reggie, who patted my shoulder in a calming gesture. Reggie was good at calming gestures, and Brittle brought the line of inquiry back into focus. "What day did you loan your car to your brother?"

"August twenty-eighth. I remember because I had a hearing that morning. I had him meet me at the courthouse in Hayward and drop me off."

"And that was the last time you saw your car and your brother?"

"Yes." I handed Brittle my cellular phone, a base model that came free with my calling plan. "You can check my call logs. I've been calling him almost every day, but his voice-mail is full."

"And you weren't worried that your brother is missing?" Detective Dortman interjected. He looked like he'd watched too many of those shows where they depict the cops as gray-haired, overweight, incompetent chain-smokers, and then deliberately emulated it to the extreme.

I glanced at him with a tired glare, mentally attempting to rear-range his name into a nasty anagram. It didn't work. I'd already been having a weird week, and it just kept getting weirder. I felt Reggie inhale slowly beside me, a tacit method of his to remind me to do the same. It worked.

"Not until you called to tell me you found my car," I admitted with a sigh. "Look, my good friend, my employer, died suddenly

this summer. He left me as his beneficiary but there's a dispute over
the will. I've been trying to take care of the business, manage his
affairs, and keep my head above water while still remembering to
eat, drink and sometimes sleep. My brother has never exactly been
Mr. Reliable. Once, he took off across country on foot, hitchhiking,
and we didn't hear from him for four months. That I haven't heard
from him didn't worry me. That I had things to do and didn't have
my car worried me."

"But let me be clear." I paused, meeting both detective's gaze
with candor. "I am worried now. Very worried."

"Do you know this woman?"

Oh, I'd been expecting it, but it was still a shock. The picture
was an eight-by-ten shot of head and shoulders, a print-off from a
digital camera. The lady in it was very much dead. She'd also been
in the water a few days if I had to guess. She had that kind of puffy
and waterlogged look that my goldfish had when it died while I
was in India visiting my dad and didn't find it until I got home. Her
eyes were shut, sunken back into the sockets and she had blond
hair, dyed with streaks of blue and silver. The dead woman, not my
goldfish. My fish was orange.

"Reservoir must be cold," I muttered.

"Excuse me?"

I couldn't break my gaze from the not-so-glam shot on the
table. "I mean, she doesn't look very decayed. Either the reservoir
is cold, or she wasn't in it very long."

"Just answer the question," Detective Dortman snapped. "Do
you know her?"

Yes, sir, Mister Doorknob. Somehow, I managed to keep that
response silent as I studied the picture a moment longer. She
had thick pale brown eyebrows and a tousle of blond hair shot
through with dyed silver and blue strands that suggested she
was something of a wild child. There was a tattoo on her neck,
black ink. Was that a dragon? An eagle? The shape was familiar somehow, but I couldn't recall where I'd seen it. She had a
wide jawline, but it was hard to guess her weight for how puffy
she looked. "No," I said finally, when I was ninety-nine percent

sure I had no idea who she was. "I don't think I've ever seen her before now."

"You don't *think* so?" Brittle asked, and I revised my opinion of him from a nice cop to an annoyed cop, and probably one who could be vicious when annoyed—like an angry Rottweiler.

"No, I don't think so. She's not familiar to me, but I don't think she looked quite so bloated and, well, dead, when she was alive. Do you?" I growled, and felt Reggie's hand on my shoulder, chilling me out. It mostly worked. "Look, I'm a paralegal. I do research, background checks, take depositions, interview witnesses. I'm a student at Cal State. I meet thousands of people. I could have run across her, seen her maybe at court, or on campus, or at the cafe. I could have seen her, well, pretty much anywhere. I don't have a good memory for faces, and that picture probably doesn't look much like when she was alive." My voice was raising slowly in frustration and I gave up trying to rein it in. "So, while I'm pretty darn sure I have no idea who she is, that doesn't mean that I haven't seen her. I'm not going to say that I've definitely never seen her before in my life because I don't need you jamming me up later over some stranger that I may have served a nonfat decaf latte at Reese's five years ago."

Brittle and Detective Dortman stared at me. I stared right back. Cops are experts at the stare-down. I have a kid brother and I live with a cat. I was a pro. These detectives had nothing on me—at least in the staring department, anyway.

"Right." Brittle sank down into his chair. The good cop had returned. "Okay. Let's all just take a step back here for a minute. No one's trying to jam you up, Kami. We want the same thing you want. We all want to know who that woman is and how she got in your car."

Reginald spoke up for the first time, and I sat back and let the legal expert do his legal thing. "I think we're done here for now, Detectives. My client was not in possession of her car when the victim was associated with it. She has no knowledge of her brother's whereabouts, and no knowledge of your victim. I'm taking my client home."

"To work," I corrected calmly. "When the good detective decided he needed to question me, I was working. Now I'm even further behind."

"I don't think I need to tell you not to go far?" Detective Brittle asked, and by the twinkle in his eye I could tell he meant it as tongue-in-cheek. He knew I didn't have anywhere to go—unless I called Dad for a ticket to India. Dad would love that. He knows dozens of eligible bachelors associated to the pharmaceutical company he worked for in the Sikkim Himalaya that he'd love to introduce me to. *Hmmm.* If it came down to a choice between going to jail or fleeing to Dad, jail sounded really good.

"And I was so looking forward to a Caribbean cruise, too." I gestured my cellphone, still lying on the table where he'd set it down. "You have my number. And you know where I work."

"Where are you living? Your landlord said you'd moved." Detective Dortman's smile was tight, like a rubber-band wanting to bust. "That doesn't look good on your part."

"Neither would defaulting on my rent and being evicted. If I'm not at my office, I'll be at my . . ." *Ugh* . . . I didn't want to say the words, "my mother's" and fortunately I didn't have to.

Reginald, apparently, thought that I was going to look homeless and irresponsible. "Oslo and Burroughs accepts responsibility for her," he said crisply, writing an address on his notepad, ripping off the page, and sliding it across to Brittle. "She'll be at our property in Alameda."

I started to protest. I wasn't some delinquent! But Reggie gave me a warning glance and I shut up. One thing working for a lawyer taught me is that if a lawyer suggests you not say anything, it's probably in your best interest to keep your mouth shut, no matter how much you wanted to tell a couple of pompous-faced detectives exactly what they could do with their batons. And that desire was growing more graphic and detailed in my mind by the second.

The detectives exchanged glances and Brittle stood up. "Well, I think we're done here. For now, at any rate."

"Not quite," I said, breathing through my nose and holding up a palm to stop Reggie before he could stop me. "What are you doing to find my brother? I'm hunting for him myself, but I want to know what you're doing?"

"We're . . . ah . . . putting all of our resources into . . ." Brittle's partner started.

"Into dragging me in here to show me pictures of a dead girl. Who is clearly not my brother."

"Kami, please . . ." Reginald's tone was both cajoling and despairing. One glance at him was enough to hold my tongue. Face it—Reggie could use that sweet accent to tell me to walk across a path full of poisonous snakes, and I'd do it—in strappy high heels if he wanted. I just like snakes, I guess.

"Keep us apprised of whatever you find, and we'll keep you apprised of our discoveries," Brittle said quickly. "Sorry for the inconvenience but please understand that we have to follow procedure."

I tried to make my "Thank you, Detective," as heart-felt as possible before Reginald steered me out of the room. He was stopped by Detective Dortman's raised hand.

"You said you knew Hannah Raye?" the detective asked.

I paused, drawing back to meet his thick-lidded gaze, a churning in my stomach as I registered what he said. "Detective, you just said 'knew', not 'know.' Are you telling me that Hannah is dead?"

He froze, his gaze suddenly finding interest in the tabletop. "I didn't say that."

"But that's what you meant. Past tense." My stomach hit rock bottom.

Detective Brittle stepped in, his voice low, crystal blue eyes softened with empathy. "I'm sure you know how it works, Miss White. The first twenty-four hours are critical, and . . ."

". . . And law enforcement didn't start looking until after forty-eight, because that's how long it takes them to get involved with a missing adult." I conceded, sorrow thick where there should have been anger. "I get it. Most missing adults are gone of their own recognizance." They jump on buses in their wedding gowns and disappear until common sense returns. I knew all about that. But Hannah went missing from the University parking lot, a public place, a place I walked myself late at night. "Now the trail is cold. And if we find Hannah, we aren't going to like what we find. That's what Detective Dortman is saying."

Detective Brittle looked pained. It was easy to see that he'd been on the wrong side of the forty-eight-hour policy in the past.

"To answer your question," I shifted to face Detective Dortman head on, even though Reggie shook his head slightly. "Hannah is in the law program at Cal State East Bay, the same as I am. I'm a returning student, and mainly take night classes. Hannah is a full-time student, but she's trying to finish in three years, and some night classes fit her schedule. I saw her in class, and she was on my project team for legal debate class last semester. Yes, I know Hannah. It could just as easily be me who didn't make it home from class. So, no, I'm not giving up on finding her alive."

"Neither are we," Brittle reassured quickly, but Dortman hesitated, heaving himself out of the small plastic chair to come around the table.

"I'm just wondering if you think it's just random coincidence that your car turns up with a dead woman in it, and you go to school with another missing woman. That's a pretty big coincidence."

"My car wasn't at the school when it ended up in the reservoir, and as far as I know, the woman in the trunk is a stranger. So yes, it's a coincidence." I shrugged, but all three men were looking at me now with strange eyes, something I couldn't quite put my finger on.

"Come on, I'll drive you back to the office." Reggie rested a hand on my shoulder and steered me out the door. Once out of earshot of the detectives, he started his own interrogation. "What are you doing for a car? Where are you really planning on staying? What efforts have you made to find your brother?"

"Gee, Dad. I'm over eighteen," I drawled. That earned me a stern glare from Reggie and I relented nearly instantly. "I'm borrowing a car from Jack Austin, and I'm staying at the office for the most part. It's got everything I need. Besides, I have to take care of Hoover."

"I think you're probably violating half-a-dozen zoning laws staying there. You need to use the Alameda safe-house for now."

"Safe-house?" I came to a halt at the door of Reggie's black Model S Tesla. "What do you mean, safe-house?"

"Safe house. A place that is safe," he answered calmly. "You know my firm represents a variety of people; ex-gang members, rape victims, government officials; the kind of people who some other people wouldn't mind seeing dead. We have several apartments all over the Bay Area that we use as havens for them during their trials. And since you have no idea who that was in the trunk of your car, and since you take the same classes as the missing woman, I think I would feel better if you were safe."

"Not so safe of a house now, is it? Brittle and Detective Dustbrains know all about it! As far as I can tell, they're the only ones trying to get me. They'd love a murder charge, but I bet they'll settle for obstruction."

"So stop obstructing them. And it's Detective Dortman. He's a bulldog, don't antagonize him." Reggie opened my door and ushered me in, sliding the seatbelt out and putting the clasp in my hand. It was cold and I buckled it in as quickly as possible. He waited for me to pull my bag into my lap. "They've never leaked on one of my clients before, why should they start now?"

I groaned. "Because they're in communication with my mother."

He laughed and slid my door shut, then strode around to his side and hopped in, smoothly starting the engine and fastening his belt at the same time.

As he drove me back to the office, the Model S rolling quietly along the late-night streets, Reggie kept up a running stream of commentary. Come by the office and he'd give me keys tomorrow. Make sure to take different routes to and from places so I couldn't be followed. Leave a front light on in the office at all times so no one thought it was empty. Call my mother and call the police department at least every couple of days, if not every day. Stay in touch with the people around me. Let people know where I was and what I was doing. Don't open the door to strangers. Did I need a loan or was I okay for money?

"I'm fine. I picked up a research contract tonight." I hesitated to say more, but added casually, "It's an easy job."

"Do you have a weapon in the office?"

"What?" I started at Reggie. A weapon? "No! Of course not. You know the stats on weapons being used against you, right?"

"My thought exactly. So, if you do have a weapon, keep it handy, where you can get to it first, and don't hesitate to use it. You know all the legalities, so I won't expound on them."

"No weapon!" I said again.

Reggie glanced across the seat at me. "Kiddo, I think you're missing the point here. Your car turned up with a body in it."

"Yeah. I know!" Boy howdy did I ever know.

A traffic light flickered red, and Reggie slowed to an easy stop, his eyes on the road in front him. "Think about it. Your car. Woman dead in the trunk. One of your classmates is missing. What if there's a serial killer out there? What if that was supposed to be *you* in your trunk?"

I felt my breath catch in my throat, and I stared out at the night street, turned ghastly yellow in the streetlamps, brushed pink by the red traffic light. That's what that look meant. The two detectives and my lawyer, back there under the bright fluorescent glare of the precinct lights had suddenly seen me, not as a suspect, not as a potential witness, but as a potential victim. "No. No way."

"So, I'm asking you again. Do you have a weapon in the office?"

"Well, there's Evrett's sword."

"I don't suppose you know how to use it?"

"Point the sharp end away from me?" For some reason, Reggie wasn't as amused as I was by my answer. He changed the subject.

"How'd you manage to keep that metal behemoth out of Juliet's sight, anyway? I'd have thought it would be the first thing she took."

I grimaced, remembering how Charles' sister had cleaned out the office the day after his funeral. "I hid him in the shower and then told Juliet the toilet was backed up and overflowing."

Reggie was still laughing when he dropped me off, after circling the block twice and checking the rear-view mirror. I was starting to wonder how I'd never noticed before that Reggie was paranoid.

I was so tired when Reggie dropped me off that I went directly in through the front door of the office, put down half a can of wet food for an unhappy and ungrateful Hoover, and squeezed into the shoebox-sized shower, where I stayed until I felt the slime of the police station was rinsed away.

I pulled on sweats, made a cup of one of my mother's herbal teas, a chamomile-laden concoction labeled "Calming Bliss", and curled up on the sofa in what I really needed to stop thinking of as being Charles' office. The tea did nothing to calm my thoughts or turn them from worry to bliss.

Sleep wasn't a sure thing. Hoover was feeling neglected and either perched on the far arm of the couch, attacking my feet whenever they moved, or on the near arm, batting at my hair to make my curls sproing around. When I growled at him, he did his crazy kitty sprint, tearing through the whole office before leaping up on the couch to start all over again. Lying there alone, I noticed the sounds of the traffic outside for the first time. Cars were a late-night scarcity on our business-district side-street, so when one went by, I found myself jolting awake and not relaxing again until I could see the lights fading against the far wall, the engine sounds fading in the distance.

Some freaked out part of my brain that I tried hard to ignore kept galloping around, repeating over and over what Reggie had said about weapons. I finally crawled off the couch, tiptoed out to the main room, and wriggled Evrett's sword from its decorative sheath. The sword wasn't original to the armor suit, so I didn't think he'd mind, but I whispered a quick, "Sorry, Ev. Can I borrow this?"

I took his lack of response as approval and slipped back to the couch, tucking the sword under the edge, within easy reach. Somehow reassured, I drifted off soundly and slept through until the sounds of the morning traffic called me back to consciousness.

CHAPTER 8

~

Wednesday Morning

M Y ASSURANCE THAT IN THE MORNING when the sun was out things would make more sense, look brighter, and feel more hopeful, were dashed. The Indian Summer heat wave had broken overnight, and a Pacific cold front had slipped in, coating the Bay Area sky with thick gray drizzly clouds. I should have been relieved that we weren't looking at another year of drought, but all I felt was tired. If I wanted cold and drizzly, I would have moved to Anchorage or London or Moscow or somewhere else that spends most of its time being wet and miserable.

I yanked a black hoodie on over my T-shirt before feeding Hoover and scooping his litterbox. That was the easiest chore on my task list. The rest of my list felt like giant boulders squashing me down. The only bright spot was signing the paperwork Jack had dropped off for me. I read it through, and as always, was impressed by the work both Jack and Oslo & Burroughs had done. Nothing to do there but sign and hope for the best. Juliet Hanford had a legal army on her side, but I had the actual law on mine. All I could do was pray the courts saw things my way.

I needed to hunt for Kenny, but I was running low on ideas and on energy. It was time, I decided, pushing slowly to my feet, to do something drastic—or at least something that involved a hot

caramel latte and a toasted onion-seed bagel with cream cheese—
and as much as I want to say that I told Reese "Non-fat milk and
light cream cheese", the conversation went more like this:

"Caramel latte. Spare no fat."

"Good. Yer skinnier than a stir-stick. Have you been eating anything at all?" Reese's special brand of honesty only shows that she
cares, right?

"That's why I need a bagel, too. With extra cream cheese."

"I was gonna smack you if you said plain." Reese pointed to an
empty table, and I settled in with my laptop and opened my two files.

Kenny. Where was he? What was he doing? I knew the police
would be processing my car thoroughly. Maybe I could ask for an
itemized list of the contents. If there was something in the car that
shouldn't have been there, I'd know it. Did it hold clues to where
Kenny went? Come to think of it, why hadn't the police asked me
about the contents of my vehicle? Other than the body, that is.
What did they know that I didn't?

I also needed to talk to Mom, let her know that I was investigating, that she didn't have to worry. Well, that last bit would be a lie.
We all needed to be worrying right now. The other reason to talk to
the parental unit was the hope that she'd have an idea who Kenny
had been hanging out with lately. I had no idea who any of his
friends were anymore, except Jude Booder, who hadn't responded
to my emails. If it meant finding Kenny, I was going to have to
break my silent streak with the Booder-dude.

The list for the haunting investigation got longer much faster:
Write up contract and affidavits and send by courier. Check property records. Run background checks on the occupants. It was
too much to hope that one of them had a public record of pulling hoaxes, but would I be doing my job if I didn't at least check?
Listen to the interviews again and see if I could catch anything
out of the ordinary. See if blueprints for the house were on file at
county records and compare the wiring with the EMF numbers
Nicky recorded.

I sat back and grinned at my lists. This paranormal research
stuff was easier than finding a loser brother for sure. Max dropped

a plate at my elbow with my bagel, as well as a small bowl of mixed fruit that I hadn't ordered. When I tried to hand it back to him, Reese cleared her throat over the counter and glared at me, pointed at the fruit and then at my mouth, a silent warning to shut up and eat every bite. That's Reese, always looking out for me. Rather than risk the cream cheese/keyboard interface, I pulled out the audio recorder, thinking I could do a run-through of the interview recording. I also wanted to make a copy to send over with the courier for the ghost-guys. *Ghost-guys?* This was my business now. It was time to take it seriously. They were my clients now.

I flipped the page on my notepad, put in my earbuds and started filling in the gaps between the jotted notes Nicky and I had made the night before, adding thoughts as they occurred to me, scribbling in here and there my impressions of each of the house tenants as they spoke, including what they said and how believable I felt they were.

Having lived through the conversation, I was far more interested in sucking the whipped cream off my latte (Hey, Reese takes requests for extra fat very seriously. Or maybe she only does that with me?), so I was only half listening, fast-forwarding through the brief silences. My eyes wandered out to the gray drizzly street and looked up the façade of my building. *No, focus.* What was I hearing? My brain chanted out the names of the speakers as they came across the earphones, and I jotted the notes in shorthand as I listened.

Fiora: I can't hear it.
Me: "Nope, can't hear a peep."
Robert: "Okay, three quarters volume."
Irvin: "No."
Me: "Nope. Still nothing."
"HELP! HELP ME!"
I yanked the earphones off and leaped to my feet, fight or flight, ready to help whoever was . . .
The rest of the café had stopped to stare at me.
"Did you hear that?" I asked, feeling vaguely stupid as I realized that the scream was on the recording. I was the only one who heard it.

"Good coffee, hon?" one of the taxi drivers grabbing a cuppa to go joshed with a grin. They all knew me. We'd all been coming to Reese's for years. I'd served half these guys their morning joe. He gave me a wave as he headed back to his cab.

I stood there. Staring down at the recorder. My eyes were watering suddenly, and my face felt like someone had held it to a coal fire. My hands were shaking.

What the hell.

I tried to take a sip of my latte and only succeeded in splashing it on my notebook. I hadn't heard that—I couldn't have. I imagined it—lack of sleep—too much stress.

Tentatively, not bothering to sit down, I backed up the recording. Unlike with old analog tape recorders, you can't just play it backwards 'til you get where you want to be. Like an idiot, I hadn't jotted down the time numbers like I should have, so it took me what seemed like forever to find the spot again. I pictured the scene as the sounds filled my ears.

Robert went up to turn on the TV. He called down the volume levels, we said we couldn't hear it, and then . . .

"Help! Help me!"

The cry, loud and clear as day, faded out over the next part of the conversation, but only a few seconds later a low-level sound intruded over the recording—the sound of someone crying; no, not crying—weeping—weeping as though their entire world had fallen apart.

I listened to it five times, then reached for my cellphone with a hand that couldn't seem to press the suddenly tiny-seeming buttons. It went straight to voicemail and I took a quick breath to fortify myself before leaving a message. "Hello, Irvin. This is Kami White. I was just listening to the recording from yesterday and I think you need to hear it as soon as possible. Call me to set up an appointment."

Thoroughly distracted now, I backed up the sound file to my computer, keeping the original on the recorder and hastily packed up my work. I dashed back to the office, realized that I'd forgotten my latte and ran back across the street, jaywalking through morning traffic, to grab it before Max cleared it off.

"You okay?" Reese hollered after me as I nudged the door open on my back way out.

"Yeah. No. I dunno!" I yelled back. "Talk to you later!"

Much later—because this was what Charles would call a dilly-problem. You know, like those ice cream bars that are covered in that waxy chocolate stuff? But when you take a bite, they start melting through the cracks in the chocolate coating and the next thing you know you have a serious dilly problem with soft serve dripping everywhere and making a huge mess.

I had a dilly problem. The cracks in the chocolate were letting too much through and I was, without a doubt, out of my depth. I called Nicky and got her voicemail. "Nickydoodle, got a problem. Call me as soon as you can."

Could anyone have tampered with the recorder? No. It was in my hand the entire time I was in the house. After that, it was in my case in the back of the locked canopied pick-up where it stayed the entire time I was dealing with the cops, until I got back with Reginald. No one could have touched it . . . and if they could, why would they?

I couldn't seem to shake the chill, so I hopped back into the shower and stayed there until the hot water ran out. Now that I owned the building, I'd have to see about getting a bigger water heater. When I came out, Mr. Morrimont was peering through the front glass and I opened the door to welcome him in. Morri is a spry older gentleman with a crown of gray hair, a lean narrow face with a wrinkled Mediterranean look, and a wry grin that makes me think of leprechauns. If you sit on the balcony of Reese's Café across the street, the view leads straight to his office, which is filled with magazines, newspapers, encyclopedias, and three computers, one of which is constantly streaming the BBC World-Service. He must be a really good cruciverbalist, because every time he gives me one of his puzzles, I can never finish it. Or that might just mean I'm bad at puzzles.

"Doin' your mop impression, precious?" he asked with chortle, and I patted rueful hand on top of my wet curls.

"Something like that. How are you this morning?"

"Oh, good. Good enough. I just wanted to ask about the build-ing." His thickly bespectacled eyes glanced around the empty office. His mouth frowned down in worry. "You aren't pondering peddling our place of employ, are you?"

"Word travels fast." I managed a half-smile. "I'm not selling, if that's what you're worried about. Juliet Hanford is contesting the will, so it's going to take some time to get back everything she took. Oslo and Burroughs are on it."

"Oh!" His worn-olive face broke into a smile. "Oh, that is pre-cipitous news, then! Perfect." He peered at me through his thick eyeglasses, an owl observing a mouse. "You're a peach!"

I met his eye, feeling absurdly like giving him a hug, but he was entirely too tweedy for hugging. A tiny sniffle made its way out as I gave him a rueful smile. "I love you, Morri."

Morri gave me a half-smile, and another shake of his head. "Now that I know you aren't looking to dispose of our abode, suppose you tell me why you appear to have peered upon an apparition?

"Let me guess? Next Sunday is 'p' themed?"

He laughed. "No, lass. Last Sunday was. But my passion for the prized P and its panoply of pleasantly pronounceable prizes is one of my prides. And joys," Mr. Morrimont added with a wink. "But you've tried to distract me now. If you'd just as soon not talk about it, say the word and I'll flit away, but it seems to me you could use a friend this morning."

I hesitated, glancing to the recorder on my desk. It should be confidential, technically, but I could easily make the argument that Morri was on my team. He had the experience and the knowl-edge that I didn't. I had told the clients I would be working with a team, so this wasn't the same as putting it on the internet with big arrows pointing to it, was it? "I've got a problem and it's just your bailiwick."

Mr. Morrimont nodded, his eyes dancing. "You've a puzzle, I can see! Let Morri help you, lass! We'll sort it out!"

"Okay. But first let me explain . . ."

I ended up telling him everything: how Irvin Zettlemeyer had misread my sign, how I'd blundered my way into saying I would do the job, because, for some reason, I thought living and working with a friendly ghost qualified me to be a ghostbuster. I ended with a slump-shouldered whimper. "I'm out of my league, Morri."

"Oh, petunias and pedigrees." Morri plunked down in my chair with a bright grin, waggling his finger at me. "You're as qualified as anyone. Back in the day, I knew Sylvia Plath. You know, the famous psychic? Done my share of poking around haunted old wrecks, too. Seen enough perplexing and peculiar things to know there's more to this world than we think, no doubt about it. And no matter how qualified one might pretend to be, dealing with the veil of mysteries is never something one can rightfully proclaim expertise in." As much as his words reassured me, it was his casual wink and his next words that eased my mind. "Let's have a get-go on it together, and we'll get it sorted."

I felt a bit of the tension leak out of my shoulders and suddenly didn't feel quite so alone. "I thought for sure this was one of those crazy claims where it would turn out to be all logical and have reasonable explanations for everything. But now? I don't even know what to do."

I plugged the recorder into my computer, and pressed play. When it got to the crying, I was watching Morri's face, and he neither moved nor made any expression at all. "Back it up," he said calmly, and then, "Again."

Finally, he crossed his arms, leaned back in my chair and looked up at me, no sign of his usual jaunty irreverence in his voice. "That soul is hurting."

"I know."

"I haven't heard crying like that since I was a war correspondent."

War correspondent? I knew he'd been a journalist. I glanced to Morri again, suddenly realizing how little I knew about the old man upstairs. "It's scary. I mean, not the crying, but the soul behind it. I mean, if that's really a ghost, we can't leave them like that, can we? And if someone's faking it . . . Well, why would they? And how did they pull it off?"

His crisp gaze bored through me. "The real question is what are you going to do about it?"

I sighed. "I don't know. I have to talk to the clients."

Morri nodded. "Well, if you need me, or Father Joe, or both of us, we're here. He's good at helping send the lost on their way."

"The lost." I felt a little shiver travel up my spine. "Morri? Why does none of this surprise you? I mean, what I heard on that recording gave me chills so bad I was nearly sick, but you just sat through it, over and over, perfectly calm!"

"Oh, *chéri*, I've seen so many things in my time, very little is peculiar to me." He gave a quick crisp salute, snapping his hand to his forehead. "Now, I'm off to do battle with a locomotive. Or at least, a locomotive-themed puzzle. If you need further fuel to steam your boiler, I'll be just up the track."

I returned the salute, already feeling a ton better. "I may want to pick your brains later about this haunting thing."

"Peachy, princess." While Morri disappeared down the corridor and up the stairs, I made copies of the recording.

The office phone rang, and I leaped half out of my skin before snatching the receiver from its cradle. "Hanford Le . . . I mean . . . White Legal Services? Can I help you?"

"Morning, Kami." Familiar, warm, and smooth, the voice on the other end of the line continued, "It's Reggie. I was wondering what time you were coming by to get the keys?"

The keys? The night before had completely faded in the glaring lights of the morning's discoveries and I stared blankly at Evrett's helmet for minute. "Oh! Safe house. Right! I forgot all about it."

"Tell you what. I'll swing by with them in a bit. I have some business that direction anyway." Reggie hesitated. "I hate to ask if there have been any new developments."

"Not as far as regards the police, anyway. The investigation I'm working took a little twist this morning." That was about as much of an understatement as it comes! "I've been swamped with that."

"Don't get too wrapped up in that," Reggie warned. "If the police think you aren't taking this seriously, it could look bad later on."

Could look bad? "Honestly, Reggie, I don't see how it could look any worse."

"But it can, kiddo. You aren't considered a serious suspect. Yet." His voice dropped a half octave to hit me with the word 'yet' like a blunt object. "On the other hand, I do have some good news for you."

"I like good news," I suggested wearily, "but lately the word 'good' seems to be tied to a whole lot of bad."

"We got the insurance paperwork with the inventory from the office entered into evidence. Everything is in order and we're filing injunctions against Juliet Hanford today for return of everything she took. Don't count your chickens quite yet, but everything looks ironclad."

I couldn't help it. I did a happy dance. You know, a whoohoo wave your arms in the air like you just don't care kind of happy dance, and promptly knocked the phone off the table, which landed on Hoover, who tore off down the corridor with a disconcerted yowl.

"Oops. Sorry! Reggie? Are you still there?"

"Was that Hoover or was it you who was just howling?"

"I dropped the phone on the cat." There was a muffled noise and I could tell he was stifling laughter. "Reggie, seriously, thank you! I don't know what I'd do without you. Do you need me to sign anything?"

"Nope. As executor of Charles' will, it's all in my hands. You just stay out of trouble as best you can." He hung up, leaving me with a slightly happier feeling in my gut.

But even that couldn't erase the disconcertion that resulted from being scared half pee-less, which is what that recording had done to me. For my own sanity, I locked my recorder in the built-in safe in the cabinet in the back office, ensuring it couldn't be tampered with. Then I settled in to do background work on the house and the occupants.

I'D HAVE TO MAKE TIME TO go by the Alameda County planning office and get the blueprints for the house. In the meantime, a historical background, including news and police reports, turned up nothing out of the ordinary. Thankfully, Irvin's original claim that lots of people died there seemed unfounded. Though it was true that a number of places in the Bay Area were built on old burial grounds, pioneer cemeteries, and indigent camps, this house didn't seem to have been built on anything other than a seismically unstable hillside. As a legal investigator, I knew too well how stories grew up quickly over time, going from something that happened ten miles away to someone entirely different in an entirely different manner to something that happened, NO REALLY, right here! Migrating rumors of dead bodies didn't lead to migrating dead bodies, thankfully.

They didn't, unless they were the trunk of my car, and then who knew where they could end up.

The entire East Bay pretty much lines up with the Hayward Fault. Seismic instability could lead to stray knocks and bangs, and to objects shifting. Even a 2.0 temblor epicentered three miles away could shiver an object off the edge of a table. But those cries? I glanced at the file of the recording on my computer. The only screaming I'd ever associated with seismic activity was my own. Drop, cover, hold on, and scream. I'm pretty sure that's what the federal quake-safety guidelines say to do.

Until I had a look at the blueprints, there was little more I could do on the house. I switched to its occupants.

BACKGROUND CHECKS CAN BE TERRIFYING. YOU think you know someone inside and out, but when you run the facts, you see everything, like a kaleidoscope of light and dark pieces. Everywhere someone ever lived or worked, what schools they attended, what cars they drove: Everything would be entwined in their background check like braids of colored ribbons that could be untangled and laid out like pathways. Sometimes, you found things you didn't want to know.

What I found helps most in doing background checks is to pretend I'm researching a movie character. I know it's silly, but it helps me think forward instead of backwards. I tend to get hung up on feeling guilty about prying into people's personal affairs, even if it was all matters of public record. If John Doe So-and-So is just a fictional movie character that I'm filling in background for, then I don't get hung. I still feel a little guilty, but at least it doesn't jam me up.

I started with Irvin Zettlemeyer; a Berkeley graduate with a steady work history since graduation. His credit rating had taken a deep dive as his business went into bankruptcy and his wife came after him in the divorce. She'd tanked his business and stolen his clients. I thought Irvin's lawsuit happy ex-wife made a good hoax suspect possibility. She was smart, tech-savvy, and seemed to have a grudge against poor Irvin. He was paying exorbitant alimony money to keep her happy, even though she was the registered owner of two new tech companies, both of which were in the financial black. Otherwise, Irvin lived a quiet, mousy sort of life. His only large recent purchase had been a computer so expensive that it could probably be used to hack a small government if he wanted to. There was nothing in his background check that would suggest he might want to, thankfully.

Next, I looked at Robert Daltry. Younger than the others, it seemed he was crucially careful with his money and his relationships. At least, he didn't really seem to have any intimate relationships that I could find. His financial records showed money paid out in support of a few fandom-promoted charities. His big financial splurge had been the new Corolla, his first car that didn't have his mother's name as a co-signer and his first new vehicle— a pride-and-joy car with special-order paint and interior colors. Surprisingly, Robert had an arrest record. A quick legal check showed it was a role-playing event that got out of hand. Someone reported sword-fighting in the park and the police arrested them only to discover that the swords were all plastic. They were all charged with creating a disturbance and got off with minimum fines. High spirits and active imaginations didn't always mix well, especially when beer and swords were involved. But it didn't make him a criminal, or a likely hoaxer.

Fi's background was hazy until her move to the United States from Venezuela. Before coming to the US for school, there was only a birth certificate on file in a small community hospital in Venezuela, and a marriage license. *An ex?* I dug further and saw that it was tagged with an annulment notice. She entered the US on a scholarship visa to Cal-State San Diego and was recruited by a start-up right out of college as an H1B visa worker. Since then, her records were clean and precise, steadily working her way up from an internship position at a start-up to her current position as a software designer. She had started the naturalization process and was working on becoming a US citizen. Fi sent money to her family in Venezuela regularly and fed the rest of her cash into high interest saving accounts. Maybe this was saving to bring more family to the US—or saving up to return home where there would be fewer job opportunities?

I traced the name on her marriage certificate, but he was in Venezuela, married with two kids, and operated an organic yogurt company. *Yum. Yogurt.*

I felt a little guilty as I pulled up Dillon's information. Sure, he was handsome, sexy, and charming. That didn't mean that I had to be interested in him, right? If I was interested, wasn't it better to know the whole story about the guy?

Dillon was born and raised in Louisiana, did undergraduate work at a community college before transferring to Missouri State with a major in computer science and a minor in criminal justice. So, computer security guy had a background in justice? That was a good thing, right? He worked a few standard jobs before breaking off and going freelance. I was surprised to find that he was on regular retainer with a few firms and companies, some with names I recognized. He flew all over the country, and even out of it to places like Hong Kong and London, with various firms footing the bill.

"That must be nice," I told Hoover. "Maybe someday we'll be that good."

He twitched his tail at me. He wasn't a fly-around-the-country kind of cat. I glanced at my watch. I had time to get to the county planning office and run the other errand—the one I'd been putting off.

WHEN YOU LIVE IN THE BAY AREA, you quickly learn that rainy days are no place for fragile umbrellas. A sturdy warm hat that keeps the rain off and a coat with a collar are the only way to go. I crammed my still-damp curls under my green military-surplus cap and donned my denim jacket. It was time to run an errand that I could no longer avoid.

I CAUGHT HOOVER, AND WITH THE HELP of a few freeze-dried shrimp treats, convinced him to let me put his little striped sweater on him. I strapped on his harness and leash and carried him out to the pick-up. Not so much because I thought Hoover wanted to go out, though he's quite adventurous for a spoiled all-indoor cat, but because I didn't feel like being alone. I did leave him alone in the pick-up at the planning office office, leaving him with a treat-ball full of crunchies to keep him occupied. He was contentedly napping when I got back, only waking up when I pulled out onto the freeway headed north.

We all have places we don't like to wander into without someone at our side. For some people, it's strange bars on shady corners, or doctor's offices, or funeral homes. For me, it's a pale green single story faux-Eichler on a eucalyptus-lined street in a tired grassy-lawned neighborhood on the far southern edge of Oakland.

Jack's little pick-up handled well for its size, even on the freeway, and before long I was pulling up in front of the house. Hoover gave a small curious mew, poking his nose against the glass of the window and leaving a smudge. He looked back at me, and then curled up on the seat as if to say, "Whenever you're ready to leave, I'm game."

"Oh no, you don't." I told him, wrapping the leash around my wrist and tucking him up onto my shoulder. "If I have to go in, you're coming with me."

The cat gave a long-suffering sigh and sniffed my ear.

I never bother to knock at Mom's. Even after my parents' divorce, when I stayed for a year with Granny Jazzy and Grandpa Dan, she insisted that her home was my home. I had a key, but her green Beetle was parked in front, so I knew she was home. I pushed open the door and called, "Mom? You home?"

There was a slight click from behind the door, and then a loudly relieved sigh. "Oh! Kamera!"

Holding Hoover by his harness, I leaned around the door. My mother, the hippy pacifist herbal tea-making, organic-gardening maven in a flowery print blouse and broomstick skirt, was pressed back between the door and the coat rack with a bright yellow canister of mace pointed directly at my face.

"Uh, yah. Mom. It's me. You can put that down."

She glanced at the can in her hands, her blue eyes widening as though she wasn't even sure what she was doing still holding it. "I'm sorry, sweetie, I didn't recognize that thing you're driving, and with your brother missing and in trouble and all, I guess I'm a bit jumpy!"

Mom dropped the mace on the little table where she keeps her keys and the pink-flowering African violet that I gave her for her birthday and gave me a quick hug before ruffling both fingers over Hoover's ears. He sniffed her fingers politely and then leaned into her petting hands. She cooed and fawned over him. "Who's a good kitty?! Who's a good kitty-kitty?"

"Not him. He's been a terror since Charles . . ." I couldn't bring myself to say the word 'died' and Mom gave me another hug. "That's why I brought him with me. And I'm borrowing the pick-up from Jack."

"Oh!" Mom gave me a sweetly vacant smile. "Are you two back together, then? He's such a good man." She drew back the curtain and took a good look at the pick-up. "I guess I didn't recognize it with the canopy on it. He had it off when he helped me with the raised beds."

"Jack helped you with the gardening?" *Dirt and Jack?* Somehow, I never connected the two words in my mind before. It was like the "one of these things is not like the other" game.

"Of course not! I do all my own gardening, you know that. He just helped me pick up the wood from the hardware store and build the beds. I'm helpless at carpentry. You're smart, so tell me why it's so hard to end up with a square when you have boards that are square-shaped? Anyway, your father's a good carpenter but I can't exactly ask him to help me, now can I?"

"So you asked *my* ex?" Why did I always feel like I was living in an alternate universe when dealing with Jaxine? I kept waiting for my evil twin to show up wearing a goatee. But Mom was dragging me to the kitchen, a warm, cozy, pink and yellow curtained affair, and pouring me a hand-cast mug of herbal tea made with ingredients from her own garden—lemongrass and something else, something I couldn't quite identify, fennel, maybe? She also fished a bag of home-made cat treats out of the fridge and offered them to a pleased Hoover. Thick as thieves, those two.

"I didn't ask. Jack offered to help when he came by to get the sofa."

"The sofa?" For the first time, I realized that Mom's old yellow and blue paisley sofa no longer graced her living room. In its place was a sleek, modern looking, dark red three-piece sectional. There was a pang of sorrow for the sofa of my teen-years. How much popcorn had been consumed on that sofa? (And how much was still imbedded in its pilled old fabric?) The night my first boyfriend broke up with me, Mom and I stayed up all night on that sofa watching funny movies. When I had to have my appendix out when I was sixteen, I spent three days recovering on that sofa, doped to the eyeballs on oxycodone and drinking gallons of Mom's herbal healing teas. I blinked. "Where'd the sofa go?"

"I donated it to that shelter Jack helped set up. He's going to have it reupholstered. I just thought, you know, with all the love we've poured into it, it certainly had to be infused with wonderful feelings and memories. In a way, maybe that can pass on to those poor women and children at the shelter who need so much love in their lives."

Do you wonder how I ended up an accidental paranormal investigator? "One of Jack's charity projects, then?"

"He's such a good man, Kam. You really should give him a second chance."

I didn't answer that; I couldn't. It was time for a serious change of subject. "Mom, when was the last time you saw Kenny?"

"I told the police all that already. Honestly, how can I keep track of you two when you don't stop by, don't call, don't even bother to send a postcard?"

"I call."

"Did you call me when Charles died? No. I had to read about it in the paper! And how he died like that? Oh, my poor baby. You could have called me, you know. I could have . . ."

"What? Brought him back? Changed how he died? I didn't want to talk about it, Mom. I still don't." Hoover jumped down from my lap and wandered around the kitchen, dragging his leash behind him. He was right—time to change the subject. "What about Kenny's friends? Who are they? Have you talked to any of them?"

"I don't know. I don't even know who your friends are. No one tells me anything."

"You know Nicky's my best friend." This is Mom's way of saying she's always so wrapped up in her own things that she doesn't hear what we tell her. "Mom, it's important. Really important. Was Kenny dating anyone? Who was he hanging out with?"

"Who do you hang out with? I'm sure I don't know." Mom poured more tea and put out a plate of what looked like wheat-germ and raisin cookies, probably made with molasses and organic stone-ground flour. She shook the cat treats, and Hoover leaped obligingly to her lap for another one. She stroked his silky ears, and he nuzzled her, best of buddies.

I dipped my raisin cookie in my tea, and it wasn't too much like composite-board filler. Yeah, I've tasted composite board. No, you don't want to know why. "I'm not the one who's missing. Mom, don't you get it? Kenny could be in trouble, serious trouble. He could be dead!"

Tears welled in Mom's eyes, and I felt suddenly horribly guilty—almost guilty enough to go watch a ball game in the bar with Jack Austin and his buddies. She pushed up from the table and went to the sink, staring out into her back garden with its neatly laid rows of herbs and flowers, their heads bending under the sprinkling rains. "He's not dead," she said suddenly. "If he was dead, I'd know it. I'm his mother. We have a bond, a connection. I would know if he was dead."

I jumped up and wrapped my arms around my mother from behind, and we stood there for a while, watching the rain come down, my mom's tears splashing in asynchronous timing into the sink. Hoover came and passed around our legs, brushing comfortingly, nudging us with his bare, wrinkly chin.

"I wasn't a bad mother, was I?" she asked suddenly, and something in the vicinity of my heart clinched.

"No. You're a great mom. The best. I can't imagine who I'd rather have for a Mom." I hesitated for a second, then pulled up my fondest teen-age wish. "Except maybe Xena, Warrior Princess, cuz she'd have beat up my bullies for me."

We both laughed at that, and I steered her back to the table. "Mom, I'm working on this. I'm looking for Kenny, but I also have to figure out whose body they found in my car. If we can't learn who she really is and how she ended up in my trunk, both Kenny and me could end up in some trouble that's going to take hard work and a bunch of luck to get out of. The police don't care about lack of evidence against us—there's enough there now to build a circumstantial case—but we can make them care about evidence that proves we're innocent. I just have to find that evidence."

Mom nodded thoughtfully and reached across the table, opening a little net-book computer. "I'm friends with Kenny on Facebook. We can see who all his friends are."

"Genius!" I didn't social network. I didn't think I had enough friends to have a social network. "I didn't know you even had a computer?"

"Jack gave me his old one when he upgraded. He showed me how to get on all the gardening sites and helped me start a blog for my herbs. I have two-hundred and fifty Twitter followers, and my organic gardening blog gets about a hundred hits a week. It's been great for business at the greenhouse."

Good god. She was blogging? "Jack. Jack. Jack," I grumbled, the comradery of a moment ago fading away. "Why aren't *you* dating Jack?"

My mother laughed. I mean, really laughed, hard enough that she had to cover her mouth. "Because he's young enough to be my son! Don't flip your wig, Kami. The poor boy lost his own mother so young. He needs a mom in his life, and since my own kids don't have time for me, well . . ."

I'd almost started to feel bad for wanting to deny Jack my mom when I knew full well how hard it had been for him losing his own mother to breast cancer when he was only thirteen. But Mom put a screeching stop on that line of thought. I snapped. "Well, if I'm not a good enough kid, maybe you deserve to have Jack instead."

"Oh, don't start, Kam. Love isn't finite, you know. I can love you and Kenny, and Jack. There's enough love to go around."

"Are you sure?" But I was teasing now, and Mom knew it.

"Oh, here we go!" Mom ignored me, turning her little computer so I could see. "Kenny's Facebook page."

I'd used social networking sites to track people before, so it didn't take long to sort out the shared joke pages and game posts from the actual friend comments. Kenny had about twenty-eight people who looked like personal friends, and a lot of artist-community connections. Most of the posts made no sense to me whatsoever, but I took note of the account names, where they'd posted, and what information was on their personal walls.

While I worked, Mom wrote down all the details she could remember from the last time she'd seen Kenny. He'd come by to do his laundry and help her paint the back bedroom, my old bedroom, which she was turning into an herb-drying station. Mom said he'd seemed just fine; said he was planning some kind of trip with friends.

"Trip? What kind of trip?" This was the first I'd heard about planning a trip. I remembered the camping gear by his door. "Was he going camping?"

"I don't know. He didn't say too much about it. I figured it was a comic book thing, or something. He's always going to those conventions. He mostly talked about his art and the comic book business and how hard it was to break into it. I don't really understand his art," Mom said tiredly. "But it was good to see him excited about something."

Kenny's hobby is writing a series of futuristic graphic novels full of things like women who are half-machine and cars with legs. It's set in a dystopian future on another planet where most of the characters are using some kind of drug that makes them invulnerable. I didn't get it either, but there seemed to be a huge market for it, based on the followers of his DeviantArt album. "Hey! That's another clue, Mom. You're on fire. Did he leave his latest for you to look at?"

She rustled into the living room and came back with a sheaf of loose art pages, Kenny's characteristic bright colors and hard lines exploding from them. "Great! I'll bring this back later, I promise."

"Oh, keep them. I don't understand it at all." She waved her hands. "You know, when I was his age, I was trying to change this world, not off writing about some future place that's the exact opposite of somewhere anyone would want to live."

"And you did change the world, Mom." I gave her a grin. "Look at me! Independent. Sexually aware. Educated. Employed. Whole generations of little girls will grow up to be their own people because of your generation."

She laughed a little. "But we're still tangled in pointless wars. Still making bombs instead of growing flowers."

"They grow poppies in Afghanistan. They're famous for it, you know," I reminded her with a wink. "Now, I've got to run. I'll let you know as soon as I hear anything. And you do the same. Watch Kenny's Facebook page, and if he posts, let me know. You can call my cell-phone."

"That thing will give you brain cancer, you know." Mom stood up and packed a small re-useable container full of her ultra-healthy cardboard cookies. She also topped off my tea and poured it into a screw-lid cup. "That's PCB-free plastic, and it's completely recy-clable when it starts to wear out."

"Thanks, Mom." I gathered up Hoover, who was sniffing hope-fully around the back door. "I'll call you tonight."

Then I escaped, casting one last sad look at the plush new red sectional. Mom waved from the window as I loaded Hoover into the pick-up from the passenger side. I waved back as I ran around to the driver-side. The rain was really picking up and I was wishing I could avoid the freeway, but Reggie had said he'd be there in two hours, and I was already pushing the timeline.

TRAFFIC WAS TERRIFYING, AS IT'S WONT TO BE during the first real rain of the year. For as often as it rains here, you'd think we'd all be far better at dealing with it. After wrangling my way around two fender-benders, one stall, and a flooded section of freeway, I finally pulled into the alleyway. I wrapped Hoover under my jacket for the trip inside—chilled hairless cats are pathetic—dashed under the eaves, crammed my key in the back-door lock and got inside just in time for Hoover to go berserk. He flew out from under my coat, leaving a long scratch down my belly, and then raced around the office, leaping from empty shelf to empty shelf, shaking himself all over.

"Well, good to see an outing agreed with you." I grumbled at him, catching him mid-leap and pinning him down to unbuckle his harness. I rewarded him with another freeze-dried shrimp which he batted under the desk before pouncing and consuming it.

There was no reply yet from Irvin, so I tried as hard as I could to put the haunting issue out of my mind and focus on the issue of the body in my car. I logged into Facebook, set up an account, and started going through the list of names Mom gave me. Of Kenny's Facebook friends, there were a few names I recognized. I figured that some of the names I didn't, like Dark Wave and Haven Lady, were artist pseudonyms for people I probably knew by names like Mike or Susie. But unless they had a public profile with a picture, it was hard to tell. I started messaging Kenny's friends, the ones who posted most often on his wall, asking if anyone had seen him, when, and where. I kept the details to a minimum, not mentioning wrecked cars or dead bodies. I kept it simple. "If you've seen him, let me know. I'm worried."

I double-checked Kenny's friend lists for anyone resembling Trunk-Girl but came up short. I also searched missing person sites. I looked at hundreds of photos of missing women between ages twenty and forty in California and four surrounding states, but none of them seemed right, and none matched up with Kenny's friend list. I expanded my search, adding a wider age-range, and came up with several missing blond women. There were four from the Bay Area alone over the past five years, including Vivian Astor and Hannah Raye, but none of them had tattoos. *No Trunk Lady there.* I gave up that line of inquiry: The police should have already checked missing persons records. Why should I double up my time to do it?

A good question was where on earth my car had been between the time that Kenny drove off with it, and the time the police pulled it out of the reservoir? I had given it to him with three-quarters of a tank of gas. How far could he have gone before he needed to fuel up? Would he have used his debit card or paid cash? I dug out a paper map of California from the file boxes and made a big circle, estimating a two-hundred-mile radius—miles and miles, hundreds of towns, thousands of gas stations—and I didn't even know which direction he might have gone.

My search ended when Reggie stepped through the front door, nattily folding his umbrella and hanging it on the coat hook. "Wet day."

"Only outdoors," I replied, half-smiling.

He came around the folding desk and looked at my laptop. "Working hard on Facebook?"

"I'm messaging Kenny's friends, not playing Candy Crush. What would it take to get a release for his phone and bank records?"

"Before the cops do? Probably a miracle. Do you have any leads?"

I looked at my computer, the little message bar empty of return messages. "Not really. Mom said he was excited about planning some trip, but she didn't know any details. He was working on this . . ." I handed Reggie the sample pages Kenny had left with Mom. "It's from his comic book."

Reggie flipped through them. "He's incredibly talented. San Francisco College of Art?"

I snorted a laugh. "Santa Cruz Junior College drop-out. I think his GPA was somewhere around a 2.0."

My lawyer gave me a narrow glimpse over the pages. "You mean this is all natural talent?"

"Our grandmother is an artist. She's a sculptor and painter. He comes by it naturally, yes, but I don't know how much talent there is."

"Believe me, it's there. That gives us a lead, doesn't it?"

"It does?"

"Jane Doe, her dyed hair, her tattoos. She had an artsy look, I think. Maybe someone Kenny knew through artist circles?"

I considered that for a moment. "Well, she's not a Facebook friend, or one of his DeviantArt followers, that I can tell, but a lot of DeviantArt users use pseudonyms and don't have profile pictures, so it's possible." But I didn't like the idea. "But that would mean she and Kenny were connected somehow—I mean, other than by the trunk of my car."

"Keep working on it, but don't get in the cop's way, and if you come across evidence we need to share with them, call me immediately."

"Umm. Mmmhmmm," I muttered noncommittally.

Reggie shook his head. "I mean it, Kami. Do not try freelancing this thing."

"Freelance is what I do these days," I rebutted, but I half-smiled in conciliation. "I'll behave myself."

Reggie put down a key ring with a keycard and two keys on it. "The keycard gets you into the underground parking garage and into the elevator. The keys are for the front door to the apartment and the laundry room, which at the end of the hall if you need it."

"Thanks." I smiled, but Reggie shook his head again.

"Why do I feel like you're ignoring my legal advice? You need to stay at the safehouse, and you need to watch your back, not just with the cops, but with everything you do. Any mistake you make could have serious repercussions later. I can't help you if you can't help yourself." Reginald Burroughs, Attorney at Law, was used to dealing with Oakland gangsta rappers and high-profile Silicon Valley executives. I was no match.

"Yes, sir."

"And you keep me informed at every step."

"Yes, sir."

"And don't 'sir' me."

"No, sir." I smirked. "Really, though, I get it. I'm taking this seriously, I promise."

He texted me the address of the safehouse. "Okay, I'll call you tomorrow. Be sure you answer."

"Yes, si . . ." I stopped myself and went for a rescue. "Siri! Call Reggie."

"You don't have Siri. You've got a cut-rate phone and plan."

"No, but I do have voice activation. See." I held up my phone and ordered it to "Call Reginald Burroughs Cell."

"Calling Reginald Burroughs," my phone intoned, and then Reggie's cell phone buzzed.

"Fair enough." He collected his umbrella. "Stay out of trouble. Please."

"When have you ever known me not to?"

He didn't answer that, and I was guessing it had something to do with my having been kidnapped in the past. Reggie was almost out the door when I suddenly remembered The Map. "Reggie! Wait."

I ran to the back room, gently unhooked the map, and as Reggie joined me, rolled it into a protective document tube. "I know Charles would want you to have it."

Reggie held the tube in both hands for a long moment, then smiled. "I love this map."

I smiled back. "Me, too."

CHAPTER 9

Wednesday Afternoon

THE OSLO AND BURROUGHS SAFE-HOUSE was in a square concrete apartment building with underground parking accessed by the swipe-card, and an elevator that took me up to the second floor. The apartment was a one-bedroom, neatly styled in modern hotel bulk-buyer furniture. I crammed Hoover's litterbox under the bathroom sink and put down his food and water bowls in the kitchen, then released him from his harness.

He ran around the entire apartment, sniffing his nose into every corner. I was quietly relieved that Hoover was on the case, seeing to my security. If there were stray crumpled papers lurking anywhere, I was completely covered. As I settled my stuff on the table, I halfway wished I'd brought Evrett, too. Not that I thought he cared much for my company, but because I missed his sword.

A quick look around included the discovery that the freezer was full of frozen dinners, and not the cheap ones either. The cupboards held canned soups, crackers, tuna, and other non-perishables. The bathroom cabinets were stocked as well: Shampoo. toothpaste, new toothbrushes, combs and disposable razors. Someone had thought of everything, and the apartment itself was surprisingly secure. The main windows looked out over the quiet street between apartment buildings, and the bathroom window stared into an alley.

There was a drop-down fire-ladder by the bathroom window and another by the living area window for making an emergency getaway if necessary.

Near the phone at the front door, there was placard with two phone numbers, one for the private security company that Oslo & Burroughs hired to protect the building and one was the non-emergency number for the local police. Beside the phone, a security panel with a screen showed security camera footage of the corridor outside the room. I would be able to see anyone coming up to the door.

Whoever had planned this place had done well. Food, water, escape routes, and personal comforts; all present and accounted for. Is there some kind of handbook, I wondered vaguely, that tells you what to include in a safe house? Was a weapon on that list? It didn't look like it. That was kind of a relief. The statistics of gun-owners having their own guns used against them made me too nervous to keep one. Being shot doesn't fit anywhere on my bucket list, and especially not being shot by my own gun.

But hiding wasn't exactly what I was doing, was it? It wasn't like there was really someone after me or anything. I was just being a responsible-looking citizen with a proper address for a few days. A little voice in my head that sounded a lot like Reggie's reminded me that there was a dead woman with blond hair in the trunk of my car. Being cautious never hurt anyone, right?

I HAD TO AGREE THAT THE SAFEHOUSE was far more comfortable than my mostly empty office. The small desk in the main room had the wireless internet password taped to the router, and I settled into the plush chair and logged into Facebook. To my relief and surprise, there were two messages from Kenny's friends. The first was from someone monikered Hose Hoser, the second from a Snake Hems. Hose's profile picture was a brown Steampunk style gear-work image. Snake's was picture of a tattoo of a rattlesnake that I was guessing he sported somewhere on his body. I didn't recognize the gear design or the snake tattoo, but I did recognize Kenny's hard lines and bright colors. Both images were Kenny's artwork.

Hose Hoser's message said his name was David Hostner, that he worked at a tech company called Genius Games, and that he'd seen my brother a week or so before. I breathed a small sigh of relief. He included a phone number in case I wanted to talk.

The message from Snake Hems was so badly written it took a moment to translate it from 'lete-speak to actual words with meaning. Roughly translated, it read that he'd been with Kenny at a festival but hadn't seen him since then. Since he didn't say when or where this festival was, I decided to start there. Maybe he'd seen him more recently than David Hostner. Checking Snake's Facebook page, I discovered he worked at a climbing gym in Fremont. I gave Hoover a hug, reminded him not to scratch the furniture, and headed out.

THE RAIN HAD DISSIPATED INTO A FAINT GRAY SKY, but traffic still seemed to think it was raining, crawling at a painfully slow rate. I made it to Fremont and found the gym, where a pair of extremely buff guys at the counter pointed out Snake, who was coiling ropes near a small climbing wall.

Snake was in his mid-twenties, a small wiry guy, with lean hands and arms and legs. Tattoos covered his arms, nearly all of them tribal style with the notable exception of Kenny's coiled rattlesnake on his left forearm. His black hair was lank under his climbing helmet. "You want?"

"What," I corrected quietly. "What do you want."

"Whatever." He turned and continued neatly coiling rope with practiced hands.

"You're friends with Kenny White?"

He stopped and looked back at me with dark suspicion. "Who wants to know?"

"I'm his sister, Kami. You answered my Facebook message asking about him?"

Snake went from bored to excited in a flash. "Oh, yeah! The Badge-Man! His art is out of this world. Dude, he's your bro?"

"Since birth. His, not mine." I confirmed. "I just need to know a few things. When did you see him last?"

Snake thought hard for a second. "Last day of the festival. We were rockin' it 'til his ride got took with all 'is spare gear in it. That sucked."

"His ride was stolen? From the festival?" I said slowly, over-annunciating as I registered the news. "It was my car."

"Oh." Snake appeared to think about this for a while as he continued coiling his rope. "Sorry about that. You get a new car yet?"

"No, the insurance takes a while to come through." Not that I was getting any, but I saw no point in admitting that to someone who called himself Snake.

"Bummer. You should get that lizard stuff. They're great."

"Lizard? Uh, okay. I'll keep that in mind. Listen, when did you meet up with Kenny? At the festival? Where was this festival?"

"Where?" Snake looked at me like I was insane. "You don't know? It's THE festival, man. The only festival. Burnin' Man! I met up with him at the gas station in Reno. My ride crapped out, and he picked me up."

"In Reno?" He'd gone to Reno? It took a second longer for the words Burning Man to sink in. I'd heard of it, but it wasn't on my radar; some arts festival that was supposed to be like Woodstock combined with a rave on steroids. "Let me make sure I understand. You rode with Kenny in my car and went to the Burning Man festival?"

"Yeah, I guess."

"Was there a girl with him? Or with you?"

Snake rolled his eyes. "I got a girl, but she be hatin' on the desert. She don't Burn. It was just Badge-Man an' me 'til we got to the Playa, then we met up with Hoser and Mudpuppy and the Booderdude. We were Rainmaker Camp, you know."

That was pretty much all Greek to me. I had no idea what he was talking about. Booderdude, I hoped, was Jude Booder. "Hoser messaged me on Facebook and I'm meeting with him later. So, from Reno, it was just you and Kenny in my car. You went to the Burning Man Festival, and that's where my car was stolen?"

"Yeah, stoled. Badge-Man had to beg and borrow water and stuff. He was sketchin' crazy fast, and tradin' art for food and . . . well . . . that kinda sucked."

"You were in my car? The blue Kia?" Was I talking to someone who could kill a woman and put her in the trunk of my car?

"Yeah, I guess. Then it got stoled, and I got a ride home with Booderdude."

"You were with Jude Booder? And who else?" *Jude.* Kenny surely would have been with Jude, right? I eyed Snake suspiciously. As honed as his climbing muscles seemed to be, I was having a hard time picturing the wiry little tattoo-bearer killing anyone and having the brains to stash them in Kenny's car and then dump the car in a reservoir. If he was with Booder, I could verify that.

"I think his name was Sane or Wayne or Same or somethin'. He had a surfboard on wheels! Like a giant skateboard that he rolled around on the Playa! Awesome!"

"Shane? Shane Davenport?" Shane was a surf-gang regular and a friend of Nicky's Rick—should be easy verify, unless they were all in it together. But there was one vital piece of information I clung to. "And Kenny stayed with you at the festival, after the car was taken?"

Snake just nodded. He gestured up the wall. "You wanna go?"

I looked up at the wide-spaced, knobby hand and foot holds and cringed back. "Not a chance, but thanks. Did you see anything unusual at the festival? Maybe some girl that caught your eye? Or Kenny's? Someone who was watching him?"

"Yeah. Like, wow! How'd you know?"

Finally! I was getting somewhere!

"She was like, brown-haired, and tall, and had these knockers, like . . ." He stopped and looked at my size B chest. "Not like yours. And she was wearing short shorts, cut to, like, whoa! I asked if she wanted to camp with us, but she was with a bunch of girls in a ladies-only camp. I said hey, that's like, discriminatin' an' all, but she . . ."

"Okay!" I held up both hands to wave him to a stop. "Enough. I meant, *like,* did you see anyone taking an interest in Kenny or in my car? A woman with blond hair with blue streak? Maybe with a tattoo on her neck?" I pointed to his throat, which I really wanted to punch at that point. "Right there?"

"Uh." Snake thought for a long second. "No. Lots of ink, but no throats that I remember. That's wicked. I would remember that. Do you have any tatts? Can I see 'em?"

I fled as quickly as I could to my car. I checked the clock and called the surf shop where I knew Rick would be working. Rick is the most laid-back, Zen type guy I've ever known, and the exact opposite of Nicky. They are more on and off than a light switch, but I think that works for them. It's not like they fight, or don't get along. When they're together, it's magic, and when they aren't, well, they just aren't together. I think Nicky really loves Rick, but she's not ready to commit to anything, and neither is he.

Rick answered the phone "Surf Surplus, Rick here."

"Hey, Rick. It's Kami. Got a sec?"

"Kami? Uh, yah. It's not busy right now. What's up?"

"I just talked to Snake Hems, and he said he came back with Shane from Burning Man Festival. Hate to play telephone-tree, but I don't have Shane's number. Have you talked to Shane since he got back?"

Rick paused a moment, thinking in his calm way. "Sure. We hit the waves yesterday. I let Shane use the Surf Surplus van to go to the Burn. He mentioned that Booder and Snake came back with him. The van was so packed full he made Booder ride on the camping gear in back."

I sighed with relief. "If I point the police to you, can you tell them that and get them in touch with Shane?"

"Sure. I can, but why?" Rick paused again. "Kami? What's this about?"

"I'm not really sure yet. But no one has seen or heard from Kenny since the festival." I decided against mentioning bodies. "My car turned up dumped in the reservoir, and the police are looking for Kenny. You wouldn't be narcing on anyone, except maybe Kenny. And since he's missing . . ." I couldn't find the words to go on.

"Of course," he replied instantly. "And you know Kenny. He's probably fine. Don't worry."

"I'm the big sister. Worrying is my job." I thanked him and told him if he saw Nicky before I did give her my love, before signing off.

I remembered the pile of camping gear and sleeping bags inside Kenny's apartment. Were they things he prepped and decided not to take with him? Or had he returned, dumped his gear and left again? I wanted to go back by his place and look. Surely, I could tell if stuff had been used and was sitting dirty by the door, or if it was clean and ready to be packed.

NEXT, I GAVE HOSER A CALL. He told me to come by his work, gave me the address, and I headed for Genius Games. I really didn't know anything about them. I played video games from time to time with Nicky, but consoles were expensive, and between work and school, I didn't have time for gaming. I entered through the double-glass doors, wiped my damp sneakers on the low mat, and approached the front desk, where two women my age were manning computer workstations. They gladly beeped for David Hostner and a moment later the elevator pinged open.

He waved me over. "Come on upstairs. We can talk in the Knock-Out Room."

In the elevator, I gave him a swift appraisal. David Hostner was a tall, lean man, around my age, maybe a little older. He was stylishly dressed in elegant clothes that I could only describe as quaint. His shirt was a white button-down, impeccably pressed. With it, he wore black slacks, a tailed black jacket, and brass-rimmed round glasses that looked like something you'd see in an old Daguerreotype.

Could he be normal—mostly? Well, I could hope. He seemed more together than Snake did, that's for certain.

The Knock-Out room, as it turned out, wasn't a prize-fighting ring. It was just a normal conference room, but the walls were covered in white boards cluttered with charts and scribbled notes. Instead of a conference table, it had a circle of comfy looking armchairs with rolling laptop stands. It was, he explained, a place for the designers to sit around and knock out ideas and plans for project development.

It was kind of cool. I had a stray thought that maybe I should give up law for game design. I settled on the edge of one of the chairs. "I'm sorry to intrude like this. Have you talked to Kenny at all?"

"Not since Burning Man, but I saw your post yesterday. Is he okay?"

"I don't know. He's missing." I tilted my head and studied Hostner, trying to get a read on him. "Can you tell me about the Burning Man festival? I don't know much about it."

He blinked behind his round glasses. "You don't know? Burning Man is an art festival in the Nevada desert, out on the Playa. It's a week-long celebration of art, music, humanity, and universal consciousness. It's insane, and yet it's the most sane I've ever been."

"And you met Kenny out there? He showed up with Snake?"

Hoser nodded. "Snake's a character, but he's a lot smarter than he seems."

I didn't comment on the intelligence of a man who couldn't even assemble a complete sentence. "When you met up with Kenny at the festival, did you notice anything unusual?"

Hoser laughed out loud. "Like a thousand half-naked, costumed people running around in the desert among giant metal statues and pedaling around on giant pineapples? Nah. Business as usual."

"That sounds crazy." I was having a hard time picturing anything he was saying.

He shook his head. "Everyone's excited to get there on the first day. It's a huge party-train of art cars headed east. And once I got there, I was running around greeting old friends and checking out the art installations. Badge-Man and I hung some, but not all the time."

But it was starting to turn my head a bit. "You saw the car that Kenny, I mean Badge-Man, was driving? My blue Kia?"

He nodded. "Yeah, seen it. Helped him move some gear to our camp, but he got screwed when it disappeared. I brought extra water and sunscreen and stuff, so he was okay. Paid me in artwork. Money transactions aren't allowed at the Burn. It's all barter system."

"So, he stayed at the festival after the car was stolen? And you saw him after that?"

Hoser confirmed that Kenny had stayed the entire week and was planning to ride home with Mudpuppy and some other friends that Hoser didn't really know. But my brain was spinning. Did the body in my car come from Burning Man? Was she already in the trunk when the car was taken? Another line of inquiry suddenly presented itself. "I have an idea. Do people take pictures out there? Is there an online forum or something where everyone posts?"

"Oh, there are hundreds of them. Most of my friends are artists of one sort or another. Everyone takes pictures. You're not supposed to post them of other people without permission, though." He shrugged. "I can send you some links if you like?"

"I think, Mr. Hostner, that you just became my best friend." I grinned and he shook his head.

"If I'm your best friend . . ." He smiled back and I was startled by how it changed his appearance from stuffy and overdressed to casual and happy. ". . . then you have to call me Hoser. All my friends call me Hoser."

"Do I even want to know why?"

He laughed quietly. "It's an MIT thing. You're safer not knowing."

"You went to MIT?" Color me seven shades of stunned.

"Yeah. Well. I didn't graduate. That place eats brains alive. I came out here and finished at Stanford."

Right. MIT to Stanford. My league's out-of pool just got a bit deeper. I gave him my email address, and said I hoped to hear from him.

"You will," he promised. He walked me down to the front doors, then hesitated. "You're really the Badge-Man's sister?"

"Yeah. Why?"

Hoser shook his head. "Just hard to believe, is all. I mean, you are nothing like him. At all."

"Yeah, well. I got the brains; he got whatever was left over." I joshed, then hesitated before asking the question on my mind. I wasn't sure I wanted to know the answer. "Why do you guys call Kenny 'Badge Man?' I mean, what's wrong with his name?" Aside from the fact that it belonged to an idiot.

Hoser stared at me in astonishment. "You mean you don't know?"

"I didn't even know he was called that until today," I admitted. Just like I didn't know he went to a desert arts festival or knew people named Snake and Hoser.

"His art is out of this world. He makes custom badges for people, and tattoo art designs." Hoser unbuttoned the top two buttons of his shirt and bared a section of his chest just below his collarbone. There was a tattoo there in brown ink, military badge shaped, with a Steampunk stylized H in the center, surrounded by interlocking gears with a dirigible behind it. It was the same as his Facebook profile image, minus the bright colors. It was, I had to admit, really good.

"I asked for something SteamPunkish with my initial in it. He knocked this out for me. It's on my business cards, too." Hoser handed me a business card and promised that he'd call if he came up with anything else that could help.

I CALLED DETECTIVE BRITTLE ON MY WAY TO THE CAR. "I just met up with a couple of friends of my brother's. He went to some festival in Nevada called Burning Man. According to his friends, my car was stolen sometime during the festival. They say he stayed the entire week, after my car was gone"

There was a moment's silence, and I suspected that he was writing down what I'd said. Then he spoke up with calm certitude. "While I appreciate that, I need something more than hearsay to go on. And Burning Man is drug-fueled chaos." Brittle said. "They won't be the most reliable witnesses."

"I think you'll find David Hostner credible." I gave him Hoser's phone number and told him where to find Snake and Shane. "David Hostner is digging up pictures from the festival now to provide hard evidence for you."

"I'll look into it," Brittle said, but I wasn't sure that *he* was exactly credible at that moment.

I changed the subject. "Look, I was thinking. What if Trunk Girl . . ."

"Jane Doe 673?"

"Yeah, Trunk Girl. What if she was at Burning Man? I mean,

what if that's why no one is missing her? That she wasn't expected back yet? A lot people road-trip to the festival from all over the country, right? What if the car thief and the murderer are Burning Men or a Burning Man?"

"Burners, you mean. The burning man is just a wooden effigy. Festival goers are called Burners," he corrected before agreeing with me. "It's possible, but I don't know of any way to figure that out."

It seemed like everyone knew about Burning Man except me. I shrugged before remembering that he couldn't see me over the phone. "I have an idea, but it's going to take time."

"Let me know when you've got something." He paused. "You realize that if your brother was last seen at Burning Man, that means he's been missing almost two weeks."

"I'm trying not to think about that."

He rang off and I drove back to the safehouse, feeling hopeful for the first time all day. Too bad that it wasn't going to last.

BY THE TIME IRVIN CALLED, I was almost ready for him. "I have something important to talk to you about. I'll meet you at your house in a half-hour if traffic allows. I'll call you if I'm going to be later."

"Of course. Do you need all of us here? It's just me and Dillon right now, but Robert will be back from his game-night in an hour or so, I think. Fi's stuck at work."

Dillon would be there? I felt myself give off a little glow. "No, no worries. Probably best if we don't tell everyone at once. Be there soon."

I gave Hoover a cuddle and told him not to tear up the drapes. I turned the TV on to the Nature Channel, warned him not to stay up too late, and headed out feeling more and more reluctant by the mile. Why hadn't I asked them to meet me at the office instead? I didn't want to walk back into that house until I understood what was going on there. My morning realization that I was in over my head was growing again, washing the rest of the day's trials away in the wake of its flood-doubts.

I ZIPPED BY THE OFFICE where I retrieved the recorder from the safe and was about to walk out the door, but something stopped me. I hate to sound like my mother and say I had a vibe, but I did. I just wasn't going to leave until I figured out a way to take Evrett with me. I gently lifted his helmet from the stand and wrapped it in my aqua blue silk scarf before tucking it into my brief-bag. It looked strange, like I was carrying a head in there. Come to think of it, with the quality of the local police, it might be just as hard to explain carrying Evrett's head as it would be to explain carrying someone else's.

I pulled up in front of the house. Once again, only one car was in the driveway, and it was Robert's brand new burgundy colored Toyota Corolla. It was decked out with Avengers seat covers and an Avengers sun-screen over the windshield. You just gotta love superheroes. I only hoped that I didn't need Hulk-strength to get through this.

When I knocked on the door, it was Dillon who answered it with a dazzling smile and a casual, "Hey, there."

He was wearing gym shorts that leaned low on his hips and a white t-tank and as soon as I came inside, he dropped down on the bench inside the door and pried off a pair of high-end running shoes. "Just got back from a run. Give me two clicks to shower and I'll join y'all."

"Need someone to wash your back?" So, I'm not so good with the subtle on most days.

Dillon flashed me a wink. "Girl, I get you in the shower and there'll be better things to do than washing."

I felt my face turn ten shades closer to fire-engine but was saved by his grin.

"So, maybe that better wait for a night you aren't working, hmm?"

Right. Work. That's why I was there.

"Exactly." I beat tracks for the kitchen where I found Robert and Irvin at the island table, an open pizza box and a gallon jug of orange juice between them.

"Pizza? Nice to see you guys live up to the national impression of Silicon Valley Geek-hood."

"It's vegetable pizza." Robert told me, sliding me a paper plate and a packet of parmesan.

"On whole wheat crust." Irvin poured me some juice. "That makes it mostly healthy."

"Besides, we only eat like this on Wednesdays." Robert perched on the edge of the stool, looking vaguely troll-like as he picked strands of red onion off his slice. "And on Fridays. Most nights we take turns cooking."

"That's homey." What else was I supposed to say? I wasn't a particularly enthusiastic cook and it rarely seemed worth the effort to cook for myself. "Who grocery shops?"

"We all do." Robert pointed to a roster on the fridge with individual items listed per individual. It had magnets that made it easy to switch names every week. "And once every two weeks, we all make a Costco run together."

"Very organized." I pretended to study the roster for a second, trying to figure out how to get from where I was to where I needed to go and vaguely trying not to wonder what Dillon looked like in the shower, with steaming water pouring off his carved-muscle body.

Irvin solved it for me. "What did you find that was so urgent? I mean, what couldn't wait?"

I took a deep breath. "I'd like to wait for Dillon to join us before I present anything. After that, you'll need to decide how you want to proceed, and I think that decision has to be made by everyone who lives here, maybe even by those who own the house."

Robert and Irvin exchanged glances, and Robert reached out tap the tabletop with his fingertips, rolling them in sequence from pinky finger to pointer finger and back again. Nervous habit, I wondered? Or was it an interrogation avoidance trick? Where would a geeky fellow like Robert learn interrogation avoidance— role playing games, maybe?

All I ever learned from role playing was how to tell a D6 from a D10 (Those are just fancy names for dice that gamers use to make them sound far cooler and more complicated than they really are.) and never to piss off the Game Master with legal arguments of the rule book. That last bit was part of why I never really got into gaming. The rule book was law, right? Real laws had interpretations. That was why law was so fascinating for me. But apparently in role playing, the rule book was cold hard fact and must never be argued. At least it was, according to Kenny and his RPG-playing friends.

Before I could decide whether or not Robert was just a habitual fidgeter, Dillon's bare footsteps sounded on the stairway and he swept in, wearing a clean plain black T-shirt and a pair of sweatpants. "Okay, so what's so important we needed an emergency house meeting called? And where's Fi?"

"She's still at work. The new rev is due tomorrow and they still don't have the data migration working right." Robert filled in around his mouthful of pizza. "I told her I'd text after the meeting."

Then they were all looking at me.

I pulled out the recorder and my laptop and laid them out on the table. "Before I turn this on, I want you three to know that I haven't tampered with it any way. I downloaded the audio directly to my laptop computer and plugged it into a sound program, but this original digital recording, still on the recorder, was locked in the safe at my office. No one could have tampered with it from the time I listened to it until the time I returned it here tonight. From the time I left here until the time I listened to the recording, it was inside my bag, right here, and locked in my vehicle." I showed them the zippered section of my brief-bag where I kept my recorder, camera and spare memory cards. "Unless someone switched recordings while I was at the police station . . ."

There was a collective drawn breath. *Oops!* I tried to wave my hand casually. "Nothing to do with this case. Completely unrelated. I actually end up at the police station a lot."

Dillon was smirking at me, one eyebrow raised, and I realized that didn't sound particularly good either.

"Never mind why I was at the police station. I don't suspect the San Amoro Police Department of tampering with evidence." I reached for the computer. "The first part of what you'll hear will be familiar to you. We were all here when it was recorded, so you can hear all of us, including Fiora, on the recording."

I watched their faces as I started the recording, the three of them leaning in to listen, their eyes following the flow of the little sound-meter on my computer.

I was trying to watch all three of their faces at once as the first scream started. Dillon was in front of me. His eyes went wide and his lips went tense, clamped into a thin line. Robert was to my left, just barely inside my peripheral vision, and when he bounced back on his stool, I couldn't see him at all. Irvin jumped so violently that his chair went over backwards, and he smacked into the tile floor with thud and a squeak, frog-crawling backwards until he hit the fridge.

Dillon went to give him a hand, but Irvin scrambled to all fours and then to his feet. He looked half a ghost himself. I'd paused the recording, but now I put my finger back on the play button. "There's more. You ready?"

I waited for their nods before starting again. The crying went on, fading out from the recording as we'd all moved back upstairs.

"It's almost a minute long, from the first scream, to the crying," I said quietly, hoping to ameliorate the panic with facts.

"Look at the meter." Robert said, reaching past me to the computer and pulling up my sound editing program, expanding it on the screen. One pudgy finger left pizza-grease smudges on the screen. "There's no spikes. No cuts or breaks. No layering. This hasn't been dubbed in or anything. It's the original recording."

"One thing you'll learn about me is that I'm not terribly savvy when it comes to technology," I told them. "I didn't tamper with the recording and I don't see how anyone else could have either."

"But we were all there. We didn't hear that!" Irvin was even more unbelievably pale than usual, and his eyes were the size of new quarters and almost as shiny. "I . . . How can that happen? That we didn't hear anything at all?"

"Someone's messing with us," Dillon interjected angrily. "And when I find 'em, I'm gonna totally mess them up."

"Are you sure you're from down south, because you sounded pretty downtown Oakland just now?" I asked him with a half-smile that quickly faded. "If someone is messing with you, it's someone inside this house. And it would have to be someone with the sound-tech knowledge to know the right frequency to record as an EVP, even without knowing what recording equipment I would bring."

I said 'EVP' with a straight face. I felt strangely proud and sadly ashamed at the same time.

"A what?"

"EVP. It stands for Electronic Voice Phenomenon. It's a term we use in paranormal research when something turns up on a record-ing that wasn't heard by ear at the time." *Hah.* I said *we* with a straight face, too. I was getting good at this stuff! "It can be faked, but, like I said, you'd have had to know beforehand exactly what equipment I was bringing and be able to broadcast on the right frequency to record below human hearing."

"But what does it mean? Who would be so sick as to put something like that on the recording?" Robert asked, pushing his glasses back up his nose with his thumb. "She sounds really scared. That's not a B-movie actress recorded off the late-night horror show. It's twisted."

"What it means is that you have justification for a full inves-tigation," I told him as calmly as I could, trying not to let it show that I really didn't *want* to investigate. Work is work, money is money, I chanted silently to myself. "If you're prepared to move forward, we'll come next Saturday and do a full investigation. I'll bring all of my equipment and, maybe, more of my team. At this point, I'm going out on a long limb here and telling you that I believe this house to be haunted. What kind of haunting it is? That I don't know yet."

"Kind of haunting? What do you mean, what kind? Like 'Paranormal Activity' or 'The Conjuring' kind of haunting?"

"You shouldn't watch so many horror movies, Robert. They're complete bunk." I chuckled, even though I felt more like rolling my eyes. "This could just be a residual haunt. Think of it like a psychic recording that's imprinted on the house that just keeps replaying night after night. With an R.H., there's nothing attached to it, no 'ghost' per se, just a piece of history that replays over and over. That's what you see with a lot of the Civil War battlefield haunts you see

on the History Channel. It's just leftover energy repeating the past."
I let them absorb that, trying to sound confident, even though I was
mostly paraphrasing what I'd read on ghost hunter sites. I really
needed Nicky here. "That's why I'm also doing a full background
check on the house. Who built it, its full history. We'll find answers
and that will help determine how we follow up the investigation."

Dillon was leaning both elbows on the table, rubbing his temples as though he was getting a headache. "First thing I'm doing is
going through the house for stray electronics. Tech's our thing. If
someone's got this house wired, we'll find it."

"Okay." I agreed. "But do it together and document every step
on camera. Do you have a digital camera?"

"Five." Irvin spoke up finally. He'd pushed away his half-eaten
food and closed the pizza box. "And that's just mine."

"I'm leaving you a copy of the sound recording." I pulled the
memory card out of my computer with the sound-file on it. "And
these." I put the copies of the blueprints on the table. "Look, guys,
I don't want this to scare you in any way. Whatever's been going on
here, you've been living with it the whole time, and none of you
have suffered any harm from it. It's probably completely harmless.
But I'll be honest. I've heard some crazy stuff, but this really shook
me up, hearing that recording the first time. I can only imagine
what it must be like for you actually living with it."

"You have no idea." Dillon said suddenly, raising his head to
meet my eye. "This is insane. How do you do it?"

"Investigate this kind of thing?"

"No, pull one over on people like this." He was staring at me
as though he'd never seen me before. All the southern hospitality
was gone, and what was left in his gaze was sub-Arctic. I felt my
stomach lurch a little. "Plant evidence so that we pay you to solve
it. What's up with that?"

The accusation stung hard, but more than that, it pissed me
off. *Fabricate evidence?* Fury roared behind my eyes as I stared
straight at him. Somehow, I managed to keep my voice even and
professional. "If you don't want my help, you don't have it." My gaze
flicked to Robert and then to Irvin, who looked like he was about

to hyperventilate. I pushed back my chair. "You have your evidence and the results of my initial research, which concludes your consultation. Therefore, I'll consider our contract concluded. Have a nice night, gentlemen."

I gathered my computer into my bag, avoiding looking at any of them. I was never a particularly good bluffer. I'd learned bluffing from my father and the one piece of advice I always failed was making direct eye contact. I was almost to the door, when Irvin's voice called me back, high pitched and pleading.

"Kami. Please . . . Uh . . . you can't . . . just go, right?"

I turned back, one hand on the fancy brass door-latch, cold under my fingers. "I told you from the beginning, all the occupants of the house have to be down with the investigation. If they aren't able to work with me, then you need to find someone that you can work with. It's good advice, Mr. Zettlemeyer. It works for lawyers, hairdressers, and therapists, too."

Before I said more, I yanked open the door and strode out into the rainy night, remembering too late that I'd forgotten my hat. It was still on their table. Well, darn it. I wasn't going back in now! One couldn't just storm right back in after making a grand exit! I reached into my bag but only came up with Evrett's helmet. Grimacing, I held it for a flash of a second before deciding to risk it. I yanked the helmet over my wayward curls, pushed up the visor, and made a dash for the pick-up, the rain making energetic pinging noises on the top of the helm. "Sorry, Ev! I'll oil and polish you the second I get back! I promise."

I yanked open the truck door and hopped in, fumbling for a moment to get the key into the ignition, but as soon as the engine roared to life, I threw the gearshift into reverse. In the periphery of my vision, something moved at the side of the house. I swiveled my head back, slamming on the brakes so hard the truck skidded backwards, the back end fishtailing slightly. For an instant, I swear I saw a dark willowy shape standing in the rain, just at the corner of the garage, looking back at me.

Yanking Evrett off my head, I kicked the headlights on high-beam and stared through the darkness and driving rain. *Nothing.*

No shadow, no image of a slender woman imprinted in the dark background alongside the concrete drive. But I'd seen her. I knew I'd seen her. My heart felt like a kettle drum was about to explode from it, and if I'd eaten any of that pizza, it would have been on its way back up. I was shaking as I got out of the truck and walked to the edge of the house. That side of the house drops down the hillside, a sheer concrete wall that goes straight down with only a waist-high concrete barrier to keep someone from a fall. No one could have come or gone from that direction.

As I turned back to the truck, I was chilled through and through, and not just from the rain. Realizing the helmet was still in my hand, I jammed it down over my wet curls, protecting me from the pouring rain as I climbed back into the pick-up.

I slid it back into gear, but before I pulled out, I took a last look at the house. The shape was back, and this time, it seemed to raise an elongated arm—almost waving. Then it faded into the side of the garage.

Silent and disbelieving, I yanked Evrett's helmet off one more time and sat for a time staring intently at the spot where I'd seen the figure. The heater in the truck was finally kicking in, but my shivers had grown worse. What had I just seen? Had I seen it at all? What the hell? *What the hell, Kam?* I asked myself over and over, first silently, and then out loud. I pulled on Evrett's helm, took it off again, and put it back on, but it was just the same as it had been in the moment before. No figure, no shifting ripples. Just the corner of the garage, the concrete barrier, and the wall of the house.

Realizing that I probably looked suspicious, having stormed out and then not gone away as I'd promised, I finally backed out and drove with extra-slow caution all the way back to the office. But the pauses at every red light and left turn gave my brain time to think between 'shift, check mirrors, watch ahead, stop early for the light'. Sure, those are pretty basic thoughts, and most of us can think around them, but my brain seemed suddenly capable of only one very slow thought at a time.

What if I saw the apparition because Evrett was showing it to me? I had been wearing his helmet both times that I saw it. Was he somehow able to part the veil? "Evrett? Was that you? I mean, did you do that?"

The helmet just sat, glistening silver, on the seat beside me.

Now that the idea had been planted, I couldn't seem to uproot it. I wanted to test it, was eager to test it. I could have a piece of ghost hunting equipment that no one else had! I could be . . . be . . . what? The crazy ghost-hunter lady with the medieval helmet on her head? Yeah, that was me.

CHAPTER 10

Wednesday Night

I TOOK EVRETT'S HEAD WITH ME BACK to the safe house, where I dried it off and rubbed in a thin coating of mineral oil. I left it on the table, popped a frozen dinner into the oven and ran a hot bath. The tiny shower in the office was adequate, but the luxury of kicking back in a hot bathtub, buried in soft white bubbles, with a plate of hot dinner to eat and the TV turned to face the bathroom door, made me feel unspeakably decadent. All I needed was some chocolate. That was something that needed to be added to the safe-house list of equipment.

I flipped through the TV-channels, looking for something amusing and brainless, stopped on a silly sitcom with people running around making foolish choices and slap-sticking their way through the consequences. It made me feel a little better. At least I wasn't that stupid, right?

I woke up with the bathwater having gone cold and a news-caster tv voice coming from the next room. I shut the shower-door and flipped the stream on high to rinse the chill off, so I missed whatever was being said. I was toweling off in the middle of the room with the heater-unit on full-blast, carefully avoiding the two nasty cat scratches I was now carrying, before I started paying half-attention to the show and realized that the voice was that of popular local news investigator, Feliz Ciaro. His show started at 11:00, so it was later than I'd realized.

Hoover chased his ball under the sofa, and lay with his paws outstretched underneath, batting like a mad fiend.

"Safe for everyone except bouncy-balls." I tilted the couch back to retrieve the super-ball, resting it on my shoulder as I reached around underneath.

My hand found something.

Something definitely was *not* a bouncy-ball.

I shoved the couch backwards until it tilted against the wall and stood up, grabbing Hoover before he could scramble in and investigate. I deposited the squirming feline into the bathroom, found my cellphone on the table and punched Reggie's contact icon.

"You've reached Reginald, I'm out at the moment. Please leave a message at the beep. If this is an emergency, please call Oslo and Burroughs service." I hung up before the recording gave me the number.

I already had the Oslo and Burroughs number in my phone and found them in the list, my eyes tracing to the clock. It was just past eleven. He had to still be up. Oslo and Burroughs answering service answered. "I need to speak to Reginald Burroughs. It's urgent."

About twenty minutes passed before Reggie called me back, opening with the words, "Kami? Is everything all right?"

"Why is there a gun under the couch?"

I didn't know silence could be so audible.

Finally, he uttered, "Come again?"

"Gun. Couch. Safe house." I thought for a second and then managed to elaborate. "How safe is it supposed to be when there's a gun under the couch?"

"Don't touch it."

"I did, by accident," I grumbled miserably. "I was looking for Hoover's ball."

"You *touched* it?" Reginald's voice said I should have known better.

"Accidently!" I justified. "I wasn't exactly expecting a gun under the sofa!"

"Well, don't touch it again."

"I can't just leave it under the sofa, Reggie. I mean, for crying out loud, what if Hoover had reached it first? He was under there pawing around for his ball. He could have shot me."

"Really? Hoover doesn't seem like a murderer. Is it loaded?"

"Hoover has committed personal assault on me twice in the past forty-eight hours. Who knows what he's capable of?" Reggie's last question confused me for a beat. "And how am I supposed to know if it's loaded if I'm not touching it?"

"Okay. Go to the kitchen, get a couple plastic bags. Put your hand in a bag and use it to lift the gun into the other bag. Then seal the bag and put it somewhere safe."

"Safe? It's a gun, Reggie, not the One Ring."

"You're right," he said agreeably. "The One Ring didn't have anywhere that was safe. That's why it had to be destroyed."

I squeezed the phone to my ear and rubbed my eyes. "I'm not taking the gun to Mount Doom. It's late and I'm tired."

"No, you're putting it somewhere safe and tomorrow I will come by and deliver it to our PI. He can trace it, figure out what it's doing there, and who it belongs to."

The Oslo and Burrough's private investigator? You didn't need to be a P.I. to trace a gun. "You know, Reggie, I could do that for you."

"No, you can't. You're my client. You can't work for me right now." He was starting to sound a little grumpy. "Now, I'm going to bed. You need to go to bed, too. Do. Not. Touch that gun!"

"Yeah, Okay." I fetched a couple of gallon sized zip-lock plastic bags from the kitchen drawer. Gun safely retrieved, I placed it on the table and looked it at for a long time. It was a .38 Glock semi-automatic; small, and compact—the kind of gun I would own if I wasn't so afraid of being shot. Through the plastic, I pressed the clip release, slid the clip free and pulled the chamber. Fully loaded, ten rounds plus the chambered one. I slid the clip back in, switched the safety on, and then put the bag in the freezer under a stack of frozen dinners. That's when I noticed the pint-sized ice-cream containers, resting in a bed of glittering ice crystals towards the back of the freezer.

Was this my reward for putting the gun away? Fate was awesome! I grabbed a container of double-fudge ice cream, found a spoon, and took it to bed with me. Who keeps a safe house with Egyptian cotton sheets? Oslo and Burroughs do, apparently. I nestled into luxurious smoothness, cradling my ice cream. There was a set of rules on the side of the bed: no smoking in the apartment, no eating in the bed. *No eating in bed?* Well, how were they going to know?

Sugar-craving satisfied, I went back through the apartment checking the door and windows and ensuring they were locked. I checked Hoover's food and water, and then headed to bed. They tell you that you can't sleep alone in a strange place, but I slept for a long and dreamless time.

CHAPTER 11

───❧───

Thursday Morning

THE NEXT MORNING, I WOKE EARLY, gathered Hoover into his harness and for the first time in three days put on a clean pressed suit, and pinned down my unruly mess of hair. I tried not to think about the gun in the apartment—or how bad the house-keeping service had to be to not have discovered it. *Eww.*

It was blearily early, barely coming on light, so I could avoid the traffic getting to work. I dropped Hoover off in the office and returned Evrett's head to his suit with a warning. "We need to talk, old boy. Don't get too comfy."

At Reese's, I ordered a bagel with egg salad and a Reese's Brown Bottom. The Brown Bottom is a cup of Reese's regular house coffee with several pumps of hot fudge in it, topped with cream and a shot of espresso. You need waking up? The Brown Bottom will not only wake you up, it'll triple your productivity. There's also the slight possibility that it'll give you the jitters for three days. Big deal—what's a little eye-twitch now and then?

That is, I thought gloomily, if you have something to be productive about. My one paying job was over. Of course, that meant I could focus all my energy on Kenny and the Trunk Girl. I believed Kenny was innocent of anything other than extreme stupidity, and really, don't we all do stupid things once in a while?

But I had to find him. He'd been alive two weeks ago, so where was he now?

Bagel nice and toasty in one hand and my Brown Bottom safe and secure in the other hand, I headed back across the street to the office—only to groan when I saw who was standing in front of my office.

Irvin Zettlemeyer, looking skinnier and paler than ever; Fi Espinoza, looking more bushy-haired than ever; and Robert Daltry, somehow managing to make even his stylish long leather trench-coat look extraordinarily geeky, were standing in front of the building, waiting for me with downcast eyes under the dark red awning.

"Morning, folks," I said with a grin that I hoped was breezy as I juggled my bagel and coffee to unlock the door. "Good to see you."

They exchanged deer-in-headlights looks and followed me into the office. I kicked on the thermostat, set my coffee on my desk and switched on my laptop as though they weren't all standing there watching me go about my day. I unwrapped my bagel and took a large bite, chewing as calmly as I could while they shuffled around me. I was encircled by a coven of geeks. If they started chanting, I was going to call Brittle and turn myself in. He was a smart man; he could find something to hold me on.

"Come on, say something," I gulped enough food to finally encourage. "We discussed this last night. I can't work if I'm being accused of fabricating evidence. That constitutes a hostile environment. I won't have my reputation damaged by false accusations. And honestly, I think all you have is a little residual haunting from some old event in the house. You can probably check news records yourself and figure out what it's all about. You don't even really need me."

Except that from everything I'd read, residual haunts didn't result in full-scale apparitions that waved at you. I thought it best not to mention that little event to the former client base.

"Yes, we do." Fiora said quietly. "We do need you."

Irvin was huddling in his coat and wouldn't meet my eye as he tried to explain. "Dillon's like . . . he's kind of strung, you know.

Suspicious of everything. It's what makes him a good security pro, yeah? He's sorry."

"Sorry? He accused me of fabricating evidence in order to extort money from you. I don't need that. And neither do you. I don't need this job." I lied, and this time I made direct eye-contact with each of them in turn, beginning and ending with Zettlemeyer. Take that, bluffers of the world! "You need to find someone he can trust to work with. I have to think of my reputation."

"Please, just come back. Help us out. This is driving us all crazy," Robert pleaded, his short-fingered hands wringing together. "You're like . . . You're our mage. Every party needs a good mage."

"And a barbarian." Fiora added, a half-smile finally approaching her face. "Think of Dillon as our barbarian."

"A suspicious, accusatory barbarian," Irvin muttered. "Not a berserker wild one."

I think that was all a role-playing reference, but I didn't dare mention that I had no idea what they were talking about. At the end of the day, I *did* need the job, even if it came with a hefty dose of accusatory barbaric behavior. "If you want me back on the job, I want an anti-defamation clause added to the contract," I said with slow-syllabled clarity. "And I'm bringing in more team members. Nicky you know, but I'm also bringing in Morri Morrimont. He's got more experience dealing with this kind of haunt than I do. I also have a priest on standby if necessary."

All three of them relaxed so quickly it was almost as if the air fell out of their lungs.

"Thank you!" Irvin enthused. "Thank you! I mean, I don't know what we woulda done. You are a godsend! An angel!"

I held up both hands, palm out. "Hold on. I'm not finished. I want a personal apology from Dillon."

The three of them exchanged glances and their smiles faded faster than the BART train that you just missed.

"And if he doesn't want me to continue the investigation, I'm out. Find someone else. I can reach out to my connections and can recommend some people if you'd like."

"He will agree," Fiora stated with a confidence that didn't show on her face—or, for that matter, in the faces of the others. She smiled that trapped-looking smile again. "Won't he, guys?"

"Yeah." Robert agreed, sounding quite sure of himself for a change. Irvin nodded, a little less enthusiastically.

"I'm a researcher," I intoned cautiously, while giving an internal whoop of triumph. "This is what I do. I think you have a fascinating case and I'm happy to continue the investigation. But only if everyone agrees."

"Dillon will fall in," Robert encouraged.

Irvin looked like he'd already fallen into something, and it wasn't something pleasant.

I sighed. It was bad enough that I was about to gain a reputation as a paranormal researcher. Did I really want to be thought of as a crooked one? But then I considered hourly rates for an overnight investigation. Even if I split it evenly with Morri and Nicky, my bank account needed this. "Okay. I'll do it. I'll be your mage. But no funky wizard hats or rainbow cloaks, got it?"

"What about a crystal staff?" Robert asked, but he was smiling. I assumed he was joking.

"Just my magic helmet." I assumed they'd take that for a joke, too, even though that was one thing I was dead serious about.

They all nodded enthusiastically so I edited up a new contract on my laptop and printed out five copies, signing and handing one to each of them. Dillon's, I handed to Irvin, since he was the one I'd originally dealt with. "If Dillon doesn't sign it, I'm out."

"He will." Irvin said quietly.

"I also talked to HR and Corporate Resources," Robert added. "They said whatever we do is fine, but if there's going to be TV crews involved, they need insurance waivers."

"No television. No newspapers" I declared. That was the last thing I needed! But I did need Morri. "No other groups. No publicity. No nothing. Just me, my partners and our equipment. I promise discreet and respectful investigations, and that's exactly what you'll receive."

Because no way was I going to tell anyone that I was a professional ghost hunter now.

They all looked quite a bit more relieved as they trooped out into the rain and climbed into Robert's Corolla. I was half jealous. I wanted a shiny new burgundy Corolla, with or without the Avengers seat covers. Some things just aren't fair.

I LEAPT INTO THE PROBLEM of finding my brother. I needed to find him and protect him, which was ironic considering that only two days ago, I'd been very much interested in sending him to prison for grand theft auto. That is, providing the blue book value on my Kia was greater than $950.00, which was doubtful.

But I didn't want to see him jammed up over a murder that I was positive he didn't commit. While my brother could be accused of many things, being organized enough to put a body in a trunk and drive it into the reservoir—after faking it being stolen to throw his friends off the track? All of it was entirely unlikely. Kenny was more the sort who would find one of his buddies dying, put him in the backseat meaning to drive him to the hospital, then decide that he was hungry, stop for a burger, and then, on realizing that his friend wasn't answering what kind of burger he wanted, speed to the hospital and get pulled over by a traffic cop and then arrested for driving around with a body in the back of his car. My brother wasn't known for his actual organizational skills. He was more free form.

I called Detective Brittle; still no identity on Jane Doe #673, aka Trunk Girl. "Poor Trunk Girl", and I meant it. How awful to be dead and no one's even reported you missing. Then again, Kenny had been missing for almost two weeks and I hadn't bothered to report him missing. "I can't believe nobody's looking for her."

"I am." Brittle corrected me with a hint of professional pride in his voice. "Jane Doe Number 673 has a family somewhere. She has a name. Someone wants to know what's happened to her. We'll find them."

"Yeah, maybe. Have you talked to David Hostner?"

"Yes, and Hems."

"And they both confirm that Kenny was there?"

"Yes, and you were right. Hostner is credible. Not sure about Hems. But their stories hang together. We've pulled the security camera footage from the gas station in Reno where Hems says he met up with Kenny to try to confirm his story."

"Yeah. I'm not sure Snake Hems knows Reno from Renoir. I wouldn't want him on a witness stand." I filled in warily, but the rest gave me sudden hope. I hadn't even thought about security cameras! "Is Kenny on the footage?"

THERE WAS A LONG PAUSE, and I knew Detective Brittle wasn't sure how much he should tell me. "Well, it's a busy older gas-station and there are six cameras, one on each of the pumps and one on the cash register inside. We have what may be your car rolling up to a pump, and but no clear footage of your brother. Not yet, anyway. There's a lot to go through and we're still combing the footage for clues. The station attendant doesn't remember either of them, but there were hundreds of cars going through on their way to Burning Man. He said that they all started to look alike."

"They all looked like freaks, you mean?" I sighed. There just wasn't a break to catch, was there? "Would it be okay if I looked? I mean, I know I'm still a suspect, but I would know Kenny, even if he's blurry and pixelated."

To my surprise, he agreed. "You're right. You might see things we'd miss. I'll talk to the tech person going over the footage and have them call you to set up a time."

"Thank you. That means a lot." That was all I could say. If I could look, I was sure I would see Kenny. I would prove he was there. "Okay. I'm going to continue trying to track down people who might have been with my brother. If I learn anything vital, I'll bring you in immediately, but I have a feeling they'll be more likely to talk to me than to you."

"And what's wrong with me?" I could hear the laughter in Brittle's voice.

"Absolutely nothing in my book. But they might take offense to the badge. And the hair. Guys named Snake tend to have problems with guys with good hair."

"I have good hair?"

"Good day, Detective. I'll call if I learn anything." I hung up, half-way snickering. I was kind of starting to like the guy.

His partner, on the other hand, needed to be backhanded with his own badge. I fantasized about that for a few moments. Too bad no one would ever do it. Detective Dortman was the sort who would retire from the force in twenty years with his gold badge and his pension fund and tell stories about what a great cop he was and how much rookies had learned from him, never realizing that what rookies had learned from him was not to be like him. We all want to leave a legacy. Just sometimes it's not what we envision.

CHAPTER 12

———

Thursday Afternoon

I HAD A MISSING BROTHER, A MISSING CLASSMATE, and a dead body in the trunk of my car. There was possibility that I was a murder suspect, or a potential victim. It was a mess . . . and what was I doing about it? I was sitting at my little folding desk with Hoover, watching videos of birds on YouTube. I like my cat. He likes chickadees. But I had no idea what to do next. When the office phone rang, I jolted upright. This was it. I answered it with a brisk, "White Legal Services. This is Kami. How may I help you?"

"Kami? It's Hoser. You get my emails?"

I hadn't even checked my messages since lunch. "Hold on half-a-sec." I stalled while I closed Hoover's video and opened my email. There were client messages, spam messages, and two emails from Hoser. It only took opening one to see that Hoser had come through in spades for me. Each message contained eight links to online albums full of pictures of the desert art festival.

"Hoser? I think you just officially became my hero."

"Nice. I've never been anyone's hero before." Hoser hung up and I grabbed a fresh cup of tea and settled in for the long haul

An hour later, I was half-blind. Or at least some of the pictures made me wish I was. But I had to admit that some were intriguing to the point where I would forget that I was looking for a face in the crowds. I'd catch myself looking at pictures of incredible art installations; raw metal, wood, or brightly colored fabrics, all framed against dusty-yellow playa sands and blaze-blue skies, admiring the composition of the photo, and, in some cases, wondering what could possibly have inspired someone to build *that* and take it *there*?

I'd looked at six albums worth of photos when I gave up. There are only so many mostly-naked, dusty, weird people one can stand to look at in a day, and so far there was no sign of Trunk Girl at Burning Man. Of course, she could have been in a mask or full costume, or running around in a pedal-powered spaceship and would I even recognize her? Especially having only seen a head and shoulders shot of her sodden corpse; all I really had to go on was blond hair and a neck tattoo. I stretched out full-length on the floor to think while Hoover clambered all over me, rubbing his jaw over my hair and kneading my belly with his hard little paws.

Tallying up what I had, and what I didn't, I scooted Hoover aside, grabbed my cellphone and called Detective Brittle, hoping I wasn't making a terrible mistake.

"I'm sorry, Detective. I'd hoped that my idea would pan out, but it didn't. I was wondering though . . ."

"Go ahead." It was the long-suffering sigh of a detective with too much on his plate.

"Was there anything else in my car? I mean, besides Trunk Girl and whatever might have belonged to Ken?"

The detective was quiet for a long moment, and I was just about to reassure him that I wasn't in any hurry, when I heard the shuffling papers and realized he had the materials list right in front of him. "Our guys took the whole car apart, looking for whatever evidence we could recover. Inside the trunk there wasn't anything really unusual, besides Jane Doe, that is. Let's see. There were three boxes of MREs and several gallon jugs of water . . ."

"We know Kenny's food and water for the camping trip was stolen with the car," I filled in.

"Confirmed by eyewitnesses," Brittle agreed before continuing. "Road safety kit with flares, jumper cables, wrenches, screwdrivers, and a Donald Duck blanket?"

"Mine. Duck was on sale at Wal-Mart. Great for picnics."

"Yeah." I guessed the homicide detective had heard so much that nothing surprised him anymore. "Ummm, bag of miniature Snickers."

"Darn! I wondered where I left those!" Suddenly I needed a sugar fix, but not badly enough to want those Snickers. In fact, just thinking about the bag stuck underwater in the trunk with a decaying body, I wasn't sure I'd ever eat a Snickers bar again, mini or otherwise.

"Shovel with broken handle . . ."

I held up my hand, taking a beat before I remembered that he couldn't see me over the phone. I pretended to pat down my hair, just in case Evrett was watching. "I don't own a shovel."

"Check. Not your shovel." Brittle continued, sounding business-like but I could imagine his amused smile. "Pair of boots, men's size twelve."

"I'm five-and-a-half ladies. I don't know what that is in men's."

"That would be a kid-size. Not men size." Brittle's dry humor carried through the phone line. "Anyway, according to your mother, Kenny wears a size 12. We're assuming they're his boots. They were too waterlogged from the lake for analysis, as was most of everything recovered. That's all that's on the list."

"Is there a chance the shovel is my brother's? I mean, camping in the desert, you need a shovel, right?"

"Maybe. The lab is doing prints, but being underwater like that, it's not certain anything will turn up. We also don't have your brother's prints for comparison." He paused again. "As soon as the lab is done with your belongings, you can have them back. Whatever isn't directly connected to Jane Doe, that is."

I thought for a second. "No, I don't want them. Not after . . . I mean . . ."

"Ew?" Brittle laughed again. "I didn't take you for the squeamish sort, Miss White."

"Squeamish? No. Not interested in anything that's been at the bottom of the reservoir, that's all. Gonna miss Donald, though." I changed tacks, charging into the next unknown on my list. "Is there cause of death yet?"

"On Donald Duck, or Jane Doe?"

"My god, Detective Brittle, was that a joke?"

He chuckled, and I was surprised to find myself smiling in turn. "Don't get used to it. To answer your questions, the medical examiner's report should be back this afternoon that. I'll know more then, but you understand that I may not be able to share details with you."

" Oh, I get it. Being a suspect and all myself." I didn't like it, but I got it. "Well, If I come up with anything else . . ."

"I'll be the first to know," Brittle sighed. "Miss White, maybe you should just sit back and let us detectives do what it is we do? I mean, you aren't considered a suspect at this point. You're doing what you said in helping find your brother. Why dig yourself into this mess?"

"I don't know, Detective." Honestly, why did I care? What difference did it make? So long as Kenny wasn't guilty of anything more than not reporting that my car was stolen—and unmitigated stupidity, which, sadly, wasn't a prosecutable offence—why did I care whose body that was and how it got there? All I knew was that I did care. A lot. "I guess it just bothers me, you know. It's a mystery. And I know my brother didn't do it, whatever else might point to him."

"Mysteries are for detectives, you know. Paralegals usually come in after the mystery is solved."

"That shows how much you know about paralegals," I clipped back and hung up before he could push me into explaining. Anyway, I had a legal degree. I was just a stint at police academy away from his job—not that I wanted to go to police academy.

I gave up lying on the floor and forced myself to sit up and resume flipping through more pictures of painted naked desert people. I had to admit that a lot of the art was amazing, but my eyes were too tired to glean faces. My detective work had led me to a gigantic black hole.

I could hear Hoover playing in the file room and was reminded that those files on the floor weren't going to box themselves. I snapped my laptop closed and headed for the back room. At least working would give me something physical to do.

I worked up a sweat, filling boxes in order, labeling them, and stacking them neatly against the wall. When I was finished, the former file room was now the box room. This seemed to excite Hoover to no end, and he leaped from box to box, stack to stack, pouncing on invisible dust bubbles. I wadded a blank page into a ball and threw it for him, sort of an apology for turning off his birdy video. He ran and tackled it, rolling around on the natty old carpet, shaking it until he deemed it dead. For all that he's very much an elite, pampered all-indoor kitty, Hoover has the finely-honed hunting instincts of a paper-shredder.

The office phone rang and it was Hoser.

"Did those jeeps help at all?"

"Jeeps?" I thought back through the pictures. I didn't remember any jeeps.

"J-pegs. Pictures."

Oh, right. JPG, digital format pictures. I rolled my eyes at myself. I might live on the edge of the heart of the tech industry, but my own tech-savviness was nonexistent. "Not really, but thanks anyway. They just didn't pan out." I wondered if there was more Hoser could offer me as a direct eyewitness to the affair. "Looks like it was a pretty strange time out there."

"It was. Strange and awesome. This was my sixth year. I love it, even though it gets more crowded and commercial every year." Hoser hesitated before continuing. "But that's not why I called. I think I found something you might be able to use. There were a bunch of aerial photos taken of the whole thing. There's several of them, taken on all different days of the festival. You can see all the cars parked. The online version isn't high-res, but I know the photographer and she's putting together a file of the high-resolution images for us."

"All the parked cars? Hoser! You rock!" I grinned.

"I assure you I don't." Belatedly I remembered that his Facebook profile said he was in a western steampunk blues band. I couldn't tell if I'd offended him or not. "Anyway, if you want, I can bring them by your place?"

"Bring them to my office." I gave him the address. "We can look at them together."

"Okay. Sure." He rang off and I did a little jig. This might be the break I was looking for.

I jogged back over to Reese's and, not knowing what Hoser liked, got two small lattes and a couple of bagels. I really needed to step up my diet, I thought. Maybe add in some vegetables or fruit or something. Well, there was fruity stuff in the bottom of my yogurt. That counted, right?

My mind kept straying back to the body in my car. More than where she might have come from, it was the identity of the dead woman that was driving me crazy. Waiting for the ME report was like lying awake at 3 am on Christmas Eve, except without the surety that the surprise would be worth the anticipation. People didn't just die in car trunks every day. Usually someone had to put them there, right? While that person who put her in the trunk might not necessarily be looking for her, why didn't it seem like anyone else was looking either?

I searched the state missing person's database again, then did a general search for finding missing women. It was possible that her family was looking for her but that the police had labeled her missing of her own accord or had refused to file a report with no evidence of foul play or something. There were a dozen reasons that the cops could fail to look into a missing person situation. Just as I was giving up hope, Hoser arrived with his laptop and a portable hard drive.

I think I have a decent laptop. I bought it on sale through one of those discount websites, and it's never failed me. It's black, with a full keyboard, and a sixteen-inch screen. It's decent. Compared to Hoser's machine, my laptop was some primordial creature that had failed to evolve in the swamps of technology. Slick and silver, with a keyboard that glowed blue as he opened the screen, Hoser's computer resembled a science fiction techno-beast.

His screen had far better resolution than mine, so we sat side by side, tapping our way through the images. We zoomed in as close as we could: not this one, not that one. Do you know how many blue cars there are? Apparently after a day or two on the desert flats, they stopped being blue and just turned a brownish color with a blue tint.

"Why, oh why, didn't I buy a bright green car with yellow racing stripes across the top?" I lamented aloud.

"Because that would be tacky. You don't strike me as tacky," Hoser said, eyes scanning down me in a way that from someone else might have been creepy, but from Hoser, it just seemed curious—kinda cute.

"Tacky, no. You're right. I'm not rich enough to afford tacky." My eyes turned back to the screen. We had the images blown up beyond the screen-size and had to scroll back and forth as we scanned the cars in batches of five at a time. "Wait! What's that?"

"That's not blue."

"No. It's burgundy. It's a burgundy Corolla. A brand-new burgundy Corolla." It was a new Corolla with an Avengers sunscreen and custom painted Avenger's 'A' emblem on the roof.

"I thought we were looking for a blue Kia."

I shook my head. What difference did it make if Robert went to Burning Man? Because, I thought to myself, that guy shouldn't be seen naked *anywhere*, especially not out in the desert. "We are. I just know who owns that Corolla. I didn't know he was at Burning Man."

"Lots of people go who don't talk about it back in the normal world." Hoser shrugged. "I mean, my bosses don't care, and I save my vacation time so I can go. But there are a lot of careers that could be ruined by this kind of thing. I mean . . ." He pointed to my computer screen, displaying a group of scantily clad women waving flaming firebrands. It sort of looked like fun, in a dangerous set-yourself-on-fire kind of way. ". . . Would you want to know if one of them was your gynecologist?"

"Point taken." I grimaced and turned back to the car picture. "It's not here, is it? I mean, what's the chance. It was just a hunch, anyway."

Hoser shrugged and started to close the photos. "Sorry. We tried."

"Yeah, we did. Thanks for trying." I tried not to feel despondent. My one clever thought had turned into not clever enough. I took one last look at the picture of the parking area. "Wait . . . What's that? There?"

"Dust cloud. Someone driving away."

"Blue! It's my car!" I leaned over Hoser and moused in, centering the image and zooming in until I was positive. "That's my car!"

Hoser cropped the driving away car and pasted it into his graphics program, making it cleaner and closer. His hands were amazing, long-fingered and delicate-looking and they practically flashed as they flew from keyboard to mouse and back again. "There, that's as clean as it gets."

The top back edge of my Kia, faded blue, disappearing into a cloud of dust, my neat row of college parking permit stickers across the top of the rear window and the smashed bumper leaving no doubt in my mind that this was my poor old, tattered wreck of a car . . . and there was something else. Donald Duck was draped over the backseat, not in the trunk—draped as though he was covering something. My heart jolted sickly.

"What day was this? What time?"

Hoser printed the picture and saved it to disk for me. "Day two. Why does someone leave on Day Two? I mean, if you're coming all that way and spending all that money for tickets, why leave? I know a lot of people come later in the week, or just show up for the Burn. They're trying to discourage that, though."

"They leave because they didn't find what they were looking for," I mused, turning the words over in my head. "Or because something went wrong."

"Like someone got sick or hurt?" Hoser asked, pointing to the smashed bumper of my car. "It's not unusual out there, you know. It can be a dangerous place if you're careless, and people die of stupidity sometimes. Dehydration is a big factor, especially when you combine in drugs. One year, a girl got hit by an art car in the dark because she wasn't wearing proper lighting, I think. Accidents happen."

But if it was an accident, why put her in the trunk? It didn't make sense.

"It's also not unusual for people to have to make a supply run to Gurlock." Hoser continued. "They come out unprepared, without enough water or sunscreen or food, or just suddenly decide they need to make a Twinkie run."

"Most importantly, after this date, when my car was pulling out, Kenny was with you, right? With you and Snake?"

"Yeah, and Mudpuppy. I took quite a few pictures myself and they're all date-stamped. I already sent them to that detective, so I'll be able to prove Kenny was with us. Here, you'll want those, too." He pulled out a flash-drive and started copying pictures over to it. "What now?"

"I don't know. I need to talk to . . . someone." *Who, though? Reggie? Detective Brittle? Maybe both.* There were still a lot of pieces missing, but at least now I had a corner piece, somewhere to start from. He handed me the flash-drive and I saved the pictures and the cropped and zoomed image of my car to my laptop. "You've been a huge help, Hoser. Thanks for everything. If there's anything I can ever do for you . . ."

"Thanks for the coffee. Listen, you want to get together sometime, hang out? I know a place that does great cheesecake."

"Yeah. Sure. That'd be nice." I grabbed my suit jacket and shrugged into it, tucked the memory card into my pocket. "I'll call you. Or you can call me. You have my number, right?"

I love cheesecake. I had long ago made it a policy not to get involved with my brother's friends, but this might be an exception. I hustled Hoser out the door, and ran around back to the pick-up, already dialing Reggie on my cellphone.

"The PI will be by to pick up the gun this afternoon and deliver it to the police," were the first words out of Reggie's mouth.

"What gun?" My brain stuttered before it remembered. "Oh, that gun. Never mind that! My car. It was at Burning Man. I have pictures of it leaving the festival on the second day."

"Meet me at the cop shop."

"Cop shop? Are you a lawyer or a movie character?"

"Station," Reggie grunted, exasperated. "Don't go in or talk to anyone until I get there. In fact, just don't talk to anyone, period. Not a word."

I'D BEEN WAITING ONLY A FEW MINUTES when Reginald's car pulled up next to the pick-up and we walked into the police station side by side. It was a far cry from being dragged up in the back of Detective Brittle's car. This time, I was dressed in my legal best: black knee-length skirt and sleek gray jacket. My black low-slung pumps were clicking on the cement as I clipped up the stairs beside Reginald, who looked sharp in his expensive blue suit. We were legal. We were upholders of the law—supporters of the law. We were here to make a difference.

I patted down my curls with one hand as we approached the glass doors, trying to make sure I looked presentable, and then Reggie swept the door open and I ducked under his arm into the raw papery smell of police stations everywhere.

Detective Brittle was walking towards us, and we spoke simultaneously.

"I have news!"

Turning aside, he ushered us into a small conference room. It wasn't all that different from the interrogation room I'd been in before, but instead of a two-way mirror, there was a picture of the San Francisco skyline on the wall and the chairs were nicer. I was disappointed to see that Detective Dortman was waiting for us as well, but I barely bothered to meet the man's eye. *Today, you are beneath me. I'm on the other side of the table.*

"You first." Detective Brittle waved to me, gesturing for us to sit.

I flipped the print of the picture I'd made from my small ink-jet printer onto the table and opened my laptop, turning it to display the original and the cropped and zoomed images side by side. "That's my car. Leaving Burning Man on the second day of the festival. This is a close up from some aerial photos that were taken and the images are the original jpegs with the exif data attached, including data and time. There's no doubt it's my car." I right-clicked and showed the exif data. "The dates and times of these pictures show that my car left while my brother was still at Burning Man. Here he is in date-stamped photos taken with friends that same evening."

"So, your hunch was that the car left Burning Man without your brother?"

"It occurred to me. I mean, most of the festival folk are artists and art-lover hippyish types, all full of the love-spirit, but there must be a criminal element that would be attracted to a place like that, right? How hard it would be for someone to hitch along with all those cars into the middle of nowhere, just full of easy pickings? Is there any real security out there?"

Brittle nodded. "We've talked to eyewitnesses that say your brother was with them for most of the week. Unless the witnesses are lying and those photos are tampered with, which I'm still not entirely convinced of, it's getting difficult to believe that he left on the second day with your car." He tapped the photo I'd printed and glanced to Dortman. "And this could explain a lot."

"What's your news?" I asked, glancing to Reggie. He said nothing, and nothing in his expression indicated he wanted to take control of the conversation. He merely waited.

"Autopsy report." Brittle smiled. "Jane Doe died of drug overdose, complicated by dehydration. And there was dust in her lungs."

"Playa dust?" I pointed to the picture of my car. "You think she died at Burning Man? I hate to ask, but do you think she's what the blanket is covering in the back seat? Her . . ." I couldn't force myself to say 'body.'

"With the evidence you just provided, that seems very likely," Brittle said quietly.

I was staring straight at the autopsy photo as Brittle, Detective Dodo-man and Reginald discussed quietly the implications for and against Kenny being involved with a death at the festival, and more pointedly, the likelihood that I was involved somehow. Brittle and Dortman were cagey with the direct answer, but from Reggie's point of view it was pretty clear that I was no longer a suspect. When the topic turned to Kenny possibly being involved in the cover-up, if not the actual death of Jane Doe, I had to speak up.

"My friend told me this afternoon that it's not unusual for people to die out there, or have accidents they have to be rescued from." I filled in. "Do we have any reason, I mean, other than that she was shut in the trunk, for it to be suspicious?"

"Putting a body in the trunk of stolen vehicle and dumping it in a lake is a strong indicator of suspicious circumstances," Brittle's voice was wry.

"We also don't know that she was dead when the car left." I pointed to the picture again. "If she's under the blanket in the back seat, it could be she was still alive and whoever stole my car was trying to get her to a doctor."

"And then put her in the trunk? How does that make sense?" Dortman barked at me, but I barely heard him.

My eye was stuck to the photograph, eyeing the neat 'Y' of stitching where the ME had done his best to repair the damage his work had caused, studying the curve of the throat, the closed sunken eyes, and the faded ink on her neck. There was something about the tattoo. Something was so familiar. I reached out and unclipped the photo from the report, tilting it this way and that. *A lion? A dragon? Wings, head . . .*

"Oh. Omigod!" I was blind—an idiot. How could I have missed it?

The detectives were staring at me, and Reggie's hand reached for my arm. For a minute I couldn't stop gasping. It was staring at me. Had been staring right at me the entire time.

"Her tattoo. It's not a dragon! It's a phoenix! She's a Phoenix."

"Phoenix?" Brittle reached across the table and spun the picture around. "Yeah. That could be a phoenix, maybe."

"Like, 'Order of the Phoenix?' Is this a Harry Potter thing?" Reginald asked, disbelieving, and the detectives both chuckled.

"The Ensemble d'Phoenix! They're an artist's group, like a guild." I stopped and took a deep breath before they decided to fifty-one-fifty me. "The map! Reggie, the map. Yours and Charles' map? Do you have it?"

"It's still in the car." He stood up and left the room, leaving me alone with the detectives.

"I've seen that symbol nearly every day for the past five years," I told them. "I'm not sure why I didn't recognize it right away."

Maybe because it was all stretched and waterlogged? And on a dead person? Now Detective Dortman was giving me the stink eye over the table, like I'd been holding out on him and was now back on his suspect list.

Reggie came in with the tube and wriggled the map free. Spreading it out on the table, we all peered over it. "It came from a vacation we took together," he explained. "Charles Hanford and me."

The familiar map rolled out before me, and I knew in an instant that I was right. I pointed. "There! South of France!"

Over a black dot on the seashore, a small black phoenix was drawn, exactly matching the tattoo. "That coastal village is the original home of the Ensemble d'Phoenix. A safe haven for artists seeking respite from persecution since 1642. Trunk Girl was an artist!"

"Since 1642?" Brittle looked down at the map, then back at the tattoo on the woman's neck. "Is this some kind of Templar mystery code?"

"Not at all!" Oh, thank heavens for my insatiable curiosity and research skills. My brain might be full of useless trivia, but every now and again, something comes in handy! "The Phoenix Ensemble isn't any secret society or anything. They started in France during a time when most art had to be approved of by the Church. Artists who colored outside the lines, so to speak, were ostracized, even accused of heresy. They smuggled elicit works out of the reach of the church and protected the artists. Later, during the Nazi years, they helped artists and their families escape persecution. After the war, they helped track down artworks stolen by the German regime and return them to their rightful owners. These days, they're worldwide."

"What do these red and green lines mean?" Detective Dortman touched the map and I resisted the urge to slap his hand away.

"That's me . . ." Reggie pointed to the red one first and then let his finger brush the blue one. "And that's Charles. We were playing a kind of international Hide and Seek, you might say. Charles would trace where he'd been on the map, and then leave it for me to find, and I would trace where I had been and then leave it for him to find along with a clue to the next city to meet up in. It was a game, a treasure hunt." His eyebrows raised and he smiled sadly, "One of many, many games. The map was our souvenir. It went all over Europe with us."

I reached for Reggie's hand, impulsively, unprofessionally. He squeezed mine back, then let go.

"Trunk Girl," I returned us to the problem at hand with confidence. It was good to feel confident again. "She was an artist who went to Burning Man. She died of an overdose and rather than do the right thing, her fellow Burners dumped her in the trunk of my car and hid it."

"Why do that?" Dortman barked. "Unless they have something to hide?"

I blinked and tried to keep from snickering at him. I answered deadpan. "You mean like drugs, an overdose, and a stolen car?"

Dortman didn't look at me after that.

"The Ensemble d'Phoenix is a guild. It takes formal memberships. Members have to pay dues. They have ties to artist's retreats, auction houses, public exhibition halls; All kinds of places." I was remembering now and speaking as fast my vaguely recalled research would allow. "Someone involved with them will know who she is."

Brittle nodded. "We'll look into it. It's a possibility."

"Possibility, yes." Reginald said, and then continued in a tone that indicated we were finished here. "This M.E.'s report, however, is certainty. The woman in the trunk of your car died, most likely in Black Rock City in the Nevada desert, of a drug overdose complicated by dehydration. My client was here, in the Bay Area, where she had no access to her vehicle, nor access to the drugs necessary."

Both detectives nodded, but it was Brittle who spoke up. "We can certainly agree to that. Her brother . . ."

"Is still under suspicion since he was at the festival. My client, however, had nothing to do with Jane Doe . . ."

"Trunk Girl . . ." I interrupted ceremoniously. "And please let's not forget that Kenny is still missing and is a potential victim himself.

Reginald ignored me. ". . . with Jane Doe's suspicious death and the unfortunate location of her body."

We shook hands with the detectives, Reginald rolled up the map, and we started to take our leave, but Dortman called out, "Miss White, where exactly were you at the time and day that your car was photographed leaving Burning Man?"

I pretended to think about it for a moment, but the date was stamped on my brain in unrelenting detail. "I was at the Alameda County Courthouse." Good doggy, I wanted to say. Reggie's hand reached for my shoulder, his hand comforting and warm. "In a preliminary hearing regarding the contestation of Charles Hanford's will. It's public record. You can look it up."

Dortman hitched his head back a little. "You failed to mention that little fact."

"Because it wasn't relevant. And still isn't." Reginald snapped coolly. "We will send you a copy of the court docket for that day. The witnesses who saw her are of impeccable character, but I'm sure Judge Harbough won't mind being subpoenaed if you find it necessary. The point is, she was here, in the Bay Area. Not in Nevada."

Being reminded of Juliet Hanford and losing Charles was like being kicked in the gut. I stood and walked out.

Ron Brittle followed us out and dashed around to get in front of me. "I'm sorry. Dortman can be a little oblivious."

"Dorkbrains can go to hell." I probably shouldn't have said that, but I'd felt so high going in, and coming out, I felt as though that flabby law-enforced bastard had jabbed me in the gut and let all my air out.

Detective Brittle held out his hand. "I won't apologize for him, but I am sorry we were insensitive. We would be nowhere on this case without you."

"I've just about reached my apology-accepting quota for this week." I stared into his eyes, and realized they were startlingly pale blue.

"Kami." Reggie sounded exasperated.

I gave Ron Brittle's hand a firm shake and tried to smile. "Apology accepted, Detective."

Brittle smiled back at me, and it was his nice smile again. "Thank you. Call me if you think of anything else?"

"She will." Reggie took my elbow and steered me away across the parking lot. He leaned down to me in an aside. "Why can't you just behave yourself?"

"Well, I'm just glad I'm off the hook." Darn! If I was off the hook . . . "Does that mean I'm out of the safe-house?"

Reggie shook his head, a half-grin starting across his handsome face, as though he knew exactly how I felt about it. "Nope. Case isn't closed yet. Until it's closed, you need a permanent address on file."

"Gee, darn." Hot meals, hot baths, comfy bed—I tried to sound unhappy about it. "That really sucks."

Reggie grinned ear to ear, then got into his car, and drove away. I don't think he bought it. For someone who wants to be a lawyer, I'm a terrible liar.

BACK AT THE OFFICE, I WAS STRUCK AGAIN by the emptiness Juliet Hanford had left in her wake. I circled my barren office, missing anew the Oriental rug, the decorative tapestry, the wall cases with their priceless artifacts. The law was on my side, but it seemed all too often that the law was terribly slow. I started shoving things around, readjusting my little folding desk, café chair, even Evrett, trying to make it look less empty. Hoover ran into the back office and hid under the sofa.

Morri's key clicked in the back lock and he stuck his head in. "Are you herding elephants down here?"

"Elephants would make it less empty. Do you have any elephants, Morri?"

He stood silently watching for me a moment, then went through to the kitchenette, fixing me a cup of tea. I watched in bemusement as he sorted through Mom's hand-labeled tins before selecting one. He handed me the cup and gestured toward Charles' old office and the sofa. I sat cautiously, not sure what Morri was up to. Hoover immediately crawled out and headed for Morri's petting hand.

Morri scooped Hoover up and settled them both at the opposite end of the couch. "Dare I ask how your haunting research coming along?"

"Awkwardly." I explained about Dillon Cheshire's accusations. "Pardon my language, Morri, but he really ticked me off."

"Understandable, but you can't let it get to you. Those who don't believe won't believe until they experience it themselves." Morri sipped his tea as though we were discussing a picnic in the park.

"I get that, but he has experienced the happenings, he's heard the noises, seen the problem firsthand. I guess that's what got to me. I finally gave them confirmation that they weren't crazy, or hearing things, and the first thing he does is accuse me of fabricating evidence. And there's more . . ." I let my words fade out. Morri was the only one I'd talked to about my experience with Charles' spirit. But this wasn't a message from a mutual friend. Would Morri even believe me?

"Well, don't prevaricate. Speak." Morri's eyes danced behind his thick-lensed spectacles.

"I think I saw an apparition, standing beside the house. Waving at me."

Morri paused with his cup nearly to his lips, then slowly lowered it. "A full-bodied apparition?"

"It was smoky, like mist. Now, keep in mind it was raining hard and I saw it though . . ." I glanced at Evrett. I wasn't ready to say I was wearing his helmet. ". . . the windshield of the pick-up. It may have actually been mist."

"Except?" Morri cocked an eyebrow and waited.

"Except that I would swear it waved." I clarified. "This was right after I pulled my grand exit, storming out and jumping in the pick-up. It looked like it raised an arm and waved, not goodbye, but like this . . ." I raised my own hand to demonstrate. "Like it was waving me back."

Morri didn't say anything for what seemed like eternity. "That could either be a particularly good sign. Or a particularly bad one. Proceed with caution, poppet."

"Nothing to proceed with unless Dillon Cheshire apologizes," I grumbled. "The thing is, I can't shake the feeling that whatever is in that house needs me. But I'm not setting foot back in there without a full apology. And assurance that my professional reputation isn't going to be tarnished by this."

"Needs you. Or wants you."

"Wants me?"

"It gestured you back. That could mean this is something malignant. If this gent does the proper thing and apologizes, I want you to make me a promise."

I blinked. Morri never asked me for anything. "What kind of promise?"

"Promise me that you will not go back into that house without Father Joe at your side."

"Morri, the apparition was on the outside of the house. Does that mean it could move? Attach itself to me, the pick-up?" *Evrett?*

"If it was waving you back inside, then no, I think it's stuck there somehow." Morri paused, then continued with something more akin to his usual aplomb. "Investigating a haunting is about more than science and equipment and evidence, poppet." Morri gave me a wink. "You'll need to get that spunky temper of yours under control before you go anywhere near that place again. Spirits can feed off emotions. If you're angry, or scared, why, they can use that to cause all kinds of problems. And if the spirit is angry or malevolent? Well . . ."

I glanced towards the corridor, wondering if Evrett was listening. "They act up?"

"Oh ho! You've been stirring the old soldier?" Morri's eyes twinkled knowingly. "Your Evrett is a decent fellow, honorable in death as in life, is my wager. But there are spirits not so kindly nor so benevolent in the world. And if you dash into a situation with your emotions all riled up, you're likely to bite off more than you can chew, so to speak."

"I would never bite a ghost."

"Don't get pert and peppy with me, pop-sweet!" Morri reached out and ruffled my hair. Not that you could tell at all. My hair was permanently unruly. "I'm being serious here. You get angry or scared on an investigation, and they'll feed on that. Gives 'em strength."

"Then why doesn't Evrett act up when I get upset?"

"He might do, but as I said, he's not trying to stir things up. He's content. A spirit that feels trapped, or lost, or scared? That doesn't understand what's happened to them? Why, they could perpetuate a plethora of perplexing problems."

"Like silent screams and slamming doors." I considered that carefully. "Okay. I follow. So, if I hear from Dillon Cheshire, and he apologizes, would you be up for helping me on Saturday night?"

"Consider Mrs. Morri and I ready and available. Saturday is her bingo night, but we can convince her to give up her prize-winning streak a bit earlier than usual, I think." Morri fished in his pocket. "I'll call Joe and make sure he's up for it. I have him on speed-dial on this little gadget."

Morri owned a cellphone? Why was I surprised? I took it from him and added my own number to his quick-connects. "Okay. If I get the apology, we're on for Saturday night."

"Saturday." Morri grinned suddenly. "You know, I'm really looking forward to this. Haven't done this kind of thing in years." He gave me a farewell wave. "I'm off home. Stay out of trouble!"

"Me? I'm innocent as a lamb," I teased. "You stay out of trouble, sir."

After Morri left, I felt settled enough to finish my school paper, emailing it to my professor with a note that I wouldn't be in class on Friday. With the police still baffled about what happened to Hannah Raye, it was too scary being alone on campus at night. He emailed back almost immediately. He was cancelling on-campus class for Friday. None of his female students had shown up for Wednesday night class. He would post the lecture Friday morning, and would expect our responses in the class chatroom by Monday morning. Well, that was a relief. What wasn't a relief was that I couldn't remember if I'd double-checked my citations before emailing my paper.

School taken care of, I sat straight in the little café chair. I couldn't get it out of my head, that misty figure, willowy and soft, but solid in the rain. I'd leaped to the conclusion that it was a spirit, waving at me. I hadn't yet eliminated the possible. "Hey, Evrett. Want to go for a ride?"

He didn't answer. I didn't think he did. The late afternoon marine front had brought overcast skies and muggy dampness, so I pulled on my denim jacket. From the duffle bag, I took the pocket-sized digital camera and the EMF detector. "I'll be back in an hour and we'll go to the safehouse, okay, kids?"

Neither Hoover nor Evrett showed any sign they'd heard me. Hoover was curled up on the empty bookshelf with his tail over his nose. Who knew where Evrett was.

CHAPTER 13

⁓

Thursday Evening

I HAD PROMISED MORRI THAT I WOULDN'T go back in the house. I hadn't said anything about staying outside of it. The apparition was outside the house. Yes, but if what Morri said was true, it was likely unable to leave. For the sake of my own sanity, and for evidentiary purposes, I needed to go back, but Morri had planted solid doubts in my mind, and they echoed loud and clear as I drove south and then east into the hills.

The afternoon was waning into evening, but it was still early enough that I was certain they would still be at work. I was relieved to see no vehicles parked in front of the house. I parked the pickup two houses away and walked up, studying the spot near the garage where I'd seen the apparition—or what I had supposed at the time to be an apparition. I took pictures of the spot, the side of the garage, the concrete wall and the steep drop-off on the other side. I looked for a dryer vent or heater pipe that might have emitted steam, smoke, or mist, but there was nothing. There was a drainage grate from the driveway through the concrete wall, but it was nowhere near the edge of the garage. Even if it had been steaming, it couldn't have created the mist I'd seen.

With the EMF detector, I took baseline readings, but they were flatlined at zero. I took out the digital recorder and set it down, letting it record while I took more pictures. I'd halfway convinced myself that there would be an explanation, that in daylight I'd see what I had missed before.

I stepped up to the concrete wall, looking down the slope, and then out to the view across the bay. There were roiling black clouds covering the Peninsula. Another rainstorm was headed my way. I didn't want to get caught in traffic on the freeway, and I certainly didn't want to get caught lingering here by any of the housemates.

"If you're here," I whispered quietly, just in case there was someone there. "I'm working on it. I'll try to come back as soon as I can."

I slipped back to the pick-up and drove down the winding switchback road, keeping a vigilant eye out for any of the housemates returning. As I waited to make the left turn onto Mission Ave, a black motorcycle passed me, heading up the hill. Dillon's? I hadn't gotten enough of a look to tell. To me, pretty much all motorcycles looked like two-wheeled death machines.

With rush-hour coming on, my plan was to stick to surface streets, but I'd no sooner turned away from the freeway when my cellphone rang. The number wasn't in my caller ID but the hope that it was Kenny had me pulling in the Taco Rico parking lot and snatching up my phone. "This is Kami."

"Kami White? I'm sorry to call you like this, but this is Feliz Ciaro. I don't know if you know who I am."

The press was calling me on my personal number? My heart sank. If the press was looking for me, they knew something I didn't. Had Trunk Girl been identified? Had Kenny been found and arrested? "From Bay Area News?"

"Yes. Let me explain. I've been following the case of Hannah Raye and I saw your post on Vivian Astor's Facebook page. Would you be willing to meet with me?"

Relief hit me like a rogue wave and I was glad I was securely parked. "Off the record? Or on camera? Because I'd rather be eaten by rabid weasels than be on camera."

"Completely off the record. Promise."

The promises of reporters landed somewhere between the promises of convicted inmates and the oratory of defense lawyers, I took it with a grain of salt. "When and where would you like to meet?"

"Where are you now?"

"The Taco Rico parking lot in San Amoro. Where are you?"

"Cal State East Bay. I've just finished some interviews with staff."

"Okay. Do you know Magillies on Main?" *Better to meet on my home turf.* "I can be there in ten minutes."

"The pub?" There was a long pause, and I guessed he was putting it into his GPS unit. "Yes. I'll meet you there."

I signed off and steered towards downtown, regretfully glancing in my rearview at Taco Rico's bulletin board advertising a Thursday carnitas burrito special. I parked behind my office building, dashed inside long enough to drop my gear on the table, then walked over to Magillies. I was looking out for the news van and thought maybe I was early but as I reached the door, a plain grey sedan pulled into an empty spot across the street and the easily-recognized Feliz Ciaro got out. Only a dark blue polo shirt with the Bay Area News logo on the chest pocket gave him away as press. His hair was wind-tossed, and he had an openly casual air about him. I was used to seeing him made-up for the cameras. This unpolished, smiling man caught me off guard.

We chose a quieter table towards the back, but still in direct sightline of the TVs on the walls, each showing various sports in progress. I pretended to peruse the menu while I waited for him to tell me what he wanted—which was, apparently, a hard cider and a plate of BBQ pork nachos. I ordered a lemonade and a grilled chicken salad . . . and waited.

Feliz Ciaro was, apparently, as patient as me. We sat across from each other, sizing each other up. Finally, he said, "You got me kicked off campus."

"What? I did?" I almost snickered. "How'd I do that?"

"Apparently, they don't like it being implied Hannah's disappearance might be linked to Vivian Astor's and that the college may share some responsibility for Hannah being missing." He eyed me sidelong.

I shook my head, biting back another laugh. "You can't put that on me. I just suggested that they might be connected somehow. I didn't blame the college in any way."

Ciaro held up his phone and I could see he had Facebook up on Vivian Astor's missing person page. "But you did write this, did you not? 'I can't help but notice the physical and lifestyle similarities between Vivian and Hannah Raye, who went missing last week. Both of them were college students, at campuses only a few miles apart.' That's what you wrote?"

"Is it?" It was late and I was tired when I'd written it. "I didn't mean to imply that the colleges were responsible somehow."

"And yet, when I tried to talk to campus security at both East Bay and Chabot, I was summarily shown the door and asked not to return. They seem to be afraid of something." Ciaro smiled, then shrugged. "Do you think there may be some sort of complicity on campus?"

"No. I don't. Maybe because I can't go there without hard evidence," I answered quietly. "I just know that we're all already afraid. My Friday class was canceled because no one wants to come onto campus at night. If I had to guess, campus security doesn't know anything, and are afraid of being blamed for something that happened on their watch." I looked him directly in the eye. "Keep the focus on finding Hannah, Mr. Ciaro, not on chasing wild geese."

"I'm a journalist. I chase geese and wait for them lay eggs." Feliz smiled his charming on-the-air smile. "Anyway, since I was politely asked to remove myself from campus, I needed another angle to investigate," The charming smile turned to a warning grin. "And I know you had a class with Hannah. The night she disappeared."

"I skipped class that night. I hadn't done the reading. So, this *is* on the record?"

"This is just a fact-finding mission. If something interesting comes up, I'll ask for permission to drag you into it."

Never trust reporters or bankers is common wisdom, but I wanted to trust Ciaro. "Okay. What facts are you looking for?"

"Did you know the cameras in the parking lot weren't working the night Hannah was taken."

Taken. The first time any of us had really dared use that word instead of the ubiquitous 'disappeared.' It struck harder than I thought it would. "I didn't know. I guess I assumed that the cops either have all the footage already, or that whatever happened was out of range of the cameras." I shrugged. "Honestly, I never really thought about where the cameras were. I guess I just always assumed they were there."

"We live in a time of unprecedented surveillance," Ciaro agreed. "Whether it's a run traffic light or a burgled bodega, there's always camera footage. Which is why it stuck out to me. If the cameras weren't working, why weren't they? And then I saw your Facebook post. You know, I thought your profile picture looked familiar, but it wasn't until I looked you up that I realized why." He put his phone down and turned it around so I could see the screen. The news headline read "Prominent Lawyer's Drowning Ruled Murder." The sub-header was "Secretary Catches Killer."

"I'm a paralegal. Not a secretary." I grumbled. "You guys always get it wrong."

He didn't meet my gaze. "It's not like we try to. But catchy head-lines catch readers. Underestimated underdog saves the day is what people want to see. Anyway, you're already a hero, so why the interest in Hannah Raye and Vivian Astor?"

"It has nothing to do with being a hero. I'm no hero." I pointed at his phone. "I didn't catch the killer; the killer caught me," I explained for probably the thousandth time since that ugly day in August. "As for Hannah, you already know we had class together. There are thirty-six students in that class, over half are women. It could be any one of us missing. All I know is that if I was missing, I'd want every-one out looking, making connections. Wouldn't you?"

"What alerted you to the similarities between Vivian Astor and Hannah Raye?"

"What made you miss them?" I fired back. But then I relented. "I saw Hannah's poster next to Vivian's on a bulletin board and realized how similar they looked. Something just clicked. I thought someone might see my post, and be in a position to see if there was some connection between them. Honestly, I'm surprised that it's Bay Area News calling me. That takes some serious attention."

"You flatter me." Feliz saluted me with his cider.

"I don't mean to."

"Were you involved in any way with the searches for Vivian?"

I shook my head. "I only know her through her flier at the coffee shop. Honestly, I was so busy between work and school that I barely registered when she went missing. Hannah is different. I know her."

Ciaro started to ask something else, then paused, eyes focused on something over my shoulder. Before I could turn to look, a familiar voice sounded out. "Kam? Hey."

Jack Austin. I glanced at Ciaro, who sat back in his bench seat, a suddenly still and silent observer. I turned and grinned up at Jack. "Jack! Hi!" I glanced around but didn't see any of his sports-watching friends. "Are you here alone?"

"Just wanted to grab a snack on my way home," he shrugged. "I don't want to intrude. Just wanted to say hi."

I reached out and snatched his hand, pulling him down on the bench next to me. "Hi! You're not intruding at all." I fired him a *save me* glance. "You recognize Feliz Ciaro? Bay Area News?"

Jack's Caribbean blue gaze washed over me in surprise, then glanced across the table, and a half-smile creased his face. His tone was apologetic. "I get most of my news from the Internet."

"Mr. Ciaro, this is Jack Austin. My close friend." If I hesitated on the word "friend," neither man showed a sign of it. "Anything you have to say to me, can be said to him."

Jack gave my fingers a squeeze before disentangling his hand from them and waving for the waitress. "Have you guys ordered yet?"

Jack. Oh, wonderful Jack. He had no idea what was going on but was willing to be there for me. Just like he always was. I repressed the urge to reach for his hand again. "We have."

Feliz interjected. "I'm hoping Kami can help me with the story I'm working on."

"What story is this?" Jack raised eyebrows at me. I knew him well enough to know he was wondering what the heck I'd gotten myself into this time. "Does it have to do . . ."

"Nothing to do with Kenny," I interjected quickly. "Hannah Raye, the missing girl from campus."

"Who is Kenny?" Feliz leaped on the question and I felt Jack tense beside me.

"My brother. He borrowed my car." Technically, he was missing, too, but I wasn't going to go waving that at the press—especially not with the body of yet another missing woman involved. "And not the point. We were talking about Hannah."

Feliz's gaze remained curious but he had the good grace to pretend to move on with his not-interview. "How well did you know Hannah?"

"We had a few classes together this year. She was trying to finish the program in three years instead of four, so she was always either in class or in the library." I paused. "She's into kickboxing, I do yoga, so not much in common there. She's whip-smart, though, and I'm glad she was on my debate project and not someone I had to debate against. I'm no slouch at the debate podium, but Hannah can talk circles around me."

"You say you missed class the night she disappeared?"

"And I have the witnesses to prove it." I shrugged. "That is, if I need to prove it. Usually, three or four of us walk to our cars together after class. If I'd been there, would I have been walking with her? Would she still be here?"

"Or you'd be gone, too." Jack stated, his expression guarded.

"That was my thinking, as well. Who was in class that night? Who would have been with her? After I learned from police that the cameras were malfunctioning that night, I tried to interview campus staff about who had access to the cameras and could have turned them off." Feliz gave a chagrined smile. "And was asked to leave."

Jack had been listening quietly, but as the waitress approached with our meals, he spoke up. "I'm sorry, Kam. I didn't realize you knew the missing woman."

"As a classmate, yeah." I knew who Jack's best friend was. He knew mine. But since we'd separated, how much happened in each other lives that we didn't know? What new friends had we made, acquaintances and names, coworkers, fellow students, other people had passed through our lives? I suddenly wanted to know. I wanted to know everything about Jack's new life. I wanted to be a part of his life. But not in front of Feliz Ciaro. "I think whoever took Hannah must have been watching, maybe knew where the cameras were. She was a kickboxer, not a weakling like me. Someone would have to be either big and strong or have a way to incapacitate her." A shudder slid up my spine. "If they were looking for an easy target, why not wait and take me? Or another smaller, weaker woman?"

"Because he has a type," Feliz said. "If the Hannah Raye and Vivian Astor cases are connected and one person is responsible, that is. We have no evidence of that, yet."

"So, what's the score, then?" Jack wanted to know. "Why would you think it's a serial kidnapper or whatever you're thinking at this point?"

I raised my hand. "Guilty. I saw the similarities between them and put a tip online."

"You did what, now?" Jack was pretending to be surprised and dismayed, but the quirk at the corner of his lips gave him away. He knew better than to think I was anywhere but square in the middle of a mess.

"Yes, you did." Feliz paused, fork paused over his food. "Why? Why put up a social media post and not the police?"

Jack's lip quirked at me again, and I put on my best smile and looked Feliz straight in the eye. "What makes you think I didn't go to the cops, too? Two birds, one stone. Or rather, one bird, two stones."

"Here's what I think," Feliz continued as though he'd barely heard me. "When people go missing, the first people we look at are those close to the victim. Then, we look at who knew their schedules, their activities. Then we look for people who might be inserting themselves into the investigation. Joining searches, giving tips to the police, and the press . . ." Feliz stared at me, and I stared back.

Jack started laughing. "You think Kami did it? A ninety-eight-pound paralegal with connections to the top law firms in the Bay Area? Are you serious? Kami couldn't hurt a spider. Believe me. I've moved enough spiders for her."

"And she knows how investigations like this go, for me, and for law enforcement." Feliz studied me for a second longer, then returned to his food. "But her professors and classmates agree with you. And I can't see how she could have tampered with the cameras."

I tried to stop myself, but the words just trotted off my tongue like an unruly cocker spaniel. "You know who else has been hanging around, asking questions, inserting themselves into the investigation? And who does work with camera technology?" I paused for emphasis. "You, Feliz Ciaro. You're a little taller than Hannah, certainly physically fit enough. And that news van you have access to has plenty of room to tie up a woman. I imagine all you'd have to do is pull up and ask to talk to her. She might just hop in willingly because everyone knows Feliz Ciaro. Except Jack, that is."

Feliz Ciaro's eyes went wide, fork frozen partway to his mouth. Finally, he chuckled. "Okay. You're right. We're both possible suspects."

With a dead body in the trunk of my car, I was more suspect that he was, but if he didn't know about that, I wasn't about to tell him. "But there have been dozens of volunteer search parties at this point, people putting up fliers, planning vigils. Who else contacted the police with tips? Contacted the press with tips?"

"The whole point of most tips is that they're anonymous," Feliz sighed. "But my station will establish a new tip-line, not just for Hannah, but for other missing Bay Area women. The official police story is that there's no connection between the cases, but you noticed the physical traits of both victims right off the bat. I think you're absolutely right, but I wanted to make sure." He paused, meeting my gaze again. "I had to be certain that you weren't involved in any way."

"Only as a concerned citizen," I hesitated. "And as a potential victim if he's taking college students from dark parking lots."

Feliz Ciaro waved for the waitress and asked for a box, picking up the check and handing the waitress his credit card before Jack or I could protest. "Thinking back, is there anything you can think of in your encounters with Hannah, something that may not have seemed important at the time, but looking back, might be important?"

"No," I admitted, my words feeling small as I explained. "Since I learned she was missing, I can't stop wondering if I missed something, that if I'd just paid more attention, if I'd had class that night, or something, anything, she'd still be here. But there's nothing."

"Well, thank you for meeting me. If you think of anything else . . ." He pulled out a fresh business card and wrote a number on it. "That's my personal cell number."

"Thanks for dinner, Feliz. If I think of anything, I promise I'll call."

"Watch Bay Area Investigates on Friday." Feliz suggested, waving over his shoulder as he left.

Jack watched him go then turned to me. "Wow."

"Wow? What does that mean?"

"I can't believe he fell for that." Jack saluted me with his water glass. "You're a lousy bluffer."

"I'm improving. And I did contact the police. Just not about Hannah."

"Uh oh. That sounds like a story."

It did. I suddenly wanted to tell him everything. I lowered my voice. "They found a body in the trunk of my car, Jack. A blond woman, blond like Hannah. While I think I've got myself cleared with the detectives, they're still looking for Kenny."

Jack went still and sucked in a deep breath. "Okay, tell me everything."

Telling him everything took the better part of an hour and two lemonade refills. Somehow, I managed to both keep from running away *and* from bawling my eyes out. *Two wins.* I wrapped up with a sigh, "And now you know. Any questions?"

"Just one." He gave a small smile, the lopsided one that said he was afraid of the answer. "What can I do to help?"

That was Jack. I started to reach for his hand again, thought better, and held back. "You just did."

"Can I walk you back to your office?"

"The wind's picking up. If it starts to rain, you'll get wet."

He reached into his backpack and held up a folded umbrella. "No, I won't. And neither will you."

I couldn't help myself. I laughed, shaking my head. "Where was that the night our tent blew down?"

"Why do you think I started carrying it?" Jack stood and raised his arm, guiding me out onto the sidewalk. There, he tucked his arm companionably through mine and we crossed Main Street, and down the dark alleyway to the back door of my office.

"Coming in? I don't have anything to offer, except some of Mom's tea." I unlocked the door, and looked up at Jack. The streetlight down the alley provided the only illumination, glinting and yellow. We were in the shadows, and his expression was inscrutable. He was beautiful, mysterious, a man I knew better than any other, and yet at that moment, I was keenly aware of how estranged we had become. Time froze, the only sounds were the rustling of wind through the rooftops, and my own pounding heart.

"Kami . . ."

"Yes?"

He leaned close, and I reached up, my hand starting for his chest to push him away, but instead I reached up to cup his cheek, feeling the faint stubble there as he bent in to kiss me—soft, and warm, and so sweet. I kissed him back. Then a sudden thunderclap split the sky and the heavens opened and sheets of rain slammed down over San Amoro, drenching us both. We broke the kiss, both laughing.

"Every friggin' time," Jack groaned as he snapped up his umbrella, and pulled open the office door and nudged me inside. "Goodnight, beautiful. Stay safe."

I ducked into the doorway out of the rain and watched him go. As he reached the end of the alley, about to turn back towards Main Street, I called out, "Jack!"

He half-turned, looking back through the pouring rain, a shadow outlined against the shimmering streetlight, umbrella held low. "I'll call you tomorrow?"

"Tomorrow!" He called back before waving and turning out of sight. I shut the door and locked it, closing out Jack and the storm, but the stupid grin on my face seemed stuck there. It stared back at me in the mirror, goofy and ridiculous. I stuck my tongue out at it as I toweled my hair off and pulled on a dry sweatshirt. Then I picked up my cell and called Mom while wandering out to the front reception area. Her cell-phone went to voicemail, so I left a cheery, "Hi, Mom. Wondering if you'd heard from Kenny. I talked to some of his friends and have some leads, so give me a call back when you can. Also, I just had dinner with Jack."

I hung up fast, knowing that would earn me a call back ASAP. The stupid grin was back. I tidied my desk and swept the floor while waiting for her call back, but glancing at the time, I realized she was probably leading a workshop or gardening club event at the greenhouse. I threw myself into my chair and looked out the window to watch the falling rain.

My giddiness receded in the blink of an eye. Standing outside, hands cupped to the glass, looking back at me, was Kenny.

CHAPTER 14

——❦——

Thursday Night

I WAS GONNA KILL HIM.

Flinging open the door, I snagged him by the neck of his poncho and yanked him inside, pushing him to the center of the room before slamming the door.

He looked like hell—or what hell would like if it went out, joined a homelessness cult, ran a kamikaze mud race, and then fell into a swimming pool. His entire frame was soaking wet, his long blond hair shaggy and unkempt, hanging down in his eyes. He was grimy—not just grimy, but National Geographic wild-man in the jungles of Borneo with mud and sticks in his hair and what looked like neon-colored paint smeared on him variety of totally grody.

"Where in the universe have you been?" I ended up screaming in his face. It's a loving gesture between the two of us, really, that screaming.

Kenny just stood there, staring at me like I was the one who was missing, presumed dead. Although, all things considered, he looked it—dead, I mean—and not just because I was going to kill him.

"Dude." Kenny gave me a look that said I was clearly overreacting. "Didn't you get my message?"

"Message? What message?! You haven't been answering your

phone! Last I saw, you were driving away in my car! That was weeks ago!"

"Yeah. It got stolen. That's the message I left, like, forever ago. What's your problem?"

"Kenny? Shut. It." I took a deep breath, closed my eyes and told my phone to call Reginald Burrough's cell. Reggie answered with a faint echo and a loud background sound of traffic and I knew he was driving and using his Bluetooth. He said he was only blocks away. I hung up, relieved. "My lawyer is on his way here right now. I don't want you to say another word until he gets here."

"God, sis. It was just your car. It was insured, right?"

I held up both hands, trying to resist the urge to clamp them both over his mouth—or around his throat. "Shut up. Don't say anything. I friggin' mean it, Kenny. I will kill you if you say one more word!"

"Can I at least . . ."

"That was four. Don't you dare say another one."

"But I'm . . ."

"I don't care!" I reached back with my right hand and yanked Evrett's sword free. The knight's helmet clanked shut as I aimed the steel at Kenny's gut. Moron-Bro flung both hands up and backed into the empty bookcase behind him as I gasped one last warning. "Shut! Up!"

"Whoa. Hey." The voice came from the door, and I glanced away as Reginald walked in, palms raised. "If you kill him in front of me, you'll have to find another lawyer." Reggie fired off one of his dazzling grins. "Maybe you should put that down, hmm?"

"Fine." I angled the sword back into its sheath, sliding the hilt back into Evrett's gauntlet. Was it my imagination or did it try to push back into my hand? "But I reserve the right to draw it again if I need to."

Kenny glared at me. "What the hell is wrong with you? I take off for a couple days, and you start actin' crazy!"

"Me? Crazy! You moron monkey-brain!" I went for him with my bare hands, but Reggie stepped in to intercept and I collided with his beautifully muscled chest, waylaid by the spicy-clean scent of his cologne. He put both hands on my shoulders and set me gently aside.

"Now, why don't we all sit down, and Kenny can tell his side of things before we call the cops."

"The cops! What for? I said I was sorry." Kenny was looking more confused by the minute. "All I wanted was to ask to get a ride back to my place. And what the hell happened in here? Where's all your furniture?"

"That's why we can't sit down," I grumbled at Reggie. "I only have one chair." I clenched both hands on the sides of my head, sucking in deep breaths and hunting for elusive calm. "Reginald? Would you be so kind as to ask my brother where he's been hiding?"

"We should record this, do you have . . ."

"No. We can't. I don't have a recorder," I lied, my gaze flicking towards the backroom and the safe there.

Reggie followed my gaze, "I thought you had a new recorder. Charles told me you bought a really nice digital for taking depositions?"

"Yes. I did. But it's . . . umm . . . indisposed. I mean, it's on another job. It can't help us right now." *It's full of ghostly screams that I'm hiding from, so please, please, don't let Reggie ask me again.* I breathed a sigh of relief when Reggie nodded acceptance, pulled out his own phone and set it to voice record.

"Okay, fine. You take notes, then."

Kenny was standing with his arms crossed, looking miserable, confused and rather like a drowned pathetic thing you might find lying on the beach after a storm. I grabbed my yellow note pad, gestured the single chair, and hopped up to sit cross-legged on the cabinet. "Okay. Go."

"Can I at least, like, borrow a clean shirt? Get something to eat?"

"No," I groused. "I'm loaning you my lawyer. I think that's enough for now."

"Look, I only came by to see if I could get a ride back to my place." Kenny turned for the door. "I dunno what you two have up your hinies, but I am *so* ghost."

"Don't use that phrase, you'll offend Evrett. And you aren't going anywhere!" I glared at him. "Not until you tell us where you've been all this time."

Reggie moved to block the door and Kenny slumped into the chair.

"We have to call Detective Brittle and tell him we found you, but we'll hold off as long as we can for you to tell us whatever it is you need to say." Reggie said reasonably. "Tell us everything that happened after you borrowed the car."

"God, what are you so on about the car for?" Kenny whined, his damp hair falling over his face as he rubbed what looked like a week's worth of beard. "It was a P.O.S. anyway."

"Yeah! But it was my P.O.S.!"

Reggie waved a palm in my direction, but kept his attention on Kenny. "Just start at the beginning and we'll get through this."

I realized that I was about to watch Reginald Burroughs, Attorney at Law, getting ready to pull out his big legal-shaped stick. As always, I was impressed. I mean, sure, he always impressed me, but watching him move into Kenny's space, mimic his body language, and start to gain his trust was like watching a magician pull a scarf out of someone's ear.

"What happened after you drove off in Kami's car?"

"I took the car to Burning Man. Me an' Snake . . . I picked up Snake in Reno. We got our camp all set up, an' stuff and it was totally mind-blowing. But a couple days later, I went to get some water an' stuff and the car was gone." He rummaged in his backpack, came up with my blue and yellow smiley-face keychain. "See. I didn't leave the key in the car or anything stupid like that. I kept tryin' to call, but it was crazy."

"You say 'trying to call'," Reginald said calmly. "You said you left a message. Did you call? Or did you *try* to call?"

"I called, man! I swear it!"

"I never got a call, not on my cell, and not in the office. Not at Mom's either. You know she's worried sick, right?" I glared at Kenny. I wanted to smack him upside the head with the phone, but with Kenny's head being so thick, I was afraid I'd break it and

I didn't have another landline office phone, and this one was borrowed from Mallory Kent anyway. The risk of another monetary
obligation stayed my hand.

"I left a message! My battery was dead, so I borrowed a phone,
but signal is bad out there. It kept beeping." Kenny was glaring at
me. "I can't help it if you're too stupid to get your own messages!"

"There weren't any messages, you moron!"

"Kids, enough," Reginald sighed. "Make sure you write that
down, Kam."

I wrote, 'Ken = Moron.'

"Okay, is there anyone you suspect of taking the car? One of
your friends who knew where it was parked, maybe?"

Kenny shook his head. "Nah. If my friends wanted my car,
they'd ask to use the car. It's all share and share alike out there."

"Did you check around, maybe see if anyone saw who took the
car?"

"I didn't ask! I mean, I called Kam, told her the car was stolen.
After the Burn, I met up with friends an' hitched a ride home with
them."

"Gurlach, Nevada to San Amoro took you a week and a half?" I
asked in disbelief. "Seriously?

"No." Kenny rolled his eyes at me. "We wanted to see the Grand
Canyon before we came back here. Then the van caught on fire and
burned up, and we were trapped in Mexico . . ."

"Stop. Just stop." I couldn't write that fast. And more so, I was
that kind of confused that you get when you think you've woken
up from a dream, but then realize you're still dreaming. I was starting to get a headache. "You were going to the Grand Canyon and
then ended up in Mexico? As in Tijuana, across the border, another
country Mexico? Do you even have a passport?"

"Yeah. How d'you think I visit Dad?" Kenny rolled his eyes at me.
"We wanted to score some weed, an' Mud knew a guy who knew a
guy. But then we had to avoid border patrol and the van caught on
fire, so we had to catch a ride on a truck full of farm workers. They
dropped us off in Bakersfield and then we hopped a freight train to
San Diego. I hitch-hiked home up the 101 from there."

I glanced at my paper. The last thing I'd written was "Mexico for weed". I glanced at Reginald. He was staring at my brother like he'd never seen anything quite like him before. Then suddenly, he started laughing. "I did something similar once, only it was India. We tried to cross into Nepal without the right paperwork, had to run from the border patrol and the old Land-Rover we were driving threw a rod right through the hood. Charles was the only one of us who spoke any Nepalese at all, and he traded the busted land-rover for some ponies. We rode around with a group of yak-herders for a week before we figured out how to tell them we needed to catch a train."

"Gaaaawwwwd! Reggie, don't encourage him. Kenny? You moron! Do have any idea what's been going on here?

My brother stared around the office with a blank and tired gaze. "I just told you I was at Burning Man, got stuck in Mexico, and then I hitched home from San Diego. How the hell am I supposed to know anything besides that you're crazy pissed off?"

Okay," Reggie made an ease-up motion my way, and I bit my lips shut. "We need the names of everyone you were with. Who were you with at Burning Man?"

"Snake and Hoser."

"Hoser?" So much for letting Reggie handle it.

"Yeah. I met 'em at ComicCon last year. They're cool. Really into steampunk."

"Do you happen to have their real names?" Reggie asked tiredly, but I was already ahead of them this time.

"David Hostner and Jeff Hems," I told Reggie. "I already gave them to Brittle."

"Okay. So, who did you leave Burning Man with?"

"They were Jude's friends."

That elicited another eyeroll from me. Jude Booder's friends. That explained it. "Do you know their names?"

"Uh, kinda. The one guy who owned the van is Harley. His girlfriend was Toolie, but she got in a fight with him and was gonna fly home from Reno. She didn't come with us. The other guys were, uh . . . Toby. And, uh, Mud."

"You went to Mexico to score weed with a guy named Mud? How is it you're my brother? Seriously? I mean, I can't even imagine how you found your way out of Mom's womb with so few brains!"

"Because I got all the beauty." Kenny smirked.

"Right. Okay." Reginald took a deep breath. "Kami? Go to Kenny's place and get him fresh clean clothes, something that looks presentable. Kenny? Go in back, take a shower, and get cleaned up. Put all of your clothes in this bag. I'm going to call Detective Brittle and let him know we'll be bringing Kenny in two hours."

"I think he looks fine. I don't want to drive all the way over there in this rain." I complained, but Reggie fired his big-legal-shaped-stick stare at me. I pushed up from the cabinet and grabbed my bag. Kenny dug around in his pack and then handed me a key ring that I didn't want to touch until it'd been bathed in sanitizer. I told him, "There are clean towels in the storage drawer by the bathroom, unless Juliet took them. There's an electric razor back there, plugged in and charged."

Kenny asked suddenly, "I still don't get why the cops are involved."

I couldn't even look at Kenny. I grabbed the truck key and fled, leaving it to Reggie to explain. That wasn't fair to Reginald, I know, but I didn't want to try to explain to my brother that there was a dead body in the car he let get stolen at some hippy fest, and while he was off running from Mexican border police, I was trying to clear of him of murder.

IT WAS THE FIRST TIME I'd been inside Kenny's apartment. I realized that during the daytime, the natural light must be amazing. Every space that wasn't filled with windows was covered in Kenny's artwork, the walls plastered with huge life-sized hand-drawings on sheets of paper tacked to the walls, his characters leaping out to save the day—or destroy it. That was my brother. The destroyer of days. I gathered some decent looking clothes from the laundry basket of clean stuff on the bed. The camping gear by the door made sense now. I could see it was all clean, but most of it was older, stuff we'd had since we were kids. He picked his best stuff for his trip.

By the time I got back to the office, Kenny had showered and shaved, and his long hair was combed back into a tidy ponytail. He looked almost human. While my brother dressed in the clothes I brought, Reginald fetched sandwiches from Reese's, but I wasn't hungry enough to eat. Would the cops buy Kenny's story? Or was my brother headed for charges ranging from car theft to murder to . . . What was the charge for breaking back into the US after going to Mexico to buy drugs, anyway? If there was one, I was sure Detective Dortman would find a way to charge him with it.

Before he reached for a sandwich, my brother shoved my shoulder lightly. "Reggie said you've had my back this whole time, an' that I better apologize. I didn't mean to worry anyone. So, yeah, sorry."

"Yeah. Well. So am I." I shrugged and moved away from him, picking at my sandwich instead of looking at Kenny. "Look, Ken, just be honest as you can with the cops. Brittle's fair, he's not gonna try to jam you up so long as you're telling the truth."

"The truth ain't exactly law friendly," Kenny muttered at me. "I mean, bro, I was runnin' around naked in the desert for a week. This whole clothes thing seems just weird. And I'm not even sure why the cops are involved. It's not like I did anything wrong."

"Really?" I raised my eyebrows. Apology aside, I was back to the desire to smack him upside the head.

"I'm going to give you just the barest facts." Reginald's voice was very calm. "And then I don't want you to ask any questions, or over-think anything. I want you to get to the police station with a clear head, and not trying to come up with facts that aren't in existence. Your sister's car was pulled out of the reservoir with a dead body in the trunk. Until you walked in that door, we weren't sure if you were a suspect or a victim or both. As far as we knew, you were dead in that lake, too. Now the less you try to think about that and the more you think on specific details that you can put together, who might have seen you, who you might have talked to, anything you saw at that gas station, the better your chances of convincing the police that you had nothing to do with it." Reggie's tone wasn't very hopeful. He continued more confidently. "I'm already representing your sister, so I took the liberty of calling a friend of mine who's a defense attorney. She's willing to help me out. She's on her way over here to pick you up. Just do what she says, don't argue with her, and you'll be fine."

"Defender? Which one?" I was afraid to ask.

"Jenni Wan."

"Wan?" I hadn't heard of her. "Who?"

"She's a protégé of mine. Just out of Pepperdine. Don't worry yourself, Kam. She's good. And she'll be perfect to work with Ken."

I was doubtful—until she walked in the door.

Jenni Wan was five foot, five inches tall, black hair in a short bob, beautiful smoky brown eyes, and clear flawless skin. She was probably a size three and wore a trim fashionable black suit. She practically screamed "competent attorney" as she marched into the room. Kenny's eyes popped out of his head when she walked in the door. Uh oh, I recognized that look! Please don't let him start drooling.

"Thank you, Burroughs. I'll take it from here." Wan said crisply, taking Kenny by the arm and pointing him towards the door. He was a head taller than she was, but she somehow managed to make him look small. "Just do exactly what I say, and you'll be fine."

"Your protégé, huh?" I glanced at Reginald, and he shrugged, a gorgeous grin sliding across his face.

As much as I wanted to follow them to the police station, I didn't dare. My presence was only going to be a problem. Best that Kenny face this problem on his own, that he try to look and act like a grown-up for a change. As I watched through the glass, he paused to open Wan's car door for her, gesturing her in politely before running around to the passenger side of her tan four-door sedan. Maybe Kenny wasn't quite the immature schmuck I believed him to be. Nah, I couldn't be that lucky.

The night was growing stormier. The lightning and thunder seemed to have passed, but wind gusts were pummeling the windows as I sunk into my chair and stared at my desk. With Kenny and Jenni gone, Hoover slinked out of the back and hopped up on the desk, begging for pets.

"So, what progress have you made? Besides finding your

brother." Reggie asked, prompting a grumble from me. He picked up Hoover, sweater and all, and the cat climbed up to his shoulder, and rubbed his chin enthusiastically on top of Reggie's head.

"I didn't find him. He found me. I've been tracking down his friends, calling everyone I know, looking everywhere, and, bam, there he was, staring in the window at me. Everything I did was a totally wasted effort. My progress has been limited to suckiness."

"Maybe not." Reggie looked over my shoulder at my Facebook account and the message I sent to Kenny's contacts and the dozen or so responses I'd received. "If you can figure out who Toby and Mud are, you'll have witnesses that can exonerate him entirely."

"Eyewitnesses that say he went to Mexico to buy weed, not that he didn't kill someone, stick them in my trunk and dump them in the reservoir, you mean?" I pulled up some of the images Hoser had sent me, and sighed. "I've looked at these until I'm half blind looking for Kenny. I mean, really? People actually *do* this?"

"You should go sometime," Reggie told me. "Loosen up, have some fun. Get primitive."

I'd scrubbed both hands through my curls. "Any looser and I'll fall apart. And I don't do primitive."

"So, what do you do?" Reggie looked around the barren office, perched on the edge my desk, balancing Hoover with one hand. "I mean, for fun? Have you been out at all since . . .?"

Since Charles died. "Yes. Well. Kind of. Not exactly. Between school and work, I've been too busy. I'd rather just put my head down and work. And this indie job I took has been eating a lot of my time. I told you about that."

"You didn't," Reggie tossed out and I glanced up from the file containing dozens of pictures of dusty, dirty, costumed people, and giant art installations.

"I didn't what?"

"Tell me about your job." Reggie gave me a stern look. "I can't defend you if you're hiding things from me."

"I'm not hiding anything," I told him, "but I have client privilege to consider. This is a sensitive case, and the clients require complete secrecy at this stage."

"Oooh. Secrecy. Come on. I'm a great consultant. Consult with me."

"Reggie, what do you want?" I tried not to groan. "I mean, I appreciate the big-brother act. Really, I do, but I think I can handle a simple research job."

His eyes widened slightly, mock hurt expression dancing across his face. "Okay, you got me. I was wondering . . . I mean . . . about your brother."

"He's a criminal who stole my car and drove to Mexico to buy drugs." I told Reggie with a frown. "I mean, Mexico? Isn't Marin a lot closer? It's legal here, why risk Mexico? What a friggin' moron. Anyway, he's straight. And he's my bro. Hands off, bucko."

Reggie laughed, settling Hoover back on the desk. "I'm twice his age. And married. But you have to admit that he wasn't lying when he said he got the beauty."

"Well, thanks very much!" I glared, slamming my computer closed.

"So, what about you?" Reggie gave me a conspiratorial nudge. "What kind of man do you find attractive, Miss White?"

"Honestly? Reggie, if you weren't gay, I'd fall for you," I admitted, feeling foolish and grinning a bit too widely lest he take my words too seriously. "And no, there's no one in my life right now."

"What about Jack Austin?"

"What about Jack?" Other than the fact that I'd just had dinner with him, and was kissing him at my own back door barely an hour ago?

Reggie sighed, leaning against the wall and crossing his arms. "Look, I can only send him over here so many times with paperwork for you to sign. I'm running out of papers!"

"You've been . . . what?" I pushed back from the desk and spun to face him. "Reggie, you sneaky, underhanded wicked *lawyer*!"

"Don't get in a huff. You and Austin are perfect for each other. You're just too blind to realize it. You broke the boy's heart, girlfriend." He grinned at me and I instantly forgave him.

But not entirely; I changed the subject. "How are things with you and Skyler. I never see him anymore."

"I barely see him myself." Reggie admitted ruefully. "Opening the new restaurant is a lot of stress."

"I can't wait until it opens," I admitted. "I'll be the first in line. I dream of Skyler's cooking. So does Hoover."

"Me, too. And plenty of other things." Reggie seemed suddenly tired. "You worry about you and Jack, not me and Sky."

"I'm not worried." I felt the goofy smile coming back and bit my lip to keep it in. "I guess I just don't want to screw it up again. Is it really worth the effort?"

"Worth the effort?" Reggie shoved off from the wall and grabbed his coat. "Sweetie, you think too much. You don't know if he's worth the effort until you try putting some effort in."

"Well, you just keep your efforts away from my little bro." I handed him his briefcase.

"Yeah, okay. How are things at the safehouse? Everything okay?"

"Except for the gun under the sofa. Hoover seems to like the place."

"Well, we mustn't disappoint Hoover, must we?" Reggie opened the door and disappeared into the dark rainy night.

As soon as Reggie was gone, I slumped down and put my head in my hands. I was forgetting something—something important— the investigation? No, something to do with Kenny? Something . . .

MOM! I glanced at the clock. Whatever was going on at the greenhouse had to be finished by now.

I dialed her number and held my breath. She answered on the third ring. "Hi, Mom."

"Oh no," she said very quietly. "I just had a vibe that you were about to call. It's bad news, isn't it?"

How the heck did she do that? "No, Mom! No. It's good news! I found Kenny! He's fine. He was hitch-hiking from San Diego." I found it safest not to mention the rest of his Burning Man vacation adventures. I was afraid Mom would tell me how cool she thought that was. "He's with a lawyer on his way to the police station to give his statement right now."

"He's at the police station? Is he under arrest?"

"Probably not," I told her. "He's going in on his own recognizance and he has a defense attorney with him. But I'm trying to track down witnesses, anyone who can verify his story. It's more than a little fishy."

"Well, I can! I will! I'll go down there right now and tell them he's telling the truth!"

"No, Mom," I said as patiently as I could. "It doesn't work that way. Trying to lie for him is only going to cause problems. Just let me do my thing here and let his lawyer do her thing, and . . ."

"Her? He has a lady lawyer?"

"What's wrong with lady lawyers?" I demanded, wondering how she always managed to do that to me. Blithely oblivious, yet somehow, she managed to ram the icepick right between my ribs every single time.

"Oh, nothing, dear. I was just hoping he'd have a competent lawyer. Someone like that nice Mr. Burroughs."

I groaned and rubbed my eyes. "I gotta go, Mom. I'll call you as soon as there's more news."

"Is he going to be in the slammer overnight? Should I take him some soup or something?"

Soup? Seriously? "No, Mom. And don't say slammer."

"We used to call it the pig-pen back in the day. When I did time . . ."

"Mom . . ." I warned. Mom got arrested back in her Berkeley college days for protesting animal testing at a cosmetics company laboratory. The judge sentenced her and twenty other protestors to whole three days plus community service. The jail was over-crowded, and they were only incarcerated for one day, and it turned out the cosmetics company wasn't even using animals for testing anyway. But if you asked Mom about jail, the tale always turned into the equivalent of having spent a year in a Russian gulag in the name of social justice.

"What? You have something against social protesters?" I didn't justify that with an answer, and she leaped back to the subject at hand. "But you've seen Kenny? And he's okay, right? He's not hurt or anything?"

"As okay as Kenny ever is," I told her. "Look, I'll call as soon as

I hear from his lawyer, okay? I'm staying at a friend's place, just until things blow over. So, if you don't catch me at the office, call my cell-phone."

"A friend? What friend? Do I know him? Haaa!" I could hear her enthusiastic gasp. "Is it Jack? Are you getting back together with Jack?"

Had she already had a chance to listen to my message? "Augh! No. Not Jack. Just someone I know through the legal community. I did have dinner with Jack tonight, and we had a nice time. As friends. Just friends."

"Oh," she sighed, her disappointment clear. Then she added hopefully, "You could always stay with me, you know."

"Mom, you turned my bedroom into an herbarium. Where would I sleep? On your new sofa?" I rang off feeling a little guilty, but there was no need to worry Mom more than necessary. I was suddenly exhausted.

I strapped Hoover into his harness and locked up the office. Within fifteen minutes, I was on the freeway in slow-moving rainstorm traffic, headed towards Alameda and the safe house, with Hoover hopping from the dashboard to the seat, to the back of the seat and back to the dashboard like a rabid squirrel.

CHAPTER 15

Friday Morning

THE RAIN HAD STOPPED OVERNIGHT, and the pavement was already drying by the time I got back to the office. I was dying to hear from Jenni Wan and find out how Kenny was, but I was also worried about the building holding up against the storm. It was an older building, and probate or not, I was responsible for it. I settled Hoover back in the office, then went upstairs. Morri wasn't in yet, but in the second office, I checked the walls and ceiling for signs of water-damage. Out the back door, I checked the rain-gutters to make sure they weren't blocked. Everything seemed to be draining just fine. I walked around the building slowly, checking the stucco and the woodwork.

I came around the front of the building and was absorbed in studying the facing around Mallory Kent's mis-painted window, checking for dry rot and termite damage, and those other things that property owners are supposed to care about, and wondering vaguely just what dry rot looked like when a voice sang out the blue.

"Excuse me? Are you deliberately ignoring me?"

The voice, sweet as molasses, with just a hint of New Orleans sultry afternoon, made me jump. Dillon Cheshire was standing beside the door to my office, leaning casually against the door frame wearing a half-smile on his face, a slender-cut blue denim jacket, and black-rimmed sunglasses that screamed casual fashion all over them.

I managed to squash my jumping heart back into my chest and swallow down any nasty comments that might have been dislodged by the action. "My apologies. I was just checking for rot."

"Rot. Sure." Dillon studied me behind his sunglasses, my face reflected back at me. I looked tired, shadowed. Or maybe that was just the gray-tint of the lenses? I could hope, anyway. He gestured across the street. "Wanna get some coffee?"

I glanced at Reese's. Friendly territory, I realized. *Always meet the enemy on your own ground.* I had a brief curious thought on whether that phrase was mine or Evrett's, and I glanced through the glass window of the office door, but the armor was exactly how I'd left it. "Sure."

At the counter, Dillon ordered a straight black coffee. I could have told him to order the specialty dark, instead of the house blend, but I didn't feel like doing him any favors. I ordered a cappuccino and paid for both drinks before Dillon could get his wallet out. "Business expense," I explained with a wave of my hand, and for a moment he seemed about to argue. Something in my gaze must have discouraged him because he nodded suddenly in agreement. I hoped it was my steely-eyed determination that deterred him, but more likely it was fear of my craze-eyed caffeine junky stare. I was in desperate need of a foamy, aromatic, perfectly pulled cappuccino.

I led him upstairs to my favorite table, the one that overlooked my building in all its turreted quake-compliant, reinforced glory. I waited, giving time for him to speak first, but Dillon just leaned back in his chair, a half-smile on his face as he sipped at his coffee.

Finally, I couldn't take the silence anymore. "So. You spoke to Irvin and the others?"

He nodded slowly. He'd pushed his sunglasses up onto his head, and his rich brown eyes were anything but contrite. "They told me they asked you back."

"But I'll only take the job if you're in," I completed with a nod. "I only took this job because I wanted to help Irvin, not because

I'm desperate for it." Well, that was a bald-faced lie wasn't it? I looked him straight in the eye because the next part wasn't a bluff. It was the stark truth. "Irvin is afraid. And so are Fi and Robert. I like them, and I want to help if I can. But I don't need you, or anyone else, blighting my reputation, professionally or personally, with unfounded accusations."

Dillon gave a short burst of laughter. "Sweetheart, you took this investigation because you're flat broke. Your office doesn't even have a real desk in it. As to your reputation, you don't really seem to have one outside of Hanford Legal Services. I checked."

"So, now you're the investigator?" I raised my eyebrows but smiled. That's what I would have done.

"I have my means and methods." Dillon smiled back, almost teasingly . . . and not in a Jack Austin kind of cute-sexy way, but in an annoying kind of way.

"And what do your means and methods tell you?"

"Less than my eyes tell me." He shrugged casually, but something in the depth of his gaze shifted, lightening his expression. "The thing is, I think you just might know what's actually going on in that house."

Well, now, that was a shift. "You accused me of fabricating evidence."

"I did. You may have. You might still be, for all I know." Another shrugging lift of his left shoulder, and he tilted his head. "Doesn't matter much. Here's the thing. Before our misunderstanding the other night, I was startin' to like you, like you more than a little. And if I jumped the gun, then I need to apologize to you. So, here I am. Apologizin.'"

"That doesn't sound very much like an apology." I shook my head. I wasn't just hard-to-get. I was impossible to catch, or so I hoped. "And believe me, I've heard my share of them."

Dillon's quirky half-smiled drifted away and he straightened in his chair, leaning forward slightly to look me directly in the eye. "Okay. Let's start over." He reached out his hand. "I, Dillon James Cheshire, hereby formally apologize for accusing you, the upstanding paralegal Kamera White, of fabricating evidence. My associates and I would be most appreciative if you would continue your investigation."

He held out his hand, and I stared at it. Well, I had asked for a formal apology, hadn't I? But something still didn't sit right. I needed to raise my visor before I could see the enemy. Or at least take a second glance to ensure that they actually were the enemy. Because right now, Dillon Cheshire didn't feel like an enemy. He didn't sound like one, either. But just the faintest rumor of fabricated evidence could take a paralegal off any law firm's contract list, and I couldn't afford that, not now, not ever.

"Tell me why you think I somehow created those cries on the tape." I said evenly, trying not to give in to the urge to just shake his hand and let bygones be bygones.

"I don't know."

I pushed back my chair and started to stand. "Call me when you figure it out."

"Wait! Just wait a second." He half-rose, too, gesturing me back into my seat. I waited for a moment, feigning indecision, but finally, with my right knee protesting the half-squat, I gave in. I slid back into my chair and waved my hand in a "by all means, do continue" gesture.

"I heard that recording and I got pissed off," Dillon admitted. His eyes turned to the tabletop and his fingers toyed with the rim of his coffee cup. "Honestly, I didn't think you would turn anything up. And when I heard that tape, well . . ." His dark eyes danced with some inner fire as they raised back to mine. "Let's just say I got mad real quick. Maybe it scared me. Maybe it just freaked me out a little. Maybe something with it just didn't sit right."

"But you'd heard the cries and screams in the house before, like the others. Weren't you relieved to have confirmation?" I wasn't going to let him off with a sissy "I was scared" excuse. I wanted a real apology, but I could feel my anger pushing the demand for an apology closer to a formal inquiry. I took a sip of my perfectly foamy cappuccino and tried to rein in my instinct to try to catch him in a lie. Be fair, I reminded myself. My reaction on hearing that recording was running in naked terror. How would I feel if I thought someone had intentionally faked it?

"Relieved? No. I'm not relieved. I'm not happy. I'm not com-forted. There's no such thing as ghosts." Dillon shrugged again, (I was starting to find his casual left-sided shrugs endearing, but that was probably just the cappuccino talking.) and his tone softened. "So, yeah, I heard that recording and it got to me, pissed me off. I don't have some overactive imagination that can be easily manipu-lated, like some people . . ."

"*Some people* being Irvin Zettlemeyer." I smiled knowingly.

"That guy really thinks your cat is from outer space." Dillon rolled his eyes.

"My cat *is* from outer space," I answered without blinking. "If you ever met him, you'd agree. But that's not the point. The point is, do you still think I faked the evidence?"

Dillon studied me for a moment, his steaming coffee cup held in his right hand, the wispy tendrils of aromatic steam wafting around his face. "No," he said finally. "I don't think you faked it. But I think someone is messing with me."

"Just with you? Not your house-mates?" I leaned in, curious. Was Dillon the target of a prank by the other three? But then, why call me in to verify it?

"With us. The house." Dillon put his cup down and fired a cha-grined smile my way, giving a single shake of his head. "Those three have plenty of brains between them, but Zettlemeyer couldn't bluff his way into a faked orgasm at a whorehouse. Fi's brain is strictly fact-based. She doesn't have the imagination to fake a haunting. And Robert spends too much time in imaginary role-play worlds to pay attention to reality long enough to pull a prolonged prank."

"Is there anyone else you can think of who would want to do something like this? If this is some kind of hoax, it's an elaborate one."

Now Dillon seemed less confident. "I don't know. I mean, I can't even think of any of my friends who could pull something like this off."

"It's not necessarily a friend," I reminded him. "What about Irvin's ex-wife? She sued him over the business they lost, didn't she? She's technology savvy, and she would know that Irvin is impressionable."

"She's a control freak, for sure." Dillon frowned as he thought. "She's crazy to blame Irvin for the cock-up with their business. They had the right idea at the wrong time in a competitive market, is all. But as far as the haunting thing goes, she only calls Irvin when she wants to guilt him for money. She's too busy dashing back and forth to LA trying to kick off her new start-up company."

"And this kind of hoax would take more time and attention than she has? That's what you're saying?"

"Well, yah. It's been going on for months." Dillon nodded in agreement.

Ah ha. I kept the smile off my face. "It's been going on for months. And if you've researched me, then you know that I'd never even heard of you until Irvin walked through my door."

"Which is why I'm sittin' here, across from you, apologizing." Dillon smiled across the table at me, and I felt a little shiver of something that I hoped wasn't attraction, because I still wanted to be mad at him. "All I'm asking for is a second chance. Forgive me?

I hesitated. When had I gone from needing this job to wanting it?

"Please?" His smile was like caramel topping on an ice cream sundae, luscious and sweet. He held out his hand again.

Finally, I lost the argument with myself and reached out to take his hand. It was warm, strong, a little calloused, and despite myself I liked it as much as I had the first time I'd shaken it. I gave it a firm squeeze and let go as quickly as was polite. "Apology accepted, sir."

I smiled then, as much as I could manage. "But I won't be accused again. I'm as bewildered by the evidence as you are. I don't know how what I heard ended up on that recording. It's the first time I've come up with anything like it. Most EVPs are a single word, a whisper, a murmur; a faint sentence sandwiched between static and background noise." I saw no point in mentioning that I'd only ever recorded one EVP before, and that was from Evrett. But I'd listened to plenty that were uploaded online since I took this job. Second-hand research but research all the same. "Dillon, all I want is to do is get to the bottom of this."

"Well, then." Dillon took another swig of his coffee and stood up, his smile breaking into a warm grin. "We'll see you Saturday."

"I thought you were going climbing?"

He winked, his voice pure tease. "And leave you all alone with those crazy housemates of mine? No way."

I stayed there, listening to his footsteps on the stair, and then Reese's voice calling, "Thanks! Come again." As he left Reese's, I had a clear view of Dillon as he walked down the street to his car. He raised the remote and held it high to click it, glancing back over his shoulder at the balcony windows. As the beep-beep reached my ears, it was hard to be certain from the angle and the light, but I thought he smiled again. I sat and enjoyed my cappuccino while I watched him drive away. The job was back on, and I was starting to feel just a bit better about Dillon.

CHAPTER 16

Friday Evening

THE WORKDAY PASSED NORMALLY, THANKFULLY. Miss Maifax
called with some minor questions, a lawyer across town asked
me for some files from a case he'd worked with me in the past. But
there were no calls from the police, or Reggie, or my brother, or
even my mother. Maybe life was returning to normal—except for
the whole ghost hunting thing.

There was one email from my father, asking if we'd heard from
Kenny yet, and I replied with a thankful yes, and that he was safe,
but not many more words than that. To say the least, my relationship with my dad is strained. My mother claims we left him, but in
my mind, he left us. He chose to stay in India, choosing his career
over his family. He called on birthdays and holidays, but I hadn't
been to see him in three years, and he hadn't been back to America
in that time, either.

With space in my schedule, I went over the final plans for
Saturday night. Nicky was in, Morri was in. Oh, and I'd made
Morri a promise, hadn't I? I called Father Joe Talbon.

"Kami? It's good to hear from you."

"Hi, Father. How are you today?"

"You can skip the small talk," he said jovially. "I saw Morri last
night at chess."

Right . . . Thursday was chess night. I should have remembered. "Did you win?"

"Against Morri?" Father Joe gave a disparaging chuckle. "Never. But humility is good for the soul, and he makes me a better player. Now, tell me about your job. Morri had some concerns."

"So do I. Morri seems to think this might be something . . ."

"Evil?" Father Joe filled in. "Truthfully, malevolent spirits are farther and fewer between than the paranormal community at large would have you believe. But I'm happy to be there and help however I can. Morri said the house is in Hayward? I can be there around 9:00."

"That would be great, thank you. Honestly, I really don't know what I'm doing."

"God wouldn't have put you there if he thought you weren't the right person," Father Joe reassured. "I have a feeling he has a plan for you. I think you're on the right path, Kami."

I wasn't at all sure that was true, but I didn't argue. I gave Father Joe the address, and he promised to see me on Saturday. As we hung up, I felt I was ready for Saturday night. At least, as ready as I thought I could be. I had the equipment; I knew the vocabulary. For whatever existed on the other side of the barrier of life, I had Evrett, and if trouble of the supernatural came along that I couldn't handle, I had Father Joe—nothing to sweat about, right?

"Right?" I asked Hoover.

He flopped over on the floor and licked his butt. Well, at least someone was taking this seriously.

WHEN THE CLOCK TICKED OVER 5:00, I gathered up the cat, Evrett's helmet, and my laptop, locked the door, and headed back to the safe house. The weather had cleared to overcast with spots of sun, and I was feeling pretty good on the drive to Alameda, but as the afternoon turned towards evening, I felt a growing sense of unease, and found myself checking my rear-view mirrors a little more often than normal.

The first thing I did as soon I got Hoover off his harness was check the freezer. The gun was still there. Somehow, that comforted me far more than I thought it should. I threw a frozen dinner in the conventional oven, slithered out of my suit and headed for the shower. Finally, clean and dressed in my Pokeman pajama pants and a clean sweatshirt, I sat down with dinner and opened my laptop.

I checked my email and social media messages and found several new messages from Kenny's friends who had seen or been with him at the festival. Hurrah for eyewitnesses. But would any of them look good in court? Could any of them testify with certainty that he had been with them instead of driving off in my car with a body in the trunk? After forwarding the messages to Jenni Wan, I felt content to let Kenny's fate be her problem and focused back on my own problems. The oven timer dinged, and I curled up in the recliner with my tv dinner and a curious Hoover hovering over my shoulder. My own problems included a phone call that I'd promised. Had it only been last night? I pulled out my phone and called Jack. Just as I thought the call was about to go to voicemail, he answered sounding out of breath.

"Jack?"

"Kam! Hi! Sorry. At the gym. Can I call you back later?"

Right. Gym night. I was tucked in eating tv-dinners, and Jack was at the gym. What exciting lives we led. "Sure, no problem. I'm kind of tired. Call me tomorrow?"

"Tomorrow," he promised. "Thanks for calling. Have a good night."

"You, too." I hung up, not sure if I felt triumphant or disappointed. Having time to talk meant trying to talk about our issues, and I was far happier just having him tell me goodnight and promise to talk later. But I missed his voice already. I turned on the television to distract me and was glad I did. The strident Bay News Investigates theme music was just playing, the flashy intro images interspersing shots of Feliz Ciaro and famous people and sites around the San Francisco Bay Area shimmering across the screen. So much had happened that I'd forgotten he'd told me not to miss tonight's show.

"WELCOME TO BAY NEWS INVESTIGATES, bringing you in-depth coverage of the current events that impact you." It was his weekly investigative journalism show, but this one wasn't about some gangland shooting in Oakland. The footage immediately caught my eye. It was the Student Services building at Cal State East Bay campus. The building was unmistakable, a slick glossy square, windows gleaming with a modern art-deco look, built to replace the old glass and concrete landmark, Warren Hall, that had loomed over the Hayward area for decades. The new building was pretty, modern and sleek, but it didn't have the monolithic imposition on the landscape that Warren Hall had. I missed Warren Hall.

On screen, Feliz Ciaro was standing in front of the new building, his back, and the news van in front of him, reflected in the gleaming glass building, speaking in low reverent tones about the search for Hannah Raye. I sprawled out on the thick, but not very soft, carpet and slowly worked my way through a set of yoga stretches while he covered the particulars of the case, which, really, were nothing. Her phone was either off or dead, her car was found still locked up in the college parking lot. There had been no phone calls, no emails, no ransom demands. Days of searching around campus had yielded no clues. Hannah had simply vanished. There was nothing new there, no new information or tips.

But Feliz kept talking.

"Hannah has been missing for a week now, but acting on a citizen tip, Bay News dug into this story and discovered a disturbing truth. There are other women who have been missing much longer than Hannah, and the similarities between them are striking."

Hey! I was the citizen tip! Thanks, Feliz.

"And their families are just as eager for answers as Hannah's friends and family are." The screen shifted to three pictures of young women. Like the familiar college campus setting, I recognized these pictures. They were women on the missing person's lists I'd gone through looking for Trunk Girl. The pictures shifted to each woman individually as the announcer continued.

"On a hot July night two years ago, Patricia Misanti, age twenty-eight, went missing after a night clubbing in Oakland. Her friends saw her to the parking lot of her apartment, but as far as anyone can tell, she never made it safely into that apartment. Patricia was a health sciences student at Merritt College in Oakland."

The picture shifted to Vivian Astor, with wavy curls in her hair, and a crooked smile that suggested a hint of embarrassment at being under the camera's eye. "Vivian Astor, age twenty-five, disappeared almost exactly one year later, on August eleventh, after leaving a study group with fellow nursing students at a local Shari's restaurant. Her car was found still in the restaurant parking lot. Vivian hasn't been seen since."

The third girl had a large blue eyes, a small nose, and long straight hair that was pulled to the side in a braid, and in the picture they showed, she had a crimson lip ring. "Jessica Powers was on top of the world, having just graduated from San Jose State and starting her dream job with Tesla when she disappeared in late June of this year."

Jessica Powers had been missing since late June? Why hadn't I heard of her? Where were her posters?

"Jessica's family admits that she has a history of depression and had been suffering from anxiety and stress over her new job." Feliz stared into the camera and shook his head slowly, refuting the conclusion the cops must have come to. That Jessica was gone of her own recognizance. "But her car was found abandoned in a Starbuck's parking lot with her phone inside. Family and friends don't believe she was a suicide risk."

Patricia, Vivian, and Jessica, and Hannah Raye all had similar ages and similar looks. And for that matter, Trunk Girl, too, shared the physical similarities, even though she didn't fit in the same social demographics. *But I did.*

"The question these families are asking now is if there may be some connection between these missing women." The camera switched back to the reporter. Feliz's location had changed, and he was now standing outside of the Alameda County Sheriff's station. "We've been talking to law enforcement about these ongoing cases, but law enforcement is thus far refusing to comment. They did tell us, however, that they do not believe the cases to be related, and adamantly insist that there is no serial aspect to them."

Serial killer always sounded plausible when the victims matched type, but the police said that wasn't the case . . . and we trusted the police, didn't we? On the heels of that thought came the image of Detective Dortman. I wouldn't trust him to find Waldo, let alone a missing woman. *Meh.* I needed to stop worrying about those missing women and focus on the one found in the trunk of my car. But honestly, I was tired. I was having a hard time focusing on anything at all.

The cat strolled over and hopped up onto my belly. I was lying on my back with my feet stretched straight up in the air, and he jumped directly onto my solar plexus. *Oof!* Yoga and cats don't really go together, no matter what some people might have you believe.

I curled up on my side and continued watching the show. The missing women hadn't really been on my radar at the times of their disappearances. I'd been too busy with school, work and making sure I had a roof over my head. While I'm firmly of the opinion that finding missing women should be a priority, I found myself wondering if there were fewer people like me, trying to survive in our own right, and more people who could get involved, more who could be a part of the search, turn over more evidence than our overworked police forces could uncover, these women wouldn't be missing anymore.

That line of thought dragged me back to the body in my trunk. I was still no closer to discovering who had stolen my car, still no closer to identifying the dead woman. If the police were, they weren't sharing the information with me. I was starting to feel a little bit offended, really. What kind of jerk steals cars and puts dead bodies in the trunk? It occurred to me then that he may have put a live body in my trunk and it had died there, which was even worse. I wondered if the autopsy had been done yet, and what the findings were.

In TV shows, the autopsy always happens within twenty-four hours and has clear cause of death written on the coroner's report. The DNA evidence is always back the same day, and always condemning. In real life, the ME can take days or weeks to get through the backlog of deceased citizens in need of his services and sometimes there's no DNA evidence at all. You don't hear that thousands of murders go unsolved in this country every year; hundreds of missing women are never found, hundreds of remains are never identified. Trunk Girl might very well be one of those.

I watched the rest of the show, only half paying attention to the events they recounted, but looking closely at the faces of the girls. I'm not good with faces anyway, but they were blond, blue eyed . . . fresh-faced California girls like me. Except that I never went out to night clubs with friends or went camping in Sonoma. The last time my hair fell in beautifully tamed waves around my face was sometime last never. I was a frizzle headed night-school social reject.

"See," I told Hoover, throwing his bright purple bouncy-ball again and watching him chase it off the walls, "those fancy things just get you disappeared. We're just being safe. Here in our safe house."

Feliz looked directly at the camera. "Without further evidence of what happened to these women, we may never know who or what was responsible for their disappearance. But as an investigative reporter, I can tell you that I've made a promise to the families to find out what happened to these women, and to bring the truth back to you, our audience. But right now, we need your help. If you have any tips or information about Patricia, Vivian, Jessica, or Hannah, please call the tip-line at the bottom of the screen. I will personally follow up leads and maybe with your help, we can find these women and bring peace to their families. This is Feliz Ciaro, saying good night."

"Goodnight, Feliz," I said as I reached for the remote. "What do you think, Hoover? The Late Show, or a Law & Order rerun?"

Hoover was far more interested in whatever was going on outside of the window where he was perched. His oversized ears were pointed straight up and his tail was twitching violently against the windowsill.

"If there's a spider out there, you leave it be," I warned him as I switched off the tv. "I don't want it crawling in here and eating us in our sleep."

If you've ever received a reproachful glance from a cat that then completely dismisses you, then you know exactly what Hoover looked like—only more naked and wrinkly than most other cats. I was clearly not invited to whatever party he was having. I opened my laptop and took a last look at the background checks I'd done on Irvin and his housemates.

Overall, they all seemed like pretty decent people: normal, typical—well, typical for tech-geek types—no history of practical jokes, no arrests for setting off firecrackers in public toilets. The housemates weren't pranksters. They weren't reckless. They might be messing with each other, but why and to what gain? Especially once they called me in, why would they continue the prank if they were paying me to debunk it? Were they after publicity? None of them had a history of being attention seekers, especially Fiora. She was the keep-her-head-down type, and the addition of confidentiality to the contracts made it even more unlikely they were looking for some kind of press. The only thing that made sense was that the house was genuinely haunted. I kicked back and rubbed my eyes.

Hoover was still sitting the window, his tail perfectly poised as he hunched down, his face to the glass.

I stood up and stretched. "Come on, kitty-cat. To bed."

"Mowl." Hoover glanced back at me, then turned back to the window, his eyes wide.

"Fine. But if it's a spider, I'm sleeping in the bathroom with the door locked and you can stay out here in case it gets inside." I went to the window, pushed back the drape and looked out—and my breath caught. There was someone standing at the corner of the building, looking up at the window . . . just a dark shape in a dark hoodie, but unmistakably looking up at the window.

The second they realized I was looking down, they backed around the corner. My blood froze. Were they watching me? I snatched Hoover under my arm and slapped the curtains closed. With the protesting cat tucked under my arm, I went around and checked all the windows and the door. All were locked. I checked the security camera screen by the door that showed the elevator where people could buzz to come up, but it only showed an empty corridor.

Watching me? Why would anyone be watching me? Doing background checks had made me paranoid, maybe? I dialed Reggie's number. "I think someone was watching the safe-house."

"Who?" He sounded tired.

"I don't know. I just . . . I think they were out there a long time. Hoover tried to tell me . . ."

"How much coffee have you had today?" Reggie asked, and I didn't think he was joking.

"Not enough that I'm hallucinating!"

"Is the door locked?"

"Yes. The knob and the deadbolt. And the chain."

"Is there anyone on the security camera?"

He was being so damned calm and reasonable. I took a deep breath, steadying my nerves. "Never mind. You're right. Who would be watching me? I'm . . . I'm just tired, I guess."

"You have the number for the security people. Call and ask them to do an extra sweep. Then get some sleep, okay? I'm sure it was just a coincidence, and anyway, that place is built like Fort Knox. Who even knows you're there?"

"Just the cops. Okay . . . You're right. It was nothing." I wasn't feeling very convinced.

He hung up and I checked the bolts again and called the security service. The dispatcher was very polite and yes, ma'am-no-problem'd me when I asked for a sweep. I curled up in the eight-hundred count cotton sheets, pulled Hoover under the covers with me and closed my eyes. But I couldn't sleep. I kept seeing that shadow at the corner of the building over and over in my mind.

Hoover wearied of my cuddling and crawled out. I could hear him bouncing his rubber ball around the linoleum flooring of the kitchen and relaxed. If Hoover wasn't bothered, why should I be? My eyes drifted closed to the faint bap bap bap of the rubber against the cabinetry. Bap bap bap bap.

"MRRAAAAAAAAAAAAWR!"

Hoover!

I threw myself out of bed, gasping in the darkness as my feet landed under me and my hand hit the light switch, casting a triangular glow out into the main room of the apartment. "Who's there?"

The words had barely escaped my lips when I bit them closed. *Stupid!* Why do people do that? They always do it in stupid horror movies. *Hey, killer monster with the chainsaw? Is that you out there? Let me make some noise so you know exactly where I am!* I reached for the first weapon I saw and crept out clutching my black low-heeled pump. (Yes, I know stiletto heels make better weapons than flats. You ever tried wearing them all day?)

Hoover was standing on the door mat, back arched, staring wide-eyed at the door, yowling fit to kill. His teeth were bared and if he'd had any hair it would have been sticking up. An unearthly growl echoed from his throat, half whine, half snarl, and over the sound, I could hear retreating footsteps in the corridor. I grabbed the phone and dialed the security company while I checked the video feed. The elevator corridor appeared empty and the elevator doors were closed, just as they had been earlier, but I didn't believe that.

"Someone's in the building! Someone was at my door," I gasped to the dispatcher. I tried to pick up Hoover and move him back into the bedroom with me, but he struggled and clawed, leaving raw scratches as he slipped out of my arms.

"We've just done a sweep, ma'am," the security dispatcher reassured. I started to move for the bathroom to lock myself in. If only I had a weapon . . .

"Well, do it again! Someone was just outside my door!"

"Are they still there, ma'am?"

"What? Do you want me to open it and look? I heard someone outside, just now!"

"Calm down, ma'am. Use the peephole and tell me if you see anyone."

"For me, this is calm!" I put my eye to the peephole. The corridor was empty, as far as I could see, but someone could be to either side of the door, or out of sight around the corner by the elevator. They could be anywhere! "I don't see anyone. But I can see the door of the other apartment. Is it occupied?"

"No, ma'am." The dispatcher sounded annoyingly calm.

I flung open the fridge and gasped with relief to see that Reggie's man hadn't picked up the gun. Holding the phone to my ear with my shoulder, I used both hands to free it from the plastic. The steel was ice-cold in my palm, and I grabbed a dishtowel to protect my hands and keep my fingerprints off the weapon. Did freezing a gun hurt it much? I didn't know, but I jammed the clip home, feeling a satisfying click. "Look, please, just do another sweep!" I begged the dispatcher. "Someone was outside the building earlier, and now they are inside. I heard their footsteps running away from my door."

"I'll have someone right there." The dispatcher hung up and I considered calling 911. Instead, I called Reggie.

As soon as I heard the click of the pick-up, I stammered out, "Someone was just at the door. Security says they did a sweep, but I swear someone was here."

"What? Who . . . It's late. Is this Kami?"

Oops. He'd been asleep. I was having a hard time feeling remorseful about that. "Someone was inside the building! They were right outside my door. Security says they came by, but someone's here. In your safehouse! How is this safe?" I was pacing back and forth, careful to stay away from the windows. Hoover was pacing, too, dashing agitatedly from the window to the door, playing guard-cat. If he only knew how silly he looked.

Reginald groaned. "I'm on my way. Don't buzz me up until you see me on the video feed, got it?"

"I'm armed." I warned him. "Call me from the elevator so I can see you on camera."

I hung up and waited, every nerve on edge. The gun felt like a steel iceberg through the thin terrycloth towel, and I desperately hoped that a gun this cold could still fire. I mean, in movies, they drop them in the snow and stuff all the time, don't they? They always seemed to work fine in movies no matter what, though. I couldn't tell if I was shivering from the cold or the fear.

Logic said I was being paranoid. There were only three people who knew I was at the safehouse: Reggie, Detective Brittle, and Dortman. *Unless someone followed me.* No one was out to get me.

Unless I had enemies I didn't know about. There was a keycard swipe to get into the garage, a key for the elevator, and the key to the apartment door. Someone would have to have all three to get in. But someone had. *Hoover knew there was someone in the hall.* I finally sat down on the edge of the couch, gun between my hands, every nerve awake and listening.

My cellphone rang and I snatched it up.

"I'm downstairs."

I went to the video screen and Reggie waved at the camera. I buzzed him up, noting that he turned and stepped backwards into the elevator, his eyes scanning the garage as the doors closed. I stood by the door, one eye to the peephole, and the gun literally cold steel in my right hand. I'd only fired a gun once before in my life, and it was a little .22 caliber pistol at a shooting range. I only did it to impress a guy. We never went on a second date, so I assumed I hadn't impressed him. Or maybe he could tell that taking me to a shooting range for our first date hadn't impressed me.

The elevator opened and Reggie stepped out, but I waited until he was at the door to unlock it. I opened the door with the gun held low, like a TV-show super cop . . . if they ever answered the door in their pajamas.

Reggie entered, his gaze rippling from my bare feet to my flannel Pokeman pajama pants to my pink tank top to the gleaming gun in my hand. "Nice look."

"No. Not nice! Your safe-house isn't safe!" I shut the door behind him and snapped the locks back in place.

He ran a hand through his dark hair, leaving it tousled beautifully around his forehead. "You look safe enough. Even if they got inside the building, this is a fire door with multiple locks."

"If they got inside the building, how hard would it be for them to get through this door?" I was totally unconvinced. "Someone was watching me from outside. And then they were in the hall."

"Did you see them?"

"Out the window. Not inside." Reggie's eye-roll told me what he thought of that admission, but I wasn't deterred. "But I heard them! And Hoover. He was the one who warned me."

"Hoover? You want to chime in here?" Reggie glanced at the cat, but he was prowling back and forth, tail erect, moving from the window to the door. At the sound of his name, he glanced up at Reggie before dismissing him with a tail-twitch. Reggie looked at me and shrugged. "Your witness appears to have withdrawn their statement, counsel."

"What can I say? He's a cat."

Reggie glanced back at the gun. "Maybe you could put that down? Relax."

"When the security people come and sweep the building, I'll relax." But I did put the gun back on the counter, on top of its baggy. I didn't release the clip and I left the safety off.

"You know what you need? A nice cuppa." Reggie walked into the kitchen, filled the teakettle and put it on to boil, found cups and tea in the cupboard. Oh, the British love for a cup of tea, the best cure-all ever invented. "Did you see who was looking at the building? Can you describe them?"

I snagged my black over-sized sweatshirt from my duffle and pulled it on. "No, he was in the shadows by the corner. When he saw me looking, he backed around the corner."

"So that's a no."

RRRRING! My heart jumped. The rest of my body doubled it.

"Whoa. Good thing you put the gun down!" Reggie answered the phone in crisp tones, went through a brief identification process with the security dispatcher and hung up. "The security people are sweeping the building now."

I went to the door and watched on the monitor as two uniformed security guards let themselves into the elevator. I would have waited for them to reappear, but Reggie pointed me to the table and put a hot cup of tea into my hands. "Sit. Relax. Calm down."

Now that the adrenaline was fading, I felt a little bit weepy . . . like you get from watching Hallmark commercials. "I don't know. Maybe I over-reacted. Too much time alone or something. Maybe everything's just getting to me."

Reggie's tone turned understanding. "It's no wonder, kiddo. But look, your brother is safe. We're convinced of his innocence. There's no reason to believe that the people who stole your car even know your name. Tell me why you think anyone would be after you?"

"My registration and insurance card were in my car. They'd know my name and the address of my old apartment." But Reggie was right. There was no reason to think they would care. "I don't know. Maybe it's Juliet."

Reggie's laugh lasted a good five minutes and he was wiping tears from his face by the time he was done. "She's not exactly a superspy ninja, Kam!"

"Well, no, but she's rich enough to hire one," I muttered determinedly. "Have someone follow me, try to ruin my life. Not that there's much there to ruin, but I should be the one to ruin it."

Kindly, Reggie didn't laugh again. "Kam, can you take some advice?"

Fortunately, I was rescued from answering by a knock on the door. I stayed by the gun, and let Reggie answer it. He demanded identification from the security team before opening the door.

I was expecting the usual rent-a-cop-not-quite-good-enough-for-the-force types, but these two had military bearing, with short-shorn heads and tidy gray and black uniforms. I silently christened them Privates Tall and Taller.

"We did a sweep of the entire building," the taller one informed us. "If anyone was here, they're long gone."

"Did you look at the security tapes?" Reggie asked, all business.

"We did, sir, but nothing seems out of the ordinary. The external camera shows someone coming around the corner on the sidewalk about two hours ago, but nothing inside."

"Did you see anyone get on the elevator?"

"Not until you arrived, sir . . . but . . ."

Tall elbowed Taller and Taller fell silent.

"There was nothing on the feed, sir. No strange cars, no one entering the premises who doesn't belong," Tall finished.

Reggie gave them both a dark look, compounded by the deep sleep-circles under both eyes. "Why do I think there's something you aren't telling me? I'd hate to have to call your supervisor at this hour, but if my client's safety was compromised . . ."

"No, sir. Nothing like that," Taller interjected, but he looked sidelong at Tall.

"It was our supervisor, sir, who recommended that we not say anything," Tall admitted. "When we arrived, the security room door was unlocked. We're sure it was just an oversight on our coworker's part. We've notified . . ."

"I want to see the video." Reginald gave me a look that said 'stay', but I was already clipping Hoover into his harness and pulling my denim jacket on. Either he was close to throwing me out the window, or he was just too tired to argue, but Reggie let me tag along as we followed the security team down to the elevator and then to the first floor.

One of them pulled out a color-coded key and opened the security room door. It was a basic doorknob lock, not a deadbolt or anything. I could probably pick it if I were inclined. Kenny had locked me out of the house enough times that I'd honed a few break-in skills. Inside the security room, they showed us the alarm settings and then pulled up the video feed, scrolling through it from when I arrived to when they appeared on the feed.

"You see. No one came in or out of the elevator except for you two, and us."

Reggie glanced at his watch, then back at the screen. It was frozen on the image of Tall and Taller standing in the elevator. "Take it back to the 10:50 mark and slow it down."

Tall and Taller exchanged sour looks. No one likes to be told their job. "Just do it," I told them. "I can only imagine what Oslo and Burroughs pays to keep this building secure. You like your paychecks, don't you?"

Tall tapped the keyboard, backing up the recording and then replaying it on slow.

The three of us were watching the feed, which showed nothing—just an empty elevator and a section of the parking garage. Reginald, however, was looking at something else and when he spoke again, the growl in his tone was furious enough to make me cringe. "You're telling me that you see nothing wrong here? Look at the timestamp."

The timestamp read 10:52:16; it read 10:52:16 for the next eighteen minute's worth of video.

Tall and Taller stared.

Reggie turned to look at me. I was staring at the video, a cold prickly feeling running down my spine and rooting my feet to the floor. Reginald shifted his gaze to the security team and uttered coldly, "One of you please escort my client back to her apartment and stand guard. The other, get your supervisor on the phone."

The look Reggie gave me wasn't conducive to argument. I carried Hoover cradled to my chest, but he was relaxed and purring, no sign that anything was amiss. My escort (Taller) did a sweep of the apartment when we arrived, leaving me alone in the hallway, and then allowed me inside.

"Lock the door behind you," he warned as he took up his post.

As if I needed to be told?

My tea was cold, so I heated it in the little microwave while I waited. The fact that I was justified in my belief that someone had been in the building did little to comfort me. Okay, so I wasn't crazy, and now, no one else thought I was either. I sat staring at the gun on the table until Reggie returned.

"Those two are probably out of a job," he told me when I opened the door.

"Darn. They were kind of cute in an incompetent sort of way." I sighed as I threw all the bolts back into place.

"I'm sorry I didn't believe you."

"Yeah, well, I was hysterical. And armed. Why would you have believed me?"

Reggie didn't answer that, but he smiled faintly. "They'll have someone swing by the building once an hour and will replace all of the common area locks tomorrow, including the garage keycard and the security room. They swept the building and checked with other tenants. Either way, I don't think your stalker will come back tonight."

He leveled his best break-the-witness stare at me. "So, who knows you're staying here?"

"Just you and the police. I haven't even told my mother. I just told her I was staying with a friend."

"Kamera." He sat down across from me, both elbows on the table, studying me with dark eyes. "Who might be stalking you?"

I didn't know. "My mother?"

But Reggie didn't smile at my joke. "So far, your two suspects are women of a certain age, with neither the prowess nor skill to break into this building and alter the security feeds. Be realistic. A former client maybe?"

"My mother has a criminal record, you know." Reggie laughed. He knew. I sighed. "I research insurance claims, Reggie. I don't defend violent criminals." I pointed at the gun on the table. "What about your former clients? Maybe they thought someone else was staying here. I mean, the former resident left a gun under the sofa for a reason. It could be that they weren't even looking for me."

"Tomorrow, we'll see about moving you to a new location, but you're right," Reggie conceded wearily. "Kami, has it occurred to you that the person who stole your car and killed Jane Doe was actually looking for you? That Jane Doe was a substitute for you?"

It had. Feliz Ciaro's report had only reinforced that. I protested half-heartedly. "I don't look anything like Trunk Girl."

"Would someone who only knows that you're blond and drive a blue Kia know that for certain? Mistaken identity happens."

I didn't like that thought. I pointed to the gun. "I'm keeping that here."

"Tomorrow, it goes to the police." He slid it neatly back into the baggie.

"Maybe." I yawned, glanced at the clock. It was quarter past one. "Probably just as well. I've got an investigation tomorrow night. I'll need to sleep in and be rested."

"You going to tell me about this investigation? As your lawyer, you know anything you say to me is confidential." He glanced suspiciously towards my laptop and the small pile of papers beside it.

I considered for a minute. I didn't want to get into it, didn't want to even mention the whole paranormal versus paralegal mess that I was mucked up in. But I owed Reggie something. Beyond cleaning the illegal weaponry out of his safe house, I mean. "I have four computer geek types who suspect that someone is playing a not-so-pleasant prank on them, making it seem like their house is haunted. But . . . I've gone over all the background checks and the house diagrams and everything that I can think of, and . . ." I averted my eyes, feeling my face heat up, "I don't like the conclusion I'm coming to."

"Which is . . .?"

"That there is no prankster. That the house is actually haunted." I sat still, waiting for the laughter, but either Reginald was too tired to find it amusing or he was too stunned to laugh at me. "I've been to the house, Reggie. I've seen and heard things that I can't figure out how to quantify. I've seen shadows. I recorded screams during interviews that no one heard at the time . . . Not things I can just explain away with science."

Reggie opened his mouth, the muscles under his right eye flexing. "Well . . ."

I held my breath, waiting for Reggie to give me the sound advice I so desperately needed. To be my voice of reason, my solid rock in the churning tide.

"Good luck with that, kiddo." Reggie shrugged and turned towards the door.

"Reggie!"

But he was already gathering his coat. "Hey, none of my business. You're not doing anything illegal. If it's within the house, it's likely none of your prank suspects are doing anything illegal. And if it's not a prank and the place really is haunted, I'm fairly certain the only law that falls under is God's, and I've made tremendous effort in my life not to negotiate with that kind of authority." Reggie winked. "I'm your lawyer, not your preacher."

Darn it.

It wasn't until after Reggie left, and I was curled up on the bed, wrapped in the comforter, listening for the security patrol, watching for the lights of their car on the ceiling, that I remembered what Feliz Ciaro had said. Whoever took Hannah had messed with the cameras in the parking lot on campus. Was it the same someone who had messed with the cameras in the building? As exhausted as I was, I didn't sleep.

CHAPTER 17

Saturday Morning

A T DAYBREAK, I PACKED MY STUFF, collected Hoover's things, stuck the gun back in the freezer, and got the heck out of the unsafe safehouse. I went straight to Mom's house, but her Beetle wasn't in the driveway. I hoped she wasn't at the police station bugging them about Kenny. I let myself in with my spare key, and wrote a quick note, asking her to look after Hoover for me a couple days. I told her I was fine, staying with friends, and I'd call her as soon as I could. I went to magnet it to the fridge and spotted her magnetic dry-erase schedule. She had Sunrise Yoga at Chabot written for Saturday morning. She would be at the park with the yoga folks.

I took off Hoover's harness, put down a bowl of kibble and his water dish. "Okay, buddy. Be good for Grandma Jax. She'll be back in an hour or so, probably. I bet she'll have treats for you. And probably a new sweater, too." He ignored me, going straight to the sliding glass door to watch the birds in the birdbath. He was fine.

I wasn't fine. I hadn't slept. As tempting as it was to stretch out on Mom's plushy new red sectional and take a nap, I didn't dare stay anywhere that I'd been in the weeks since Hannah had gone missing, and if someone was stalking me, I didn't dare go anywhere alone. My gaze strayed back to Mom's calendar: Sunrise

184 E.L. OAKES

Yoga—a public place with plenty of friendly places. I headed for Lake Chabot.

Sunrise Yoga was happening in the small park area in front of the little marina. A couple dozen people, many I knew from my yoga collective, were in neat rows, easing into Warrior Pose. Jaxine was near the front, so I slipped into place at the end of the last row and found my footing. Sunrise is not my favorite time of day, but there was a brisk breeze coming off the glittering lake, the sun was edging over the hills, and I breathed deep of dew-damp, eucalyptus-tanged air, checked my balance, and slid into Warrior Pose, front leg extended, arms raised. Through the haze of sleepless stress, my body responded by opening my lungs, drawing more sweet air down into my center. The adrenaline packed into my muscles dissipated as I stretched and flexed. Surrounded and secure, fear eased away and focus returned. Here I was safe. No one knew I was here, no one here meant me harm. There was only my breath, and the warmth of the rising sun, and the shimmering of blue-green water.

As the meet-up came to a close, I stood to the side and waited for Jaxine. She was chatting with friends, and hadn't seen me yet, but as soon as she did, her eyes went wide with surprise and she hurried over.

"What's wrong? Is your brother okay?"

"He's fine, Mom." I smiled faintly. "I just dropped Hoover off for you to babysit, saw the note on your calendar about yoga, and thought I'd come up and join you."

Mom looked at me through narrowed eyes. She was wearing an orange flowered t-shirt and matching yoga pants, her silver-streaked hair was tied up in a French braid and her cheeks were bright from the early morning chill. "You don't do sunrises."

"I do today."

Mom looked like she wanted to say something more, but instead gestured towards the Marina Café. "Want breakfast?"

"Do I ever!"

Over omelets and toast, I gave Mom the abbreviated, mother-safe version of why I was there. "So, I'm just laying low for a couple days. I mean, maybe it's all just a coincidence, but I really think someone was looking for me at my friend's place last night. So, I'm leaving you in charge of Hoover for a couple days, if that's okay."

"Of course it is!" Mom seemed relieved. "I love having that little miscreant around." She paused, English muffin halfway to her mouth. "When I saw you standing there, I thought for sure something really bad had happened. You scared me."

"Sorry. I just thought after everything that's been going on, breaking my usual patterns and doing something different seemed like a good idea. I mean, even if someone is stalking me, which, in the light of day, seems kind of silly, who is going to try to snatch me when I'm surrounded by yoga fanatics?" I chuckled to make light of the situation.

"We'd beat them to death with our yoga mats!" Jaxine laughed, too. "And then throw them in the lake."

"What happened to peace and love and how sacred life is?"

"Peace and love have their limits. So, what's your plan for the day?"

"I hadn't decided. I have plans later this evening," and I saw no point in telling her I was going ghost hunting with Morri and Father Joe. "But I think I'll feel safer if I hide out. Just haven't decided where."

"You can come with me to the greenhouse. I've got a pile of tomato seedlings that need to be potted up for sale."

"Thanks, but I think everyone in San Amoro, and probably half of Alameda County knows the greenhouse and that you own it. I've been seen there. A lot." Not as much as I probably should be, if I was a better kid to my mom and if I liked gardening better, but in the genetics department, I seemed to have missed getting the green thumb. "I really need to get a nap. But I'll call you later."

I had no idea where I was going to take that nap and let Mom's voice fade off as I tried to figure out where to go.

"... phone off, you never know ..." Jaxine was saying.

"I'm sorry. What?" I jerked my attention back to her.

"Maybe you should turn your phone off. You hear all the time about those smart phones getting hacked and people tracking your every move."

"I would," I told her sincerely. "But for one, my phone isn't very smart. And for two, if I do go missing, you'll want the police to be able to ping my phone to find out my last known location."

She waved both hands at me as we walked back out into the sunlight. "Well, I'm sure you know more about than I do. Technology and I just clash all the time."

"Really? How many hits did your garden blog have this week?" I teased. I gave her a quick hug. "I'll call you later. Have fun with your tomatoes."

Jaxine paused, looking up at the treetops, then out to the lake. "Let's do this more often."

I suddenly wanted to. "Yeah. Let's do that."

I walked her to her green Beetle, then made my way to the pick-up, keeping an eye on the cars coming and going from the lot, the dog walkers, mountain-bikers, and joggers filling up the park on one of the last nice days at the start of autumn. Faces were vaguely familiar, faces I'd never seen before, cars that could be cars I'd seen on the street outside the office, or in the school parking lot. I jumped into the truck and took the most circuitous route I could find back to the office. I parked in the public lot on 3rd and walked the back alley to the back door. I slipped inside, bolted the door behind me, and stopped, listening. It was Saturday, so no Morri. No Mallory. I unlocked the door to the file room, and, without turning on any lights, snuck into the shadows of the back office, curled up on the sofa, prepared to listen for every clink of the pipes, every pop of the old beams, but there was nothing. The building was silent. I shut my eyes and slept dreamless hard sleep.

CHAPTER 18

Saturday Evening

A FTER A SOLID NAP AND A HEARTY SANDWICH and salad from Reese's, I felt fortified and ready for the evening. I went over all of the equipment, packed it up along with extra batteries, and headed for the Hayward hills. At the house, Dillon's leased white Stanza and black motorcycle were in the driveway, as was Fi's older model Honda Fit. I couldn't decide if I was glad or not that Dillon had cancelled his Yosemite climbing weekend. Part of me didn't looking forward to seeing him, especially if he felt like accusing me of fabricating evidence again. Despite the apology, I still partially suspected that he was the one fabricating the evidence. I just couldn't quite figure out how he was doing it, or even why he would.

I knocked on the door, and Dillon answered it. He was wearing black jeans and a gray micro-fiber shirt with the sleeves rolled up . . . and dear god, he looked good. "You done being mad at me?" he asked as I stepped in.

I stepped around him. "Mostly. Don't expect me to apologize."

"I won't. Don't expect me to accept it if you did." His grin was heart-stoppingly beautiful. "I was kind of an ass."

"There we are then."

I strolled through to the kitchen and set my brief bag and the black duffle on the table. I nudged my laptop open and started laying out gear. "Where are the others? Still can't believe you can-celled Yosemite for this."

"The kids? They're fetching pizza and ice-cream. Apparently, you can't hunt ghosts without pizza and ice cream." A smile charmed and devilish crossed his face. "And Yosemite's been there a long time. It'll be there a little longer. I wouldn't have missed tonight for the world."

"Waiting for me to falsify evidence?"

"If that's what you wanna think." Dillon leaned over my com-puter, scanning the recording programs that were opening. "So, you think we got a ghostie-ghoulie? Or you think the boys are havin' one over on us?"

"I think," I met his eye over the back of my laptop, "that I'm keeping all avenues of investigation open until I have enough evi-dence to draw specific conclusions. Also, ghosts don't like being called ghoulies. Ghoul is a different class of haunt entirely."

He fell back a half step and crossed his arms, head tilted as though ready to wait out a lecture. "Really?"

"Oh, sure. And 'ghost' isn't politically correct anymore. They prefer 'disembodied entity.'" I flashed a grin across the table, letting him know I was joking. "So, do you stay in this house every time you work in the Bay Area?"

"Why do you ask?"

"Well," I flicked on the K2 meter and held it up, checking its little lights. "If you've stayed here every time you've worked in the area, that gives you years of history in this place that the others don't have. But you never saw or heard anything out of the ordi-nary until now?"

"Out of the ordinary." Dillon smiled again, and I remembered why he'd originally caught my eye. He was one gorgeous man. "No. Unless you count all the crap you see and hear living with oddball assortments of tech-heads."

I laughed a little. "They do have their quirks, don't they?"

"Face it. Brilliant people can be perfectly normal, but some-where, somethin' has to break, you know." He leaned forward, both elbows on the table while he watched me. Finally, bored, he reached for the K2 himself and flipped the switch a few times, toying with it. "So, what does this do?"

"It measures electrical fields. Spirits need energy to manifest. Some can actually use their energy field to communicate using the K2." I turned on the digital video camera, checked the memory card in it, and held it up, testing it with a slow run around the room. It came into focus on Dillon's face as he came around the table, and I backed up a step, moving further back to open the space between us and keep him in frame.

"Really?" No masking the sarcasm there, was there? "So, what else is in your magic bag?" He asked, putting his hand down on the duffle bag. I complied by opening it further, making it clear that I had nothing to hide.

"Cameras. Recorders. Flashlights. Batteries." Evrett's helmet was wrapped in a silk scarf in the bottom of my bag. I didn't point it out. "I'd like to run downstairs and see if there's a good place to set up the stationary video camera on the mini-tripod. The more I can get set up before my team gets here, the better shape we'll be in."

"Sure." He stepped back, picking up the K2 meter, charming grin dancing across his face. "Maybe we can try this out while we're down there. You can show me your thing."

"My *thing* doesn't show on command. We may not get any response at all," I warned, ignoring the double entendre. Yeah, he was sexy as hell, but he had also insulted me along with my honor and integrity. No man who pulled that crap was gonna see my things without some serious groveling.

"Come on. I wanna see it in action."

"I think we should wait for the others, shouldn't we?" I glanced back towards the door, but Dillon shrugged.

"Think of it like a test run. Be a real shame if all this fancy gear goes kablooee in front of the others."

Kablooee. Kind of like my career. "Yeah, okay." I gathered everything up and followed him down the stairs. To tell the truth, I was kind of eager to try the gear without the rest of the gang there. If I screwed up, I wanted as small an audience as possible. But I could feel a shiver of excitement creeping up my spine. The solution to the voice on the recording and the shadows in the driveway might be only hours away. Sure, all the ghost hunter sites warn you that you can go years without ever capturing hard evidence of a haunting, but I just had a feeling. I knew tonight was gonna be a night to remember.

I set up the tripod on a bookshelf near the patio doors of the 'quiet room', making sure that it covered as much of the room and stairs as possible. I hooked it up to my laptop and made sure it was recording the video directly to my hard drive.

"Aren't we supposed to turn out the lights? Light candles? Set up a Ouija board?" Dillon laughed and I laughed too, despite myself.

"No. This is the 21st century." I put the K2 meter on the table. "I prefer a more scientific approach. I don't believe in ectoplasm or channeling. But go ahead and turn off the lights and let's test the K2 response."

I placed the K2 meter on the bean-bag chair in the middle of the room. The beanbag was perfect, I reasoned, because any movement or pressure would make the Styrofoam bead filling shift, making noise, and the chair visibly move in response. If anyone was trying to use strings, sticks or sleight of hand to trick the K2, the bean bag would help to give them away.

Dillon leaned over and switched off the light, and we were plunged into darkness, with only the faint ambient light coming in through the windows. I studied the lighting for a minute, looking at the camera screen. "Those reflections from the windows are bad. Tricks of the light and all. We're going to get all kinds of weird reflections."

Dillon reached behind me, flipped a switch, and motorized blinds slid closed, plunging us into darkness. Standing close behind me, he leaned towards my ear and whispered, "What now?"

"Now?" I pulled out the recorder and held it up in my hand, "Let's see who's home. Speaking of, maybe we should wait for the others? I don't want them to miss anything if we get something good. And my team should be arriving in the next hour or so."

"You're recording everything," Dillon answered. "The roomies said they'd text when they were on their way back. Anyway, I'm sure they'll be back soon. Though, with those three, they could take all night just to pick out what kind of pizza sauce they want."

"I suppose you're the decisive kind?" I joshed, flicking on the recorder. Before he could answer, I gave him a 'shush' motion and gave the starting cue to the recording.

"This is Kami White and Dillon Cheshire, in the Quiet Room, at 7:38 pm, Saturday."

"If there's anyone here with us, we'd like you to try to make contact."

Dillon was watching me, not the K2, standing just off my shoulder, almost too close for comfort. I tried not to sound nervous as I addressed the open space in front of me. "There's a recorder in my hand, and if you talk to it, we can play it back and hear you. You can say whatever you'd like. Also, there on the bean-bag chair is a little device with a light on it? You can try making those lights light up?"

There was a long tense moment, both of us with our eyes focused on the K2 Meter. Nothing happened. Not a blink. Not a wink. Okay, nice try. "All you have to do is get close to it. It can't hurt you." I encouraged, but in my heart, I think I knew it was a total bust. I let out the breath I was holding, feeling deflated.

That's when the K2 meter lit up full-bore.

"Holy crap," Dillon muttered.

I felt a smile bust across my face so fast Dale Earnhardt Jr. wouldn't have been able to outdrive it. "That's it! Good job! You did it! Okay, let's try this. I'm going to ask a question, and if the answer is no, step back. Don't make it light up. But if the answer is yes, you can light up the lights."

The lights went full bright again. *An intelligent haunt?* "It could still be a coincidence." I cautioned Dillon. "There might be some kind of electrical interference. Maybe from the motor for the blinds or something. Don't get too excited."

He shook his head and gestured for me to continue.

"Are you the only one with us tonight?"

No lights.

"Are there two of you?"

No lights.

"Come on. It was a fluke." Dillon said quietly, though to my ears he sounded off-key.

"Three?"

The lights went bright.

"There are three of you?"

The lights flashed once, twice, three times. My heart was racing as fast as the lights.

Wow! Holy cow wow! I looked at Dillon, he stared back at me, and I could feel the tension in his body, a fight or flight response I was entirely too familiar with when it came to this house. We stared at each other for a second and then he nodded encouragingly.

I tried to remember my list of carefully prepared questions. "Did you die in this house?"

The lights flashed bright again.

I glanced at Dillon, clearing my throat. "My research on the house didn't find any record of deaths here. Nothing. That doesn't make any sense." I started to ask how they died but remembered that I was limited to yes/no questions.

"Did you die before this house was built?"

No lights.

"So, you died in this house after 1979?"

Full lights.

I was starting to feel a little creeped out.

"Do you want to stay in this house?"

No lights.

"You want to leave?"

Full lights.

Why can't you leave? How did you die here? How can you be trapped? There were so many questions that didn't have yes and no answers! I wanted to reach for Evrett's helmet, and put it on, see if I could pierce the veil with sight. Talking to disembodied entities was a lot more difficult when they were strangers—just like with live people, I guess. "I know someone who can help you leave, but it may take some time." I said quietly, hoping I wasn't lying. "Is there anything you need to tell us?"

The lights went full bright again.

"You can try saying it to the recorder. The recorder has heard you before."

I held it up, let it run for a full timed minute, then said aloud, "This is Kami and Dillon, closing EVP session."

Suddenly I realized I was cold, shivering in fact, goosebumps raised on my arms. "Dillon? The lights?"

He didn't reach for the light switch but clicked the toggle to the motor that opened the blinds, letting the ambient light from the city below fill the room with a hazelnut glow.

I shrugged my shoulders, trying to shake the chill, and plugged the recorder into the computer, transferring the file and putting it on playback.

"Is there anything you need to tell us? You can try saying it to the recorder. The recorder has heard you before."

I had steeled myself for the sounds of hopeless weeping, for the cries for help. I was ready for them this time. I was a professional paranormal investigator. Nothing could shake me. I was a rock.

"Get out. GET OUT!"

The otherworldly scream grated from my computer speakers with terrifying accuracy.

"Kill you! Kill you!" the voice said again. The repeated words faded in volume slowly, petering out completely before I turned off the recorder.

"Kill you?" My lips felt numb, my entire body was shivering again. "Kill us? Who would kill us? Or do they mean them? Kill them?"

"Not us." Dillon's voice was low in my ear. He was standing directly behind me, his chest against my back as we both leaned over the computer. "Just you."

Just . . . The words sunk in too slowly. I threw my hands up as I turned towards Dillon, trying to push him away from me, but there was a sudden jab, a sharp sting at my neck, and I froze stiff, my entire body tilting towards the floor. "Ow . . . what . . . you . . . What the hell did you . . . do . . ."

The last thing I saw before everything went black was Dillon's molasses eyes, turned hard as granite, his expression grim as he leaned over me. "You know what I did."

CHAPTER 19

—◆—

Saturday Night

WHEN I WOKE IT WAS TO TOTAL DARKNESS. I was lying on the floor and when I spread my palms, I could feel wood underneath me, like raw boards, or planks. It was surprisingly warm.

"Hello? Is there anyone there?"

Total silence.

I was thirsty and dizzy. I blinked my eyes and tried to sit up. I wasn't restrained. At least, not by any ties that I could identify. My hands and feet were free to move. I was still wearing my jacket and cap, but my headlamp was gone. *Damn.* Crawling on my hands and knees, I started to scope the size of the space while trying to figure out how I'd ended up there.

Dillon.

Dillon had drugged me.

With what? I was awake, so it wasn't fatal—or was it? Some things killed you slowly. I gave a tentative call. "Is there anyone here?"

A coldness crept over my shoulder, touched my neck and a shiver poured through my spine. If I hadn't already been familiar with Evrett's touch, I would probably have crawled out of my skin and stayed there. As it was, I jolted to my knees, arms curling defensively around myself in the darkness. I knew it wasn't Evrett.

The three lights, three entities—who were they? "Is that you? You tried to warn me? Didn't you?"

Stupid. Stupid. How had I missed the signs? Had there been any signs? I didn't know. Nothing was connecting. Nothing made sense. "Sorry. I'm not usually so stupid."

The coldness drifted back a bit.

I was in a wood-walled room, perhaps six feet by eight feet . . . a cell. I couldn't feel a door or hinge or knob of any sort. Stretching up, I waved my hands into the darkness, but if there was a ceiling, it was high. The air smelled stale and earthy, like damp wood and old clay.

My shuffling knees hit something, something that gave softly. Oh no! Please don't let that be a body! I lowered my arms, hands reaching tentatively, afraid of what they might find. They touched familiar coarse canvas. It was my duffle! Fighting nausea, I crawled further, checking for my brief bag, computer, anything else he might have hastily had to throw in with me to hide. Oh god . . .

I only found my duffle and I forced my stiff fingers to seek out the zipper. My cellphone had been in my brief-bag. I couldn't think what was in my duffle that could help me. I unzipped the duffle a bit and squirmed my fingers through the opening, feeling for the contents. I had the blueprints of the house, crisply rolled into a rubber band, a ball point pen, the black Sharpie I'd been using to label boxes at the office, the spare cell-phone charger cord, something that took me a short while to identify as the zip-lock holding the crumbly remains of Mom's cookies, and something silk-wrapped; cold, round, hard . . . Evrett's helmet.

"Oh, Evrett!" I pulled out the artifact and hugged it, feeling stupidly sentimental. I might be surrounded by ghosts, but this one I knew and loved. It remained cold and still in my arms. Maybe it was too hard for him to act being stretched across distances? I couldn't rely on Evrett to save me. I had to be smart right now. I needed to figure out how I was going to get out of this.

"Okay, so I know I'm not alone," I told whoever it was who had touched me earlier. "I don't have my recorder or anything. I can't see or hear you."

The air was still and cool, not the bone-deep cold that I associated with Evrett, and that I'd felt earlier when I'd first woken up. I took the Sharpie to a corner, and using my spread fingers as a guide, wrote my name and the date. I started to write "Tell Mom and Kenny I love them." but that felt too much like giving up, so I crammed the pen in my back pocket and started moving around the room, feeling once more for levers, hinges, doorknobs, anything that indicated where I'd been brought in, and where I might get out.

Dillon. Dillon drugged me. The very thought pissed me off. Why the hell would he do that? Just to keep me from fabricating evidence? Oh, I was gonna fabricate him right into the nearest jail cell and then legalese him into staying there for the rest of his natural born life!

Something was nagging at me, something I didn't want to think about very much: the crying, the screams for help. They were playing over and over in the back of my mind like an earworm of a song that you didn't know the all the lyrics to. Dillon had been in the house the longest, in and out over a timeframe that spanned years. I was pretty sure it wasn't the drug that was making me nauseous as I spoke the realization out loud. "The screaming wasn't just you after you died, was it? Sometimes, they were hearing you when you were still alive."

A soft thunk echoed near me, so close that I squealed as I jumped back from the wall, my free hand snapping back over my chest. As soon as the panic faded and I realized that there wasn't some hidden door opening to admit my future killer, I gasped out, "If that was you, you can do that again. I won't scream like a sissy-brat this time."

There was another knock . . . and then another, fainter than the first.

It started to occur to me that two weeks ago, I would never have considered talking to dead people as a great filler of time. But now? Oh hell. I'd been drugged and shoved in a . . . I wasn't even sure what this was! While on a paranormal investigation? Legal investigating never got me into this kind of trouble! "Okay, knocks are good. I can do knocks. Um . . . one for no, two for yes?"

"Kami?" The voice was faint, tiny, far away. It was followed by two knocks.

"You know my name?" It could speak! The ghost was speaking to me!

"Kami! It's Hannah! I'm here! Can you hear me?"

"Hannah?" My heart pounded, my mouth went dry. "You're . . . you're a ghost?"

"What? No! I'm trapped in here!" There were two more knocks on the wall. "Kami, I'm here!"

She was alive! I hit the wall twice as hard as I could. "I'm here, Hannah! I'm here!"

"Get me out, please, Kami. Help me."

My heart broke. "I'm trapped. It's dark. I can't find a door or anything . . ."

"Me, too." Her voice shivered with hopelessness.

A cold chill brushed over my neck, and I instinctively ducked away from the touch. The ghosts were here, too. A raging wildfire of revelation swept over me: three ghosts on the K2 meter, Hannah, alive, trapped like me, four missing women on Feliz Ciaro's investigative report, and Dillon Cheshire—Dillon Cheshire, whose work had taken him in and out of the Bay Area for years, but always here in summer, always here when women went missing.

Dillon did this. But why me? Why now? I suddenly remembered his denial of the haunting claims, the way he didn't meet my eye when I revealed the sound on the recorder, and then his accusations. "Dillon thought I was onto him." I realized. I had no idea whether the dead were still listening. "He thought I planted your voices to try to trick him out! The background checks . . . all those dates, your missing dates, his work dates. They all lined up! I should I have seen it."

"What are you talking about?" Hannah sounded so far away, so tired, her voice faint through the wood planks.

"Dillon. He thinks I came here alone tonight. He'll tell Irvin and the others that I didn't show up, or that I called to reschedule or something. He'll text Nicky back from my phone, tell her not to come. But he doesn't know about Morri and Father Joe. Morri won't take no for an answer. If I don't pick up my phone, he'll get the cavalry involved. You'll see."

There was one knock from the other side of the wall, and an overwhelming wave of hopelessness in the air around me. Hannah had lost hope, and so had the ghosts.

Where was I? I needed light. I needed to see the blueprints. I dragged them out of my bag and spread them out on the floor, but unless I had a light, I was screwed. I pushed up my sleeves, frustrated when one hung on the oversized diver's watch I wore. Charles' prize watch—the Suunto Elementum dive watch with more buttons and features than I could even begin to consider using, with its alarm that I couldn't figure out how to turn off. Why was I still wearing this thing? It wasn't like . . . It wasn't like it didn't have an illumination feature? God, I was an idiot! Fumbling fingers pressed buttons until the face lit up, faint green light flaring painfully bright to my eyes.

I tilted the watch down, finding my way across the blueprints. I couldn't see how Dillon would have had time to move me out of the house or off-site. According to the watch, it had only been an hour or so since I went downstairs with Dillon. I didn't weigh much, and Dillon was a built man who'd obviously had experience moving unconscious women in the past, so it was plausible that he'd managed to move me anywhere in the house, or even to the garage, or a close-by outbuilding. It was almost 8:30. Morri and Father Joe would be there in half an hour, and Nicky wouldn't be far behind.

The walls were solid, probably insulated for soundproofing. There didn't seem to be any air coming in from anywhere, but I hadn't suffocated yet. It was warm. Perhaps I was near the furnace? I moved slowly over the blueprints. Dillon would have had plenty of time over the years to make modifications, but even as I recognized the fact, my gaze was drawn to the section of the drawing that showed the portions of the house that pressed against the cliff-face. There were maintenance spaces, central heating ducts, and small open spaces behind the frame of the house. Most had crawl spaces that led in from the sides of the house or from inside closets. Inside closets including the one in Dillon's private apartment area.

"Kami?" Hannah's voice came through the wall. "Are you still there?"

"I'm here, Hannah!" I raised my voice. "I'm going to get us out of here, just hold on!"

As best I could figure, we were probably in the crawl space behind the Quiet Room, a space that could be accessed from Dillon's closet. He'd obviously modified it over the years to meet his needs. That wasn't good. The only way out that I could see was through Dillon's room. There should be an air duct but as near as I could figure, if it came through the room at all, it was well over my head.

I had no idea what direction I was facing, and even with the eerie green light from the watch, I couldn't see anything that looked like it might be an opening.

What I could see were all things I wished I hadn't.

The walls were covered with scratches, the kind that desperate people make with their bare fingernails: the kinds of scratches that destroy those hundred-dollar manicures purchased for the special occasion of a girls' night out, or a trip to the wine country with friends. I let go of the light on the watch and the space went dark again. I didn't want to see any more.

I was never good at sports in school. They just weren't fun to play. Softball was too slow and soccer was entirely too much running. Basketball was too dangerous. One elbow to the eye in fourth grade put me off the game totally. Tennis was like dodgeball but with a racket. No, I was never good at playing sports. But every kid who attended my high school will tell you that I was a great cheerer! I had lungs that could be heard clear across a home-coming game field. If Irvin and the others had heard those women before, they'd hear me now.

"Help! Help me! I swear to god, Dillon, I will get you for this!" I screamed. I banged both fists against the wall, but that just hurt, and didn't seem to make much sound. "You ever hear the term unlawful imprisonment? What about kidnapping? In California, kidnapping gets you decades! And not in some namby-pamby Missouri prison where you get to go break rocks all day outside. We're talking San Quentin, you jerk!"

I wondered when Dillon had decided that he wanted me. I didn't fit his type. I wasn't a pretty society girl. When and why had I caught his eye, and for how long? Had he been at Burning Man, hunting me and finding Trunk Girl instead? I remembered what Reese said about the guys being in the café. Dillon had put Irvin up to knocking on my door, I realized. He had orchestrated the entire thing to lure me in. I should have suspected him from the start! Now no one suspected him at all.

The lesser consolation for me was the knowledge that because I didn't fit his victim profile, I probably didn't have days, or even weeks. He wouldn't keep me for fun, like he had the others. He would kill me as soon as he could. Were they still in the house, back in one of the cubbies behind the foundation? Or were they somewhere out on the hill, just dumped down where no one would find them? Were they stuffed into shallow graves? Or had he chopped . . .

Chopped? Ugh! No, stupid! Don't even think about that. It was too late. I'd thought about it.

"Gaaah! I hate you! I hate you, you bastard!" I screamed into the blank wooden walls. "I hate you worse than Jack Austin, and that's saying a lot! Except that you actually deserve it!"

"Kami, shhhh. You're just gonna make him mad," Hannah whimpered through the wall, but that was my plan. I wanted to face Dillon eye-to-eye.

"You deserve whatever you get, Dillon Cheshire. Cuz you friggin' doped me and threw me in a closet! No one gets forgiven for that. No one! And all Jack ever did was love me. And one day, I'm gonna tell him that!" Oh, my God, where did that come from?

I said it.

All Jack ever did was love me, and I couldn't stand him for it. I was gonna die in a crawlspace and get chopped up and scattered in trash cans all up and down Highway 880, and Jack was never going to know how much I loved him. Would he even miss me? There was no sound as my heart broke a little bit more.

I slumped down to the floor, reaching for Evrett's head and shoving it over my own, slamming the visor closed so that I could be alone, for even just a second, with my own pathetic self.

If you don't raise your visor, you'll never see the enemy.

The thought came in the same moment the wall behind me gave way and I fell backwards.

CHAPTER 20

—◆◆◆—

Saturday Night Continued

THE VISOR FLIPPED OPEN AND I FOUND MYSELF staring up into Dillon Cheshire's crotch. Has anyone ever mentioned how good Yoga is for stomach tone? I did the hardest, fastest sit up I've ever done in my life, ramming Evrett's ridged helmet right straight upwards into Dillon's dangly bits so hard that my neck popped. Unfortunately, I was too short to do any real damage, and only succeeded in making him fall back.

I rolled fast onto all fours and launched myself towards the light I could see on the other side of the room . . . Dillon's room. I made it out of the chamber and into the bedroom before a hand clenched around my leg, yanking me back. I kicked him in the gut with my free foot and cut loose with another scream, this one echoing inside the helmet so loudly that my ears hurt.

"It's soundproofed." Dillon grunted, doubled over, one hand on his knee, the other wrapped around my foot. "My room and that room. If anyone hears you, they'll just think it's the *ghosts*, thanks to your little trick."

He forced himself upright, dragging me back towards him. My flailing fingers caught the edge of the bed, forcing him to haul both its weight and my own. He was too strong, and his fingers bit deep, grinding my ankle bone as I flailed, thinking as fast as the few neurons that weren't so terrified they'd stopped firing would allow.

That's when I looked straight at him, looking for a weakness—and gasped.

Behind him, I could see shadows, wispy shapes moving in the darkness. I went still and that must have caught his attention because he stopped jerking on me.

"You think I'm dumb enough to fall for that?"

"They're here." I gasped out, taking advantage to drag myself a few inches further away from him. "The girls you killed. They're here. Right behind you. They won't rest, and neither will I. We'll haunt you till you rot."

Dillon started to laugh, and with a sharp jerk pulled me free of the bed. "You think I believe all that crap?"

I rolled, tried to connect the heel of my sneaker with the side of his head and missed. Why did I have such small feet? "You don't have to believe it. They know it. I know it!"

His fist slammed into my stomach, knocking the air out of me.

Yeah, just for reference—if you're aiming to subdue someone, that works any time. Unable to scream, I coiled up into a ball, tears of shock biting my eyes as he wrestled me around and pinned me, knees on either side of my chest.

He hooked a finger around Evrett's helm, under my chin, and popped it off my head.

"Careful. That's 14th Century," I gasped wispily. "Oils on your hands . . . tarnish . . ."

He laughed as he jammed it on his own head but it didn't fit well. "They musta had little heads in those days."

"Or yours is just fat!" I kicked again, flailing.

Grabbing my wrists, he pushed them together and tied them with a sport sock; an unwashed sport sock. *Gross.* I was gonna have to disinfect my entire skin! "Eww . . ."

With my hands tied, he was sitting across my chest and reached across for his nightstand. From there, he took a small vial and a syringe. "This is real easy. Makes it look just like an overdose. They never suspect a thing. My own little mix for when things don't go as planned."

"Is that what happened out at Black Rock City? At Burning Man?" I asked, suddenly sure of something that hadn't even occurred to me before. "Things didn't go as planned? So you killed her and left her to be found as an overdose?"

He didn't breathe then, not for a long moment, the syringe in one hand and bottle in the other. "How the hell'd you know about that?"

I hadn't. I hadn't put the clues together at all! Hello, I'm Kami White, Paralegal. I needed a snappy slogan like "Gotta clue? Because I sure don't." Nah, it's too long to paint on the window. I nearly giggled. God, how stupid I could be? Pretending to know something you don't isn't usually an advantage in a legal context, but I was playing for my life and for the first time, I was realizing just how fast my brain could think. If they gave Academy Awards to kidnap victims, I would be in the running after this. "You went with Robert, in his car. But you couldn't let Robert suspect you, so you had to act fast. You thought you were getting me, but you got that other girl instead. You told Robert, what? That you were getting a ride back with friends? You just didn't tell him she was a dead friend. Did you know it was my car that you took?"

There was something in his gaze now that was terrifying. It was like peeling back an orange, only to discover that it was full of maggots. How I'd ever found him handsome, even been attracted to him, was completely beyond me now. I wanted to vomit.

"Oh god. You did! You followed my car to Burning Man. And when you realized it was Kenny, not me . . . you took her."

"Shut up. Just shut up!" he screamed in my face. For a second, I was afraid he was going to hit me again. I jerked my bound hands up to protect my face, but both of his hands were occupied filling the syringe with his death serum. "You think you're so friggin' clever, coming in here, trying to trap me in front of those morons. In the end, you're just as dead as the rest. Only difference is, I didn't want them to die."

The needle slid clear of the vial and he tossed the little bottle aside. Through the slotted visor, the grin that had once seemed sexy now struck me as macabre and horrific. "I loved them. All of them. You? I don't care at all about you."

"No," I said as calmly as I could, praying that I wasn't wrong about Evrett and his gift. "But they do." I raised my bound hands and pointed over his shoulder. "Raise your visor, dumb-ass."

There was a hesitation, a wary curiosity in the deep gold eyes that peered through the slits in the visor. Then, he twisted his head around and looked behind him. What he saw through the eyes of a centuries-dead crusader knight, I'll never know, because I hammered him as hard as I could with my elbows, hitting the hand holding the syringe. The needle jabbed deep into his chest.

As Dillon scrambled back, trying to get the needle out, I gained my feet and ran, breaking from his room with screams that they probably heard all the way across the bay into San Francisco. "Call 911! Call 911! Fire! Police! Fire! Help!"

I wanted to run out, but forced myself to turn back towards the hidden door and wooden cell beyond. I could now see the slotted catch that concealed the other place, and broke two fingernails prying it open. Hannah was coiled in the shadows, blinking as light flooded in. She had always been so tall and strong in my mind, but now she looked hollow, fragile. I grabbed the blanket off Dillon's bed, wrapped it around her and pulled her to her feet. "We have to go! Now! Before he wakes up!"

We stumbled over Dillon's prone body, through the Quiet Room, being anything but quiet. I screamed my way up the stairs, "Help! Help! Call 911!", slipping and catching myself on my elbows, not feeling the sting of rug burn as I pushed up and kept running.

Robert was coming in the front door of the house and I plowed past him, only catching a glimpse of his gaping mouth as I went by. "What are you doing here?" he stammered, as though he could barely register presence. "I thought you canceled."

Behind him on the step, Fi was already doing what I'd hoped, calling 911. Never cry for help unless you know explicitly what kind of help you need, and Fi paused in giving them the address to ask me. "Fire? Ambulance?"

"Ambulance. Hannah's going to need one. So's Dillon. And cops! Lots of cops." I gasped as I pushed past her. My feet resumed their exercise in fleeing. I called back a warning. "Don't go in there! Don't go inside until the cops get here!"

I didn't stop running until we'd broken from the front porch and into the driveway. My pick-up truck was gone, or I would have jumped into it and locked the doors. Fortunately, Irvin was still in his Nissan, looking for something under the seat. With Hannah, I jumped into the car before he could get out and slammed the door, pushing the lock-button frantically.

"Kami? What's happening?" His watery eyes were wide and his voice shaky. I couldn't answer. I was shivering so hard my teeth chattered. In the back seat, Hannah was crying tired, relieved sobs.

"We're safe! You're safe!" I promised her.

Irvin pointed at my bound hands. "Uh. You want me to . . . uh . . . take the sock off?"

I shook my head. "Evidence! It's evidence! Don't touch!"

"Uh. Okay. Can I get out?"

"No! Don't open that door!"

Irvin rested both hands on the steering wheel and kept glancing side-long at me. "Ooookayyyy."

He didn't say another word, and neither did I, too busy trying to catch my breath, until I heard the scream of sirens coming up the hillside. The ambulance pulled in first, with a cop car right behind it—bonus points for San Amoro Police department response time. I let Irvin roll down his car window and talk to the badge that approached. I still wasn't sorted, still not smart enough to say more than, "Detective Ron Brittle. Get him here, now! And get the paramedics to Hannah!"

The cop hesitated, started to argue with me. "Calm down, ma'am, and tell me what . . ."

"Detective Brittle! Get him. I'm only talking to him. Downstairs in the house, you'll find Dillon Cheshire. Poisoned. Get him a paramedic." I snapped. Then I rolled the window up and drew my feet up on the seat, curled into a ball, watching the lights, ignoring the cop's plea for me to open the door and tell him what was happening. It occurred to me that I should have the paramedics do a blood draw for a tox screen. Depending on what he'd used, it may not stay in my system long. But I was shaking too hard to force myself out of the safe space Irvin's car provided.

"Kami? Look? The police are here. Can I get out now?" Irvin asked, his eyes perfectly round. "It's safe. The cops are . . ." He reached for the door handle.

"No! Don't leave me!" I'm afraid I left fingerprint bruises on his arm.

"Um. Okay." He kind of huddled in the driver's seat and tried not to look at me. He did unlock the doors for the paramedics, and I finally let him get out and help them get Hannah onto a stretcher.

Another car pulled up, and I was relieved to see Morri get out from behind the driver's seat. Mrs. Morri, decked out in crystal necklace and earrings, hoisted herself out the other side. Morri immediately approached the police officer, his keen eyes dancing behind his spectacles, looking for me.

I tried to promise myself they would have arrived in time had I not been able to escape, but we'll never know for sure. I realized Mrs. Morri had a Happy Cookie bag in her hand, and it was the thought of snickerdoodles that finally persuaded me open the car door.

"Kam! Poppet!" Morri and Mrs. Morri dashed to me, despite the cop trying to hold them back. "What's happened? Nicky called as soon as she got your text, and we rushed over."

"What text?" But I knew any text to Nicky had come from Dillon, not me. "Are those cookies?"

Morri's hand came up to stop Mrs. Morri from handing me the bag. "Tell us what happened first."

An unmarked police car rolled in, and I saw Detective Brittle in the passenger seat, Dortman driving. At the same time, the paramedics came up with a stretcher carrying Dillon's body. I couldn't tell if he was still alive. I didn't want to know. Brittle jumped out of the car and ran over, taking a look at Dillon, then looking around the scene until he spotted me.

A paramedic ran over to the car, and Brittle and Dortman came up right behind him in time to hear him demand, "What's in that syringe?"

"Poison," I stammered, my tongue still struggling to form words. "He called it his special cocktail. I don't know what's in it. He was trying to kill me, I hit him and he jabbed himself." I looked at Detective Brittle and watched understanding dawn across his face. "He drugged me before. I'll need a tox screen ASAP. Hannah, too."

"You found Hannah Raye?" Dortman's pudgy face ballooned with astonishment, and I pointed to the ambulance where they were loading her in. To my relief, he ran to get her statement, whatever statement she was in a position to make.

"Talk first, hospital after." Brittle himself untied my wrists with gloved hands and bagged the sock. "Okay, tell me everything."

The words tumbled over themselves, and I gave my full statement from the passenger seat of Irvin's car as Irvin sat stunned behind the driver's seat, looking ever more ghostly as I recounted how I'd arrived early, allowed myself to be lulled into a sense of security by Cheshire, been drugged, locked in a hidden room, and the final struggle for my life. ". . . and I hit him, he stuck himself with the syringe, and I ran out. And here I am."

My voice trailed off lamely. I wasn't sure what else to say. Mrs. Morri handed over the bag of cookies. "Oh, dear. You need these!"

Irvin, rubbing his eyes, muttered, "He told us you canceled, so we were going to dinner and a movie, but Robert got one of his migraines, so we left. If we hadn't come back early . . . Oh man."

At some point in my oration, Dortman had returned and now he and Brittle looked at each other, then at me. Dortman snorted. "You say you came here to . . . hunt ghosts? As in, ghost-busting?"

"It's what I do . . ." I shrugged and held up the Happy Cookie bag. "Wanna snickerdoodle?"

I'd give them every last crumb if they believed me—or maybe not. Mrs. Morri's cookies were super delicious, even better than usual. Apparently, being drugged, locked up, and scared pee-less makes you hungry.

Then there was nothing more to believe. The officers that had gone downstairs had found everything. The hidden cells, the claw marks, the syringes, the drug vials; every bit of evidence they needed.

Ron Brittle sighed and a ran a hand through his thinning hair. "Is there someone I can call for you? We need to get you the hospital for a check-up and a tox screen."

"Jack Aust . . . I . . . never mind." Was this really how I wanted to do that? "I mean, my lawyer, call my lawyer, Reginald Burroughs."

"I didn't know ghost-hunting was so dangerous." I whimpered to Morri as Detective Brittle loaded me into an ambulance to get checked out. Morri muttered something soothing and handed me another cookie.

MORRI CALLED NICKY AND SHE ARRIVED AT THE HOSPITAL while I was waiting for my blood test results. She handed me her phone, showing the text she'd received.

Nick. I have to cancel the job tonight. Sorry.

I read it three times, gave her a dubious stare. "And you knew I was in trouble? From this? Really?"

"You called me Nick, not Nickykicks or Nickydoodle. Just Nick." She twisted her long braid in her hand. "You know I hate that. And you lete-speak and shorthand when you text me. I knew it wasn't from you. I called Morri and told him to skip the rest of bingo."

"We weren't having a good run anyway. Not a single bingo." Morri smiled, but I could see the worry behind his eye before his voice turned chastising. "I told you not to go back into that house alone."

"I wasn't alone. Dillon was there. You said not to go back because of the haunting, not because of Dillon!"

Reginald Burroughs arrived, followed closely behind by Detective Brittle. They let me know they had spotted my pick-up parked a mile down the road from the house, near a vacant lot.

"It was probably headed for the reservoir, or the bottom of the Bay," Detective Brittle said. "If you'd disappeared, chances are no one would have asked about it until long after it was gone."

I glanced at Nicky, who nodded in agreement with the detective, but I asserted, "Jack would have asked. Jack would never have stopped asking. What about Hannah?"

"She's sedated and resting now, but it's going to be a long recovery for her," Brittle said softly.

"And the other girls? Patricia Misanti? Vivian Astor?" I couldn't remember the third girl, but I could see her face in my mind.

"After finding the hidden room, we brought in a cadaver dog. He led us to an old cistern at the bottom of the back yard." Brittle shook his head. "It's going to take some time to sort out, but there's multiple remains."

"They told me there were three of them. The ghosts."

"I'm afraid you're right, even if I don't believe in ghosts." Detective Brittle said. "I'm just glad you escaped."

My eyes found Morri's again. The women were there– they helped me escape, and there was no way I could tell the cops that. "I was stupid. I should have seen it. Should have realized. He was at the coffee shop. He was at Burning Man, where my car was. He's into computer security."

Realization dawned on Reginald Burrough's face. "The safe-house cameras!"

"And the cameras on campus. He had some tech way of manipulating them." I groaned. "Probably had some way of bypassing your fancy key-card system, too. I'm an idiot."

"You're alive," Ron Brittle asserted again.

"*And* you're an idiot," Nicky slapped my shoulder. "What were you thinking, going alone?"

"Irvin, Fi, and Rob were supposed to be there," I grumbled.

A nurse came down the corridor and got Detective Brittle, who warned me not to go anywhere, then followed her off to talk to the doctor.

"How are you feeling now?" Mrs. Morri asked. "Can I get you anything? Coffee? Water?"

"I'm fine." I wasn't fine. I had a headache the size of the Ferry Building, and all the cookies on top of the drugs was making me queasy. "When can I go home?"

"As soon as your tox screen is back," Reginald said firmly. "I fully intend to see that we have every piece of evidence against Cheshire we can get."

"That may not be necessary." Detective Brittle returned, standing straight in the doorway. "He's lapsed into a coma. He went into a grand mal seizure in the ambulance, then collapsed. They're analyzing the drugs in the vial they found, but it's going to take time to sort out what it was."

"He said it was a custom blend," I muttered. "Do we know yet what he drugged me with?"

"Just talked to the doctor. It was a basic roofie. A blend of ketamine and Rohypnol," Brittle said calmly. "We found a large stash of vials in his room and sent them to the crime lab. He must not have given you much, or you'd still be out cold, but the doctor said there's trace amounts in your blood test."

"It takes a lot to counter-act a Reese's Black-Bottom coffee." I half-smiled. But I wanted to make sure I heard right. "Dillon is in a coma?"

"Doctor says he's in preliminary organ failure. He might still recover, or maybe he'll die quietly and save the State of California the expense of a trial." Detective Brittle sighed. "Not how I wanted this to end. But I'm glad you found Hannah alive."

"Yeah, me, too." I stood up and leaned on Nicky. "Am I clear to go?"

Detective Brittle nodded. "Yeah, you're clear. And with the tox screen on Cheshire matching what the coroner found in Jane Doe, so is your brother."

"When can I get my stuff back from the house? I want my duffle bag, my brief bag. And the helmet from my suit of armor. Where is that?"

Morri gasped.

Brittle blinked. "The helmet is yours?"

"Yes. The jerk was taunting me with it."

"Oh, man." The detective paused. "It was on his head. We thought it was part of his kink. It's being booked into evidence."

"That's not going to make the old knight happy," Morri whispered to me.

"It doesn't make me very happy, either," I groaned back under my breath.

"I'll see what I can do about getting it for you, but this whole case is going to take time to sort out." Detective Brittle sounded apologetic.

"The good news," Reginald inserted, "is that as long as the helmet is in police custody, Juliet can't get her fat fingers on it."

"Oh god. If Dillon killed me, Juliet would get everything!" For some reason, that thought terrified me more than the thought of ending up in that old cistern.

Detective Brittle was staring at us. "Mr. Burroughs, if you can bring your client to the station tomorrow for a full formal statement, I'd appreciate it. In the meantime, I've got to get back to work."

We waved goodbye, I checked out of the ER, and we all trooped out into the cool autumn night air. I was suddenly exhausted and fell asleep in the Frankenstang as Nicky drove me over Highway 17 to her trailer at the wrecking yard.

CHAPTER 21

The Last Night

As glad I was to get out of that house on the hill that night, it wasn't even a full month later that I found myself back there. This time, though, I was gathered with Nicky, Mr. and Mrs. Morri, Father Talbon and the remaining occupants of the house. We were ensconced in a circle in the Quiet Room, holding hands. Irvin was on my left (cold, dry hand) Robert (warm and slightly sticky hand) was on my right, and directly across from me was Morri, holding hands with Nicky on one side, and Robert on the other, Mrs. Morri completing the circle.

In the center of our circle, Father Joe Talbon, his dark brown eyes soft and kind, and his silvery gray hair shimmery, led us in prayer as we gently guided the restless spirits of the hillside house to peace. There was a swift rush of cold across my face as he encouraged them to go to the light, to move on from this plane, and to be at rest.

I wished I'd been able to bring Evrett's helmet. I wondered what I would see, looking through the veil that carried the weight of two worlds, as they left us. There was a faint sensation of a whisper near my ear, *thank you*, and I felt a tear break wetly down my cheek. "You're welcome," I answered her, wishing I knew which of the missing women it was. I owed her my life. "And thank you."

The room grew warm suddenly and the candles flickered for an instant. Then it was still.

Father Talbon closed the prayer, and we all recited our Amens. When I looked over at Fi, her eyes were closed, her lips were moving, and around her neck, I could see her communion crucifix glittering gold in the warm light.

Irvin gave a nervous half-laugh, letting go of my hand quickly to rub his together. "Well, that's it for me. I just need to grab the last of my things and I'm out of here. I'm never coming back."

"They're gone now, you know," Father Joe said encouragingly. "There's no harm that can come to anyone here now."

Irvin gave a rueful shake of his narrow head and tugged at his too-long hair. "I can't stay here. Never want to come here again."

"Where are you going?" I asked, figuring I might as well make conversation with my first real client. Maybe I'd send one of those business Christmas cards, *Happy Holidays from your Haunt Hunter.*

"For now, just to Fremont, but we have a London office and I asked for a transfer."

I reached out and shook his hand once more, giving him a friendly grin. "London? That's a great city. Absolutely chock full of haunted places."

I don't know too many men who can squeal like two-year-old toddlers, but if you ever need one for some reason, Irvin is your guy.

Robert didn't shake my hand, but he took one last curious look around the room. "I'm leaving, too," he said with a sadly hopeful look at me. "I still can't believe I trusted that guy. I went to Burning Man with him! I let him drive my car. Makes me sick."

"You didn't know. I fell for his charm, too." I tried to comfort the guy just a bit. At least he hadn't had a crush on the murderer. "He knew just how to get you to see what he wanted you to see. There was no way you could have suspected him." But just saying it, I knew that wouldn't help at all. I was pretty disgusted with myself, too. Go me, and my rotten taste in men!

"Yeah, well, I just picked up a four-month gig at McMurdo Station." Robert shook his whole body, obviously glad to be getting away completely for a while. "Maybe when I get back, I could call you? It'll be before Comic-Con in San Diego."

"Sure." I waved a blithe hand. "Call me."

"They . . . uh . . . don't have ghosts in Antarctica, do they?"

I thought briefly about bodies of centuries-old explorers lost beneath layers of ice and shrugged. "If they do, call me sooner."

Fi was staying in the house. She was making it her mission to help erase the damage done there. Dillon's apartment was still cordoned off as part of the ongoing police investigation, but as soon as the tape came down, she had the company's permission to completely tear it out and remodel the entire ground floor. "I want to remember that people died here," she said with calm practicality, "but I also want it to be a place to be lived in. I loved living here before I knew what Dillon was doing. I want to restore it to a place of beauty and safety."

"If there's anything I can do to help with that, let me know." Spontaneously, I gave her a quick hug goodbye, and then my group of ghost hunters walked out to the cars.

Morri bumped my shoulder as I pulled out the key to the pickup. "Next time, no going in alone."

"Sure." We both knew I couldn't really promise it. I had a business to run, after all. Even the staidest jobs sometimes meant being alone in less than wise places. "There's got to be easier ways to get free cookies."

Mrs. Morri smiled and said perkily, "I'm just sorry we missed all the excitement. When do you get Evrett back?"

Poor Evrett; the police had all kinds of untoward (meaning seriously kinky!) thoughts when they found him on Dillon's head. Yegads! I know cops see all kinds of whack, but there's got to be a limit to the depths of the gutter a mind can go, doesn't there? Dillon nearly ended up in the press as the Medieval Knight Killer. Thankfully, a call to Feliz put a stop to that.

I gave Morri a relieved smile. "I'm picking him up from Evidence on Monday. They wanted to keep him in case there's a trial, but when I insisted on insurance provisions and warned that they'd be responsible for any damage, they kind of changed their minds. They had all the forensics they needed from him. It's not like keeping him in a vault would help prove or disprove anything . . ."

"Why is it that when you say, 'kind of,' I get the impression nothing of the sort happened?"

I laughed, a real laugh for the first time since I'd ended up in Dillon's hidden chamber—it felt good. "Well, let's just say that sometimes the law works for you and sometimes it's against you, even when you're the police."

I hugged the Morrimonts and told them I'd see them on Monday, if not before. I waved farewell to Father Talbon, then Nicky and I piled into the little pick-up and headed back down out of the hills, but not before sitting for a long moment looking at the house. No shadows played in the corners near the garage, no lights flickered. The scars Dillon Cheshire left behind would never completely heal, and the families and friends of his victims would never forget, but the house where he had performed such horrors no longer felt afraid. It had started to heal.

"You good?" Nicky asked, waiting patiently as I failed to put the pick-up in gear.

"Yeah." I took one last look at the house and slid the gear-shift into reverse. "Yeah, I think I actually am."

After dropping Nicky off, I was at loose ends. With the police no longer considering me a suspect, I didn't have need of Reggie's safe house anymore. I drove downtown to 542 Marin Ave and parked in the alleyway, letting myself in through the back door. Hoover ran to greet me, then immediately turned his tail and pretended that he hadn't missed me a bit.

I settled down at my makeshift desk with my laptop but I hadn't been there more than twenty minutes when my cellphone rang. A glance at the caller ID warned me it was Ron Brittle.

"Kind of late for you, isn't it, Detective?" I asked, feeling slightly cheerier.

"Reese's is open another two hours. Care to join me?"

I glanced out the window to see Brittle's unmarked police car parked at the curb in front of the café. He was standing beside it. There was no sign of his partner. "Business or pleasure?"

"Business, if you want to be picky, though Reese's cinnamon rolls are a pleasure. I'm buying."

"In that case . . ." I abandoned Hoover faster than a hungry flea and hightailed it to Reese's.

Brittle did indeed buy, and though it was a little late for cappuccino, there's never a bad time for a cinnamon roll.

"So, what's going on? Is Dillon awake?"

"No, and that doesn't look likely. Still alive. There's low brain function, according to the doctors, but there is brain function, so there's still a chance he'll wake up someday. They can't just unplug him. Not yet anyway. He'll be moved to long-term care soon." Detective Brittle gave me a warm smile. "How have you been? Feeling better since last we talked?"

Last we talked, I was still pretty much having a breakdown. I'd had enough of formal statements to the police to last for a lifetime. I shrugged. "The nightmares have eased off." I cupped both hands around my hot cup, letting the warmth seep up my arms. "Not likely to trust anyone quite so easily for a long time, though."

"That's natural." He sat back and studied me. "I wanted to tell you that the Louisiana police have connected several missing women with Cheshire as well. His special drug mixes tie them all together. He could have as many as ten victims across the country, maybe more."

That took the wind from my sails a bit. "He was clever."

"There's more," Ron put a netpad on the table and swiped a file open. "We found these on a secure file on Cheshire's personal laptop."

They were pictures: pictures of the Oslo & Burrough's safe-house in Alameda, pictures of my Kia, my mother's green Beetle, Nicky's Frankenstang—and pictures of me: pictures of me at Reese's, me coming out of my office, at the courthouse, having burgers with Nicky, and lastly, of me pulling into the safe-house parking garage. I felt sick all over again. He'd been stalking me for months. "Oh my god. How did I not know?"

"We think he started stalking you before he ever took Hannah. We've found ample evidence that he was stalking her, and several other students as well. He was just waiting for the easy take."

"So why Burning Man? That seems elaborate. Tickets have to be bought months in advance. And why Trunk Girl? She doesn't fit his M.O. except for being blond." But then, neither did I.

"She's not a Jane Doe anymore. Your artist tip paid off. Her name was Annie Benton. She had an extended police record in Texas. Minor things like creating unlicensed works of art in public places. Trespassing. Vandalism. General crimes associated with a vagrant artist lifestyle." He saluted me with his coffee cup. "She was an easy target for someone like Dillon Cheshire. He knew your car very well, possibly even had spare keys for it with all of his stalking of you. It would have been an easy take for him."

"Poor Annie Benton." I sighed. "If she hadn't gone to Burning Man, she'd still be alive."

"It was a total accident that she crossed his path. Nothing but a coincidence."

"That's a hell of a coincidence." I used to not believe in coincidences. Now they were all I believed in. Everything was just too random. The fact the trunk of my car was involved was purely coincidence.

I really had to stop having those.

"There's one more thing that I think you'll be interested in." Brittle smiled and handed me a small stack of papers. "Why don't you sign this for me?"

When a cop hands you a piece of paper and asks you to sign it, you're supposed to fetch a lawyer, or at least a legal document preparer. Oh, wait—that would be me. I read it twice, then a third time. "This is for real?"

"State of Louisiana offered rewards for information leading to capture of suspect on two of the deaths they connected to Cheshire, thanks to that drug cocktail. Twenty-five grand and it's all yours. You captured him."

"He captured me, you mean." I muttered as I signed the paper and handed it back.

"It will take a few weeks to verify everything, of course." Brittle glanced over the paper. "But I think everything's in order. I'll file this as soon as I get back to the office."

Twenty-five grand. Enough that I wouldn't have to worry about much for a while. It would support me while Charles' will was being sorted out and I was getting my business going. I relaxed and smiled at Detective Brittle. "You know, you're not such a bad guy for a cop."

"You're not so bad yourself. For a former suspect."

We shook hands and parted ways, but I had a feeling that this wasn't going to be my last encounter with Detective Ron Brittle.

BACK IN THE OFFICE, I WENT STRAIGHT TO THE COUCH and curled up under the blanket, holding my phone. For a long time, I sat staring at the numbers, steeling myself. It was time, I knew, to make my own amends. People will tell you that there's something about almost dying that makes you realize what's really important to you. I still don't know if that's true or not.

What I did know was that I wronged someone who never deserved it . . . and in my darkest moment, when I wasn't sure I could make it another breath, that person had been the one on my mind. I finally punched in the numbers, and on the other end, the phone started to ring.

My heart was pounding with anticipation. My palms were sweating. I couldn't wait to hear his customary "This is Jack." at the other end of the line.

beep A generic voice intoned in my ear: "You've reached Jack Austin. He's not available to take your call. Please leave a message after the tone."

Denied!

I pulled the phone from my ear, stared at it a long time, then punched the 'end' button with my pointer finger and flung the phone across the room. "I hate that man! I hate him!"

Hoover dumped his toy catnip mouse on my foot and gazed at me imploringly.

I scooped him up into my arms and carried him out to the front office where we could sit at Evrett's sabatons and watch the streetlights glitter in the rainy street. "What do you think, Hoover? Are we paranormal investigators now?"

F.L. OAKES

He reached up and patted my nose with his paw. Behind me, I could feel Evrett's boot shift, pressing slightly against my back. "I guess that's a yes."

THE END.